BEGGARMAN, THIEF

I0674964

BEGGARMAN, THIEF

Righting our Wrongs in Small-Town America

**Continuing the Award Winning Dancing Deer Series
with Book Six**

Ron Lambert

Copyright © 2013 by Ron Lambert

All rights are reserved. No part of this work may be reproduced or transmitted in any form by any means: electronic or mechanical. It may not be photocopied, recorded, or otherwise without the prior written permission of the publisher. For information on getting permission for reprints and excerpts greater than three hundred words, contact Printers Guild Publishing House at printersguildpublishing@gmail.com.

Published in the United States by:

Printers Guild Publishing House

425 Spring Street, Suite 101
Columbus, Texas 78934-2461
(979) 732-2963
Fax (979) 733-0015
www.printersguildpublishing.com

Library of Congress Control Number: 2013904458

ISBN 978-0-9855083-6-4

Trademarks

Red Wing Shoes, the *Courier Democrat*, the *Kansas City Star*, the *Arkansas Gazette*, the *Memphis Globe*, *Grit*, Octagon Soap, Sears Roebuck and Company, Montgomery Ward, and all other trademarks are property of their respective owners. Printers Guild Publishing House, llc is not associated with any product or vendor mentioned in this book.

Beggarman, Thief is a work of Fiction

Except for some historical personages, the names, characters, and incidents of the story are used fictitiously and do not represent any actual person or event.

Some of the towns, cities, or geographic localities are real. An interested reader might find Lee Mountain, the Buffalo River, the Illinois Bayou, the Big Piney, Moccasin Gap, or even Little Creek's water crossing. Eudy's Drug and Fountain might be more difficult.

The author grew up in a small, rural community and saw wonder in all living things. He wrote this story using the hazy remembrances of a child's fertile imagination and sheer luck.

Cover

Art from Dreamstime.com

Acknowledgements

The quote at the end of the book, "I love thee, I love only thee. With a love that shall not die. Till the sun goes cold, and the stars grow old." is quoted from *Venus and Adonis*, a poem by William Shakespeare.

Permissions

The Society of Authors, as the Literary Representative of the Estate of Katherine Mansfield, have graciously granted permission for Mr. Lambert to use an extract from a 1918 letter Ms. Mansfield sent to John Middleton Murray.

Table of Contents

CHAPTER 1 11
Christmas Morning, 1945

CHAPTER 2 21
December 26, 1945

CHAPTER 3 29
December 27, 1945

CHAPTER 4 43
December 28, 1945

CHAPTER 5 51
December 29, 1945

CHAPTER 6 65
December 30, 1945

CHAPTER 7 69
December 31, 1945

CHAPTER 8 81
January 1, 1946

CHAPTER 9 87
January 2, 1946

CHAPTER 10 95
January 4, 1946

CHAPTER 11 101
January 9, 1946

CHAPTER 12 107
January 14, 1946

CHAPTER 13 .... **109**
January 13, 1946

CHAPTER 14 .... **113**
January 14, 1946

CHAPTER 15 .... **119**
January 15, 1946

CHAPTER 16 .... **121**
January 16, 1946

CHAPTER 17 .... **125**
February 4, 1946

CHAPTER 18 .... **129**
February 9, 1946

CHAPTER 19 .... **133**
February 10, 1946

CHAPTER 20 .... **137**
February 12, 1946

CHAPTER 21 .... **143**
Valentine's Day, February 14, 1946

CHAPTER 22 .... **149**
Early Evening on February 14, 1946

CHAPTER 23 .... **153**
The Evening of February 14, 1946

CHAPTER 24 .... **161**
February 15, 1946

CHAPTER 25 .... **165**
February 19, 1946

CHAPTER 26 ....**169**
March 4, 1946

CHAPTER 27 ....**173**
March 5, 1946

CHAPTER 28 ....**181**
March 6, 1946

CHAPTER 29 ....**185**
March 26, 1946

CHAPTER 30 ....**195**
May 12, 1946

CHAPTER 31 ....**203**
May 12, 1946

CHAPTER 32 ....**207**
May 15, 1946

CHAPTER 33 ....**215**
August 15, 1946

CHAPTER 34 ....**223**
August 19, 2013

CHAPTER 35 ....**229**
August 20, 1946

CHAPTER 36 ....**233**
Wednesday Evening, August 21, 1946

CHAPTER 37 ....**241**
August 23, 1946

CHAPTER 38 ....**249**
Friday Afternoon, August 23, 1946

CHAPTER 39 .... **253**
    Saturday Morning, August 24, 1946

CHAPTER 40 .... **255**
    Saturday Afternoon, August 23, 1946

Author Bio **259**
    Ron Lambert, an Examined Life

Additional Novels **261**
    The Dancing Deer Story

CHAPTER 1

Christmas Morning, 1945

James pulled into a sleepy Indiana town. He had spent his youth riding bicycles down its streets, playing marbles on bare patches of ground, and kissing the girls. Not much had changed. Several retail establishments once frequented, were now renamed. Some had been torn down and replaced with updated buildings. Others were shuttered, waiting for a visionary, someone who could reach out with their version of the American Dream: to see how a coat of paint, a new sign, and a product everyone passing by could not live without, would transform his life. This dreamer would snap up a bargain, make changes, and embark on a life of entrepreneurship.

How many years had he been away? Twenty maybe. James turned left on Piedmont Avenue, passed his junior high school, entered a residential area, and stopped in the driveway to the house he had bolted from. Would his parents be glad to see him, welcome him home, or would they tell him to go away? He had not left on the best of terms: expelled from school halfway through his senior year, a pregnant girl under the clutching wing of a distraught mother and gun-toting father, and the law creeping up with a fist of warrants.

James Merle Dandae walked to the front door of his parent's home and knocked. He had constantly thought about this reunion on his trip back. With twenty years of crime under his belt, his bridges burned, havoc and mayhem strewn along the highways traveled, he had reached the bottom of a despotic life in a little town in northern Arkansas. It was a long road back, both spiritually and physically. It was also Christmas and he had a burning desire to hug his mother.

Rays of light illuminated a weathered porch. A frail voice came through the door, "Who's there?"

"It's me, Dad—James."

"James?"

"Open the door, Dad. I've come home."

Slowly the door opened. Inside a dark foyer, piercing eyes stared out in disbelief. A hand reached a light switch, the weight of a hunched over man pressed down on a black cane, then both arms extended in a welcoming gesture with the cane falling to the floor. "James? James, you've come home! Come here, boy."

James stepped through the doorway and put his arms around his father. "Dad, I never meant to stay away so long. My whole life came crashing down and I ran."

"I know, son. I know. Will you hand me the cane? Let's go into the sitting room—we need to talk."

"Don't you think we can wake Mom? I really need to see her."

"No, James. We can't. Your mother died three years ago."

"Died?"

"Yes. Here, let me sit down." James' father leaned his cane on the armrest of his chair and gave his eldest son an appraising look. "You look good, boy. But your clothes are wrinkled and you need a shave. How long have you been on the road?"

"Two days. I came in from Arkansas. How did Mom die?"

"She caught a cold and it went to her lungs. The good woman was in bed a month. She asked me to find you, said she wanted to see your smiling face one last time. But I didn't know where to look. I went to see your friends, but no one had heard from you. I even went to Jacqueline's house. Her parents said she didn't live there anymore. They sent me to Lindale. She worked for the school. Jackie said she had not communicated with you since the night you left. It was all dead-ends. I came home. While I was looking, your mother made a time-line chart using the dates and postal marks from the envelopes of your letters. On a map, we traced your journey and determined you were headed to Atlanta. I caught a bus, but after two unsuccessful weeks in a city I didn't understand, I gave up and came home.

"Telling your mother I couldn't find you was the hardest thing I've ever had to do. She died in my arms."

"Dad, I am so sorry." James slid his hand along the smooth wood of a frame holding a stretched piece of lace. "I wrote when I could. I thought I was on an adventure. Never really considered anybody else. It's just one more example of me failing the people I loved." James sat on a corduroy sofa and hung his head. "I should've called."

"Yes, you should have. When the letters stopped, we thought you were dead. Your mother cried every time something happened to remind her of you. One time she was housecleaning and plopped down in a chair. With tears in her eyes she said, 'You know, if James is still alive he's probably married. He might even have a child or two. Henry, we might have grandchildren we don't even know about.'"

"Where's Jeff? Didn't he get married?"

"Your brother went to England in 1940 to join Britain's Royal Air Force. He had ten confirmed kills before his plane was shot down over the English Channel."

"Jeff was a fighter pilot? How'd he do it?"

"I don't rightly know. I do remember he had his mother write a letter or two and it wasn't long before he received a reply containing a travel voucher and a letter from a high-ranking congressman telling him to make his way to Philadelphia." Henry Dandae adjusted a lace doily while he thought about the woman he loved. "There for a while we got letters from Jeff trying to save the world and from you trying to live yours down."

"Jeff turned out to be the man I should have been. As a boy, he was always following in my footsteps and doing what he found lacking in me." James looked down at his shoes. Under his breath he whispered, "Jeff, you did good."

This is not how James had planned his return. "So now it's just you and me?"

"Yeah. But that's an improvement. For the last three years, it's just been me."

"Well, I'm back now and I ain't going anywhere. How were you planning on celebrating Christmas?"

"I usually spend it at church. We prepare food in the fellowship hall and invite anybody needing a hot meal. I ladle on scoops of mashed potatoes or carve the five or six donated turkeys. This year we've invited a group of missionaries. They've been touring the country preaching their message from a tent. They held services here several nights last week. You should hear Miss Agatha Parker scare her audience back into the fold. She can make Hell seem like a negative alternative no one would want themselves cast into. But we don't have to go."

"No, Dad. The church has been your life. I've not come back to disrupt. I want to make things right."

"Son, you don't know how good that makes me feel."

James carried in one suitcase and a second pair of shoes before plopping down in his mother's easy chair. When his dad had finally committed to retirement, his mother had been firm. She announced right then, "Henry, I think that's great. And I have an announcement of my own to make. If you're going to retire then I'm going to retire." She waited for that to sink in before adding, "And, I want my own comfortable chair. A smaller version of that behemoth you spend half your life in, waiting for me to walk by, so you can ask me to bring whatever you're in need of."

With two more hours until dawn and his father back in bed, James lost awareness as he relaxed in the cushiony leather of his mother's chair to wait for the day to arrive.

"James, do you have any shirts not so wrinkled?"

"No, Dad. They're clean though."

"Okay, we have two alternate roads. You can wear something from Jeff's closet or we can try our hand at ironing. Why don't you go see what you can find in your old bedroom? Jeff wore your clothes until they wore out. Your mother would see your striped shirt coming down the hall and gasp before realizing it was Jeff. They turned to rags before he would let us buy him anything. While you're looking, I'll see about getting the wrinkles out of one from your suitcase."

After a few minutes, James yelled from the bedroom he had shared with his younger brother, "Dad, what size did Jeff grow to? His shirts are too big."

"He fought your battles at school and beefed up by lifting weights. I don't think he was much heavier than you—just bigger in the neck and across the chest. By the end of your first year gone, no one said anything bad about you anymore. Jeff had become a force in the neighborhood and would not tolerate a sneer or a joke made at your expense. You never knew what an influence you had on him."

"I know I never appreciated him like I should've."

"Here, try this on. I hand sprinkled it with dissolved starch. James, I've had to learn a lot of new tricks after your mother died. I even cook a little."

James walked into the kitchen and picked up his shirt hanging on the end of his mother's ironing board. His dad was now at the refrigerator. "I usually have oatmeal for breakfast. Can I fix you some? I got toast but not biscuits. I've found making biscuits beyond my abilities."

"Sure, Dad. I'll have whatever you're having. Did you make coffee?"

"No. Rudy says caffeine makes my blood pressure go up. And I don't use salt. It was hard to get adjusted, but when Rudy told me about the alternative, I found I could make the effort."

"Rudy is your doctor?"

"Yeah, small world isn't it. He came home from college with a diploma and a completed internship to work for Doctor Pratt then took over when the good doctor retired."

Stuffing his ironed shirt into his trousers, James wondered about his father's health. He looked so old. James remembered his father towering over him saying something like, "Boy, what have you done?" He had always looked so tall, so upright and well put together.

James shaved and showered and now was wearing a shirt his father had ironed. It was good to be home. "Will I know anybody?"

"Mr. Dickey and his wife will be there. Your friend Patrick York married Cynthia Howell. He'll be in charge of the serving line and Daryl Harris will probably come. He now lives in Rockford. Most everybody else is gone."

"What does Patrick do for a living?"

"He's the head of our police force."

"How about Daryl?"

"Well, now there's a story. Daryl got a scholarship to Indiana State. After college, he came back to be the high school head coach. Our boys played in the state basketball tournament several years in a row. Then last year they were disqualified early. It almost killed Daryl. You would not believe how some people can get carried away by a team sport. He went into a depression and tried to commit suicide. We had to get him counseling. Daryl moved to Rockford to start over and now shows up here on most holidays."

"Dad, tell me about Jackie. Did she have the baby?"

"I don't know. You remember how uppity her family was. After you left, we didn't see her anymore. When I visited her house, her father wouldn't let me in. It was all I could do to get her address in Lindale. When I arrived, I called and we met at a coffee shop. She said she only had a minute that she had to get back to school. She must've been on lunch break. She still harbors a lot of resentment toward you."

"That's what I expected. What time will we be leaving for the church?"

"As soon as I finish eating. Will you mind helping set up the tables?"

"James, is that you?" Patrick thrust out his hand. "Man, it's good to see you. Do you remember Cynthia? She and I got married fifteen years ago. I got two boys now."

"I always knew you'd do well, Patrick. I'd come by to see if you wanted to get into trouble and you'd tell me no, you had lessons to do. Remember?"

"Yeah. My parents didn't much like me hanging out with you. They thought I might pick up bad habits. But I told them you were really a nice guy. You just didn't want anybody to know it."

"Yeah, I was a rebel. Someone no one could tell what to do. So fiercely independent that he couldn't conform to the established rules of behavior. And for that, I was an outsider with just a few friends. You, Daryl, and Rudy were the only ones I thought worthy."

"Are you still like that?"

"No. Patrick, I've changed. I hope you'll give me another chance—this time to be a better friend."

"James, you've always been my friend. You don't have to prove anything to me. But I'm glad you've overcome your abnormal individuality. Man is not an island. Life is so much easier if you think of yourself as part of a greater whole rather than thinking everybody is out to make your life miserable."

"So, what can I do to help?"

"We got missionaries coming. We should give them a prominent seating area. Miss Parker got her audience so incited two nights ago we had to step in to keep the whole house from storming down the street to dismantle Bathsheba's Night Club."

The front door opened and in walked a striking woman and a tall man in a long frock coat. Patrick said, "Here she is now. Let me introduce you. You can talk to her while I prepare a place for them to sit." Patrick put his hand on James' shoulder and nudged him toward the attractive woman as if he was herding a reluctant steer.

"Hello, Miss Parker and . . . is it Seth? There was someone talking when we were introduced and I'm not sure I correctly got your name, sir."

"Yeah, Seth is close enough."

"Well, let me introduce James Dandae." Patrick turned to his friend. "James, this is Miss Agatha Parker and Seth." Patrick looked at Miss Parker, who was staring at James. "James is a high school friend I haven't seen for twenty years. What a wonderful Christmas we're having."

Miss Parker held out her hand. "Mr. Dandae, I am so glad to make your acquaintance."

"Likewise, Miss Parker. Have you found many heathens in Indiana?"

"Mr. Dandae, I am prepared to talk to all questioning people. Are you a practicing Christian?"

"Yes, ma'am. My father is a retired Methodist minister. I grew up in a religious home with Christianity instilled into my very being. My father made me read a chapter of the bible every day and tested my faith on a regular basis. I rebelled at my first opportunity and came back when I finally realized it was not just dogma but a way of life with a basis beyond reproach."

"Mr. Dandae, you have skill in rhetoric. Have you thought of expressing your faith in front of an audience?"

"Absolutely not. My faith is personal. But I would like for you to tell me how you became a missionary."

"Good grief. I need air." The man named Seth threw both hands in the air and headed to where Patrick was setting chairs beside a long narrow table.

James joined Agatha for the meal. At the table setup for Agatha and Seth; James, his father, and Patrick sat across from the two visitors, with Cynthia sitting beside Miss Parker.

Cynthia said, "Agatha, do you ever feel uncomfortable speaking publicly about your beliefs in front of an audience containing men?"

"I used to. I've heard that public speaking is considered the most imagined worst of all possible phobias. As you gain experience, it becomes easier. And it helps to be adequately prepared and enthusiastic about your subject."

"Seth, do you give a testimony?" asked James.

"No."

Patrick said, "Seth is Miss Parker's front man. He comes into town ahead of the rest to get the permits, find a place to set up the tent, talk to the newspapers, and hang posters."

"It sounds like you have everything organized, Miss Parker. Will there be any more services held here or will you be traveling to a new venue."

"We have the tent secured for travel, but everyone—other than Seth and I—have headed home for the holidays. After the first of next year, the guys will return and we'll continue to whatever town Seth has arranged. I leave all those details and the financial matters to him."

"Well, Seth, it looks like you are the spring that makes the clock work."

"Yeah."

"Have you decided on your next stop?"

"No."

James turned his attention away from Seth and continued with, "So, the two of you will be staying with us through the New Year's festivities? Is one of our families supplying you with lodging?"

"Seth gets me a hotel room downtown. The three men who handle the tent sleep in it. Seth is usually on the road, but sometimes he gets his own room at the hotel. In the larger towns, we have longer runs and then Seth is not so stressed about getting our next engagement."

"And you travel from town to town on the train?"

"No, Mr. Dandae, besides Seth's car, we have another automobile and a flat-bed truck."

Henry Dandae whispered in James' ear, "Don't monopolize the conversation, son."

For the next few minutes, everyone ate with no one offering much comment." Then Miss Parker asked James, "Mr. Dandae, what kind of work do you do?"

James thought for a moment and said, "I'm a consultant."

"Really?" questioned his father.

CHAPTER 2

December 26, 1945

The day after Christmas was Wednesday. After attaching his car's license plate, James went downtown to talk with Patrick. A uniformed sergeant escorted him to a small private office.

"Good morning, Patrick."

"James, you're around early. I don't remember you being a morning person. You were always yawning or with your head lying on your desk till halfway through second period. Would you like a cup of coffee?"

"I would. Dad doesn't drink it anymore." James poured a cup from a thermos he found on a small table beside Patrick's desk. "Was I so worthless?" He waited a moment before continuing, "Well that's behind me now, Patrick. Presently I need a job. You got any suggestions?"

"I could hire you as a police officer. We got an opening or two."

"Anything else?"

"James, what's this about being a consultant? Could you use that somehow?"

"Naw, there's not much manufacturing here. I was primarily helping businesses streamline their operations. You know, following the assembly of some product to see how it could be put together more efficiently. I also worked in offices redoing their filing systems. But it takes a long time to develop a working relationship with a prospective client, and I need a job now."

"Let me think about it. You planning on being around for a while?"

"Yeah, Dad's got a bushel basket of pills. I think he's got health problems. He needs me, Patrick. Do you know how good it feels to be needed?"

"Not really. That must be a comparative issue. It only feels good after a period of time when no one needs you. I've always done things for other people and don't know what it feels like not to be needed."

"Okay, let's move on. What do you know about this Seth character? Have you done any checking on him? Agatha seems to be the real deal, but Seth is out of place. He appears to be a shady character who's latched onto a naïve bundle of goods."

"No. I think he's a monosyllable man without texture. He only seems out of character because he is in close proximity to such a dynamic and beautiful lady. Is that why you need a job? So you can spend time showing Agatha a little Indiana hospitality with money in your pocket?"

"It's an exciting possibility. But right now, I'm as poor as a church dormouse."

"James, how about coming to my house this evening? Agatha and Cynthia have become close friends. Agatha is coming over tonight to help Cynthia take down the Christmas tree and be rewarded with a home-cooked meal."

"I'll be there."

James stepped outside to a light snowfall. December in Indiana was usually a cold affair. This year was no exception. James buttoned his coat and stuffed his hands in his pockets. He still had a few dollars left from the bank robbery in Skunk Hollow and from robbing those two men in Dancing Deer. He felt bad about shooting the police officer, but this was a new chapter in his life and he was starting to like it.

At the Hotel Lexington, he asked the desk clerk to ring Miss Parker's room. After dialing, the man handed the telephone to James.

"Hello, Miss Parker. This is James Dandae. I thought I might show you around town if you have an hour or two without anything pressing."

"Good morning, James. Let me think. I could stay in my room and read, or I could sit beside the window and watch people walk by on the sidewalk; I could take another nap, or I could be escorted around town on the arm of a handsome man. Let's see. Yes, I just about have it. There it is. I think I'll read. Thank you anyway."

James couldn't believe what he had just heard. It was finalized by the click of Agatha hanging up the receiver. This certainly needed more thought. Agatha was in her middle to late twenties. Maybe a thirty-eight year old man was too old for her; thirty-eight and without a job; thirty-eight, without a job and living with a parent. Hmm.

Rudy was James' only other friend. Daryl had not made it into town for the Christmas meal and there had only been three. "Hello, Rudy. Do I need to make an appointment?"

"James, it's good to see you. When did you get into town?"

"Early Christmas morning. I've been trying to re-acquaint myself. Of our little group you and Patrick have done well, Daryl is having emotional issues and I became the . . . the . . . well, let's just say I have not fared as well as the remaining three."

"James, you were smart. You had a perfect family. Your dad took you fishing, watched your ball games and your mother doted over you. We were envious of your family. But about the time you'd get settled, your dad would pack things and everyone in your family would move to another town. Then a year or so later, you'd show up again. You lived the life of an army brat but instead of your dad being transferred to another base it was to another church."

"I know, and the schools I went to were not synchronized. I remember trying to learn algebra, and then getting moved to Kentucky where they were still getting a handle on long division. When we came back, you guys had gone through trigonometry into graphing equations of the transcendental functions. I was lost."

"I wasn't aware of that. I'm sorry. We should have given you help. Why didn't you tell us? We thought you were bored."

"No. I was too proud to let you know."

"Okay. Now that a chunk of information has been entered, let me tell you what happened when you left the last time.

"Old man Peterson went to the police and filed a complaint saying you had robbed him of his gun and a sack of silver dollars. The police put you on its list of persons of interest. Your parents were interviewed. Jackie's parents were interviewed. My parents were interviewed. Then Jackie left town and was gone for a year. She eventually came home for a week or so and left again. No one has seen or heard from her since.

"Occasionally, the police received requests for information about you. You are notorious in some circles. After a year, old man Peterson went back to the police and had his complaint removed. He wouldn't tell them why. They thought he'd found his gun and the money and decided you needed to have your name cleared.

"James, does any of this make sense to you?"

"Rudy, it's a wonder you would even talk to me without calling the police to tell them to get over here fast, that you'd try to keep me busy while they located a cruiser in the area."

"Now James, don't be like that. I still consider you a friend. I just don't understand you."

"Rudy, let's move on. What can you tell me about Dad's health? I've got a sack of pills. I think some of them are out of date. I can't believe Dad needs to take everything in the sack. If he does then he's one of the walking dead."

"Let me see." Rudy emptied the bag on his desk. "These three were for your mother. One was to settle her nerves when she went through menopause. The other two were to stimulate a gland. If he's taking any of them, he needs to stop. And these are for his blood pressure. I had to keep increasing the strength until we got to one that worked. This one is for gout. You know he had a small stroke a few months back and these two bottles are for that." Rudy set these two aside. "Here is a bottle your mother used to deal with headaches.

"This is a diuretic, this one is to replace the lost potassium, and these are vitamins. So these three are the current ones he should be taking. Let's separate them. And these two for his heart. All the others need to be disposed of."

"Holy cow, he said he couldn't read the labels, that they had faded. He would only take the ones from the top shelf. He said that sometimes when he opened the medicine cabinet a bottle would fall out and, if he couldn't determine which shelf it came from, he'd put it on the top shelf. Every day he took pills from every bottle on that shelf hoping to finish them off before getting with you for replacements."

"Good grief. Is he feeling okay?"

"Seems to be. You want me to bring the others?"

"You've got more bottles?"

"Two deep on two more shelves."

"I think someone should have been checking on him. It's good you came back."

James returned home to find his father sleeping in an easy chair. A radio was playing a college football game and a book was laying open in his lap. His father's head lay on one side and propped on top of a throw pillow usually found stuffed in a corner of the couch.

"Dad, wake up." James gave his dad a vigorous shake.

"What? What. Oh, it's you. You go into town?"

"Yeah, Dad. Rudy says most of those pills were for Mom. Only these five bottles are yours."

"Well, that explains a lot. I'd take a handful of pills and think I had to go into town to buy a purse."

"Dad, will you show me how to iron a shirt?"

James arrived at Patrick's at six o'clock. Patrick hadn't said when to be there and, since it got dark before five, James had to control himself so that he didn't show up before the man of the house. Patrick was probably like most businessmen and had to work till five to get in his eight hours.

James' knock was answered by a young boy who led James into the sitting room. Patrick was lounging in a comfortable chair while Cynthia grappled with boxes while backing down the ladder from the attic.

"James, this is Tyler, my youngest. I hang him upside down from a hook in the ceiling every evening. A gypsy told me it'd make him grow taller. He wants to be a basketball star. Tyler, this is Mr. Dandae. I have another, but he does his lessons at his girlfriend's house. Of course, he doesn't have lessons over Christmas break, so we're not sure why he keeps going over there every night. Tyler and I have talked about it, but so far we haven't come to any conclusion."

"Did you tell Cynthia I was coming?"

"No, I forgot." Patrick got out of his chair and walked a few steps toward the hallway. "Cynthia, honey, let me help you with that. Our guests have started arriving."

"Guests?"

"James, for one. You remember? I invited him yesterday at the church dinner."

"Oh yes, of course. I'm sorry, James. But I forgot you were coming and I invited Agatha. I hope you don't mind. There's plenty of food. She and I will be talking about girlie things while we put away the

Christmas ornaments. If we get too loud, you and Patrick can go to Patrick's private sanctuary—the back porch."

"Cynthia, you are such a dear. I look forward to seeing Agatha again. And I wouldn't mind helping the two of you. Maybe I could get the ornaments from the top of the tree."

"Great. That must be her now. Tyler, get the door, please. Patrick, would you carry this into the living room? I've got to get rid of the apron and check my hair."

Ten minutes later when all pleasantries had been exchanged, Agatha and Cynthia retreated to the kitchen while Patrick and James sat in the living room. James leaned over, "Patrick, you took advantage of your wife's stress. She wants everything to be perfect for Agatha and couldn't remember whether you had asked me or not."

"You're right, James. It takes years of practice to get what you want without offending. She does the same to me. Every time she fixes cherry pie I know she wants to spend money on something personal for herself. A peach cobbler is followed with a trip to her parents' house. Sometimes, when I get finished with my shower, she'll be standing there with a warmed towel. She must stick it in the oven for a few minutes. I don't know what that's for, but whatever it is I'll make sure she gets it."

"Is that what married life is all about?"

"That and a lot of cuddling. Sex plays a part, but a woman really wants to feel appreciated and safe and loved."

"Patrick, you and James need to come into the dining room. Dinner is served."

During the course of the meal, small talk was exchanged, but nothing was mentioned about Agatha preferring to read a book over being escorted around town by James. After the meal, the four adults went into the living room with Tyler retreating to his bedroom. He was glad he didn't have to help with the Christmas tree ornaments or wash the dishes.

Agatha walked around the tree. She turned on the linked strand of lights and watched their twinkling reflection in the front windows. Snow was falling with white triangles collecting in the corners of each window pane. "Christmas is such a special time of year."

"Why is that, Miss Parker?" asked James.

"Why . . . it's the anniversary of Jesus' birth."

James said, "We could have just as easily celebrated it in February or July. I understand the early church decided to put it in December because there weren't any church holidays then in that month. Sometimes they would make a new holiday coincide with a pagan ritual. It was a way to incorporate non-believers into her clutches. The churches in the east celebrate his birth on January 6th."

"That's not actually true is it? Would the church deceive us that way?"

"I don't think the church was deceiving us. They needed a date and they had done similar deeds in the past. Easter is determined by the Jewish lunar calendar and is also the day sacred to the pagan goddess, Eostre. She's known for her love of rabbits and eggs."

"Really, Mr. Dandae, you must be jesting. Do you think I am so gullible as to believe that rubbish?"

"Miss Parker, as a missionary, you have chosen to take your message on the road. To be effective, you should be properly schooled in the history as well as the dogmatism of Christianity. Anything less and you might be hurting the cause more than helping. But, then again, you might be in it for the money."

"I beg your pardon."

"Miss Parker, religion can be thought of as a business. And in some parts of the country that business is booming. Indiana, for instance, is a hotspot of religious fervor. You come to Indiana with a religious message and you get to tell it to packed houses. But if you want to convert heathens, you have to go to where the heathens live. You would not preach to standing-room-only crowds if you took your show to a country where the dominant religion was Hindu, Shinto, Buddhism, or Islamic—or an Indian reservation for that matter. How about the poorer sections of New York City or Chicago?"

"Mr. Dandae, Seth determines where we travel. And, although we have nice-sized audiences, our donations are small. Every month I have to supplement our bank account with money from my trust."

"I'm sorry, if I have offended you."

"I know the bible, sir. And the Christian dogma you refer to is just man's interpretation set forth as a series of rules."

Patrick got out of his chair, walked to the Christmas tree, and plucked off an ornament. "Honey, what do I do with this?"

CHAPTER 3

December 27, 1945

The next morning James lay in bed thinking. It was through his efforts that a bridge lay burning at his feet. A bridge that had once spanned a deep chasm, but now that same chasm presented a black void barring his way. He had rebelled against his father by studying the history of Christianity looking for problems. Until the sixteenth century when Martin Luther nailed up his ninety-five points of debate, it was wholly controlled by the Catholic—sometimes referred to as the Universal—Church. When James told his dad about things the church did to increase its influence, to convert the pagans, to control the heresies, to punish the heretics, his father would cringe and storm off to another part of the house. Did he have to do the same thing to Agatha, or was it some sort of retaliation? All she had done was rebuff his advances. If he really wanted to change, why continue with old habits?

James' father opened the bedroom door and leaned in, "James, are you up yet? Patrick wants you to come to his office this morning. He called an hour ago. Can I fix you a bowl of oatmeal?"

"Man, you are a piece of work. I invite you to my house, let you sit by the most attractive woman in our part of the country, and you criticize Christianity—to a . . . a missionary. James, what were you thinking? Are you a self-defeatist?"

"Patrick, are you a psychologist?"

"I've read the books."

James put his arm around Patrick's shoulder. "Then my good fellow, I want to be your first test case."

"Sorry, buddy. I don't have time at work and at home my better half thinks you're a cretin."

"There you go. I need your help so that you and your wife can be civil to each other again. You did stand up for me, didn't you? You knew me years before you even met that blonde bombshell."

29

"The reason I called was to offer you some work. We need to get a handle on our paperwork. I told the mayor you were an expert. He asked me to get a bid. You weren't giving me a line of bull were you, buddy?"

"Absolutely not."

"If you're sure, I'll give you the detail of what I have and a description of what I want. Then you can estimate the time you'll need and give me a price. We'll purchase any supplies you'll need so you can leave them out. Does that meet with your approval?"

"Yeah."

"We have about forty-five hundred case files going back before the turn of the century and a dozen large crates of miscellaneous papers. Then there is another pile of papers we are currently working on. James, do you need a tablet and pen to take notes?"

"No, I got it."

"We got lists of convicted felons, confiscated items, office furniture and equipment, and stored evidence. There are inter-office memos, federal and state letters, FBI notices, warrants, permits, affidavits, and—James, you're not going to sleep, are you?"

"Hell no, I got it."

"Okay, there are personnel files, performance appraisals, certification, travel vouchers, time sheets, overtime approvals, and expert witness testimonies."

"That's about enough Patrick. If you have much more than what you've already enumerated, you'll have to sneak it in. I'll have you a bid tomorrow."

"I look forward to it."

Before Patrick would let James escape he pointed out the multifarious assortment of files, folders, and loose papers. "I don't want to scare you, but all of these bad boys need a home."

"Yes you did. Your wife put you up to this as an appeasement to her new best friend and promised to make you your favorite dessert as a reward."

"Ha, ha. I'm glad you see the humor."

"But just like Hercules figured a way to clean the Augean stables, I will get this done. Give me until tomorrow morning to bring my bid—I promise it will be reasonable."

James decided to leave his car and walk the two blocks to the Hotel Lexington for lunch. Maybe he would bump into Agatha and start to mend fences.

Seated in a cozy restaurant with a dozen small tables, James decided this was a place frequented by more women than men. And after observing the waitstaff, cashier, and kitchen help he came to the conclusion that he was the only man in the entire place. He looked over the menu. No manly items. There was something wrapped in a grape leaf, dabs of meat and vegetables on a skewer, cucumber sandwiches, chicken salad, and . . .

"Well, good morning, James!"

James lowered his menu and stood to address the woman he had come to find. "Would you care to join me? I'm on my best behavior."

"Was last night's behavior your worst?"

"Yes, ma'am. Anything I do or say today will be an improvement. Please have a seat and give me a second chance."

"Mr. Dandae, America is the land of second chances—ask any immigrant."

James pulled out a chair for Agatha. "You look quite lovely this morning. May I ask what plans you have for the afternoon?"

"Yes, you may. I've been invited to sit in the audience while a group of actors rehearses a new play."

"Sounds like fun."

"Would you care to join me, Mr. Dandae?"

"I'm sorry but my afternoon is tied up. Let me order us something to drink." To the waitress standing at his elbow James said, "Miss, do you have Darjeeling tea? Right, then be so kind as to bring a pot and two cups, please. Is that all right with you, Miss Parker?"

"Splendid."

"So, Miss Parker, tell me how you came to be a missionary."

"An evangelist might be a more correct term. I'm not bringing the word to people who have never heard. My *modus operandi* is to bring back those who once believed, but have strayed."

"A major difference?"

"Yes. My adopted parents were advanced in age when I came into their lives. They were devout believers. They thought I was a miracle God had given them for being good stewards of the faith. I grew up thinking I was destined for a calling in His service. But it's hard for a woman to be accepted into any school of divinity, so I read what books I could and, when I thought I was sufficiently well versed, I gave a testimony in my church. It was well received, and a neighboring church asked if I would talk at one of their services while their minister was away. I went on from there to other churches in the area. That was five years ago."

"And the trust?"

"When my parents died I became depressed and mired in a swamp of self-pity. It was only through faith in the Savior and some kind words from a pen pal that I was able to recover. The will required their property be sold with the proceeds invested in an annuity. I now receive a substantial amount of money each month and will continue to do so for the rest of my life."

"Miss Parker, you are a marvel."

"Please, call me Agatha."

"Then you may call me Jim. I only let special people call me Jim. I consider it to be about halfway between James and darling."

"Jim, you are absolutely too funny. May I ask what activity you have planned today that is more important than spending time with me?"

"I have to do research at the library, but you are welcome to tag along."

"I don't do 'tag along.'"

"Okay, what can you tell me about the play?"

"Oh, I am so excited about it. An acquaintance in Arkansas wrote it. I say acquaintance, but actually, I've never met the man. He was mentioned in a religious magazine, from a letter he had sent in. And I wrote him to get a difficult theological concept clarified. We've written to each other for a number of years. Then one day, out of the blue, he sent a novel he had written."

"But, you said it was a play."

"Yes. I wrote back and asked if he would rewrite it as a play. So far I haven't received a reply, so I took the liberty of doing it myself."

"And you've never met him?"

"No. But he is so wise, he must be quite advanced in years."

"Agatha, I've been to Arkansas. Do you remember the name of the town where he lives?"

"Oh, yes. You can never forget a town with such an image provoking moniker as Dancing Deer."

"Dancing Deer? I've been there."

"How extraordinary. Is it a pretty town?"

"I don't remember. I was just passing through. Tell me the storyline of the play."

"All right. It's centered around a man who wants to be loved. He's middle aged with a wife and grown daughter, but the wife is a shrew. She berates his dignity, accuses him—with wild exaggeration—of his ill treatment of her, and laments how she could have done better. The abuse she flings at her husband has poisoned their daughter so that she too holds her father in contempt. The unhappy man spends very little time in their company.

"He holds down three jobs to supply his wife's many wants. And he comes into contact with several other women who have needs of their own. Quite by accident he fulfills the need each woman is seeking and each falls in love with him. But none of the women feel secure enough in the relationship to express the boundless love they harbor—which is the only thing that would make the man happy.

"Over the course of several years, the man's life with his wife deteriorates, and his romantic interludes outside of the marriage picks up steam to where the man is known throughout the land for being every woman's dream. His reputation reaches such mythical heights that women from all parts of the country descend on the town in which he lives to get a glimpse of the one man who could make their lives worth living.

"One of the women overcomes her reluctance and tells the man she loves him. He becomes ecstatic. The one thing denied him had been freely given. He is delirious with compassion toward the woman and keels over with a heart attack.

"The funeral is held in the largest church in town but it won't hold all of the women who show up. The story ends with the daughter oblivious to the entire affair and the wife and her mother looking around incredulously at all the weeping women who have shown up at her husband's funeral."

"What a marvelous story. If I were to complete my task at the library, might I be allowed to meet you at the rehearsal?"

"I'll have to think about it. I don't usually allow anyone to dictate terms or to require me to operate according to their schedule. With me, it has always been my way or the highway."

"Good gracious, lady. I am completely at your mercy."

"Well, if you understand at the outset that I take no prisoners and I will be the one to make all the decisions you are welcome to meet me should you finish your task early. The rehearsal will be in the ballroom, here, just above us on the second floor. It starts at four. And don't make any noise if you arrive after it begins."

James was mumbling incoherently when he entered the library. He walked straight to the information desk and asked if there were any books on coding.

A busiesswoman in her early thirties and a pencil stuck deep in her hair replied, "It depends on what's being coded or decoded."

"Information."

"Would you want that information coded alphabetically, geographically, chronologically, theoretically, . . .?"

"Systematically."

"According to whose system?"

"Mine."

"And what are the conventions of your system?"

"I haven't decided."

The woman shook her head. "That will be your first duty. Then you will have to decide how to store the information once it has been classified. And, finally, how to retrieve the stored information."

"Lady, how do you know so much about coding information? Is there a field of study?"

"Sir, if you will look around, you will see a large building full of information. Our cataloging system lets someone looking for a particular bit of information, find it. And the cataloging system gives the precise location of where it is stored. At the university level, that field of study is called library science."

"Ma'am, would you be interested in a little part-time work?"

"No."

"They pay you well here? You don't have a need for new clothes, shoes maybe, or a vacation to a warmer climate?"

"Well, there is a conference for librarians coming up in California."

"That's terrific. Here's what I propose. I'm contracting with the city to organize the police department, but I don't want to do it. How about you doing it, I act like I'm doing it, and we split the money sixty-forty. With you getting forty percent of the entire bill."

"You want me to do the work with you getting the credit?"

"Pretty much."

"How much money are we talking about?"

"It's a big job. I'm thinking about giving a bid of six thousand. And you wouldn't have to do all the work. I'd help, but it would be accomplished by performing according to your guidelines. I assume you have regular hours you work here."

"Yes."

"So you decide how everything needs to be coded, stored, and retrieved. And I'll work, per your instructions until you get off in the afternoon. For a few late hours each day we'll work together. During that time, you'll probably make a few changes to get us going faster with a better end result and I'll implement it the next day while you're here checking out books. I'll get the city to pay us in stages and we'll split each payment. So, can you use twenty-four hundred dollars for a couple of months' hard work?"

"How much would you pay me if I figured out the procedure and you did all of the work?"

"If you did it in elaborate detail to the nth degree, I'd give you twenty percent."

"So, if you billed six thousand dollars I'd get twelve hundred dollars for figuring out the details and another twelve hundred dollars if I worked beside you in the afternoons and evenings getting it done?"

"You are so smart."

"And I would be in charge?"

"Yep. As long as it looked like I was the one in charge. Otherwise, I don't think they would be willing to pay the big bucks."

"I won't do it."

"What?"

"You heard me. I won't do the work so a man can take the credit. See if you can find a man who can figure it out."

"Now listen here, sister."

"My name is Sam, Sam Crocker."

"Sam?"

"Short for Samantha. Now excuse me, I have people waiting to get information. Come back tomorrow when you have a better offer."

"Sam, you got an agent?"

On his walk back to the Hotel Lexington, James passed a gift shop and stepped inside.

"May I help you?"

"Just looking, thank you."

"We just got in a new shipment of picture frames. And there are all sorts of interesting gifts. Are you looking for something to give the woman in your life?"

"Ma'am, is it all right if I just look around . . . without being pestered."

"Certainly. At Elisa's Gifts, we take the attitude that the customer is always right. Let me tell you how the store is laid out so you can quickly go to the area you're interested in. Over here we have the figurines, the scrapbook supplies are in the front left corner, bead-making and stringing supplies are on that wall over there with the costume jewelry. Candles and fragrances are . . ."

"Lady, do you have a set number of words you have to get in each day?"

"What?"

"I only want to purchase some quality paper and escape with a calm spirit. Do you think we could dispense with the mindless chatter?"

"Well, I never . . ."

"The paper. Try and stay focused."

"Sir, you are a difficult man. May I offer you a cup of tea? You can't let your blood pressure go up. Here, look in this mirror. You're so red in the face and . . . what's with that finger?"

"It twitches when I get upset."

"Here . . . sit down. I'll go get you samples of the paper we have."

Ten minutes later James slinked out of the gift store with a package under his arm. What is it with the women in this town?

When he arrived at the Hotel Lexington, he took the elevator to the second floor. There may be something to the woman's observation. He was not feeling quite so good—he was in slow motion with the world speeding by.

Several ladies were filing through a door thirty feet down a wide hall from the elevator.

"Excuse me. Is this where the play is being rehearsed?"

"Yes it is. Have you come to play one of the parts?"

"Uh, no."

Agatha walked up. "Over here, Jim. I've got two seats close to the stage."

"Where are the props?"

"This is an early rehearsal. They haven't been assembled yet. Ssh, we have to be quiet."

Five women sat in chairs in a semi-circle on the stage with ten women in the audience. One of the women on the stage stood up and addressed the audience. In a rather loud voice she said, "If you refrain from talking during the rehearsal your presence will be allowed. But remember the actors have only read their lines in their homes. This is our first rehearsal and no one should expect it to be a polished production. That will come with time. After the rehearsal, we will take questions and make comments on our parts. I want to thank all of you for attending.

"When performed this will be the play's premiere performance. And we have the author in attendance. Miss Parker will you please stand?"

"Adeline, I am not the author. I altered a novel written by someone else, so it could be produced on a stage."

"Thank you, Miss Parker for that clarification. Now sit back and enjoy a wonderful new play adapted to the stage by Agatha Parker."

A pretty, young woman sitting on the stage got up from her chair and walked to the woman addressing the audience. She whispered something in Adeline's ear and returned to her chair. Adeline said, "Miss Parker, we don't have anyone to read the single male lead. Would you allow your escort to temporarily fill that role?"

"Why not ask me directly? I'm not a man under the thumb of any woman."

"Agatha, a little help."

Agatha Parker turned to James. "You remember what we talked about earlier? Now go on stage and read a few lines so these ladies can get started. It won't hurt you and I will be so appreciative."

"I now know why there are no men here."

While James was making his way to the stage, an additional chair was added to the semi-circle and a sheaf of papers placed in it.

James picked up the papers and read the first few paragraphs. "It says I'm supposed to be drying dishes."

"Just read the underlined words. Those are yours."

Adeline continued, "Okay. The first scene takes place in the kitchen of a small townhouse. Richard is drying dishes while his wife, Agnes, and daughter, Portia, sit at the kitchen table."

After a slight pause one of the seated women said, "And when you're through with the dishes, put the towel away. I don't want any dirty towels lying around my clean kitchen. And you better not break any more pieces of china."

Richard said, "I'll be careful."

Portia said, "Mom, we have to buy me new clothes. I can't start school in these rags."

Richard said, "Pumpkin, I bought you those rags two weeks ago."

"Richard, you moron, everyone knows that you have to have new clothes on your first day at school."

"But I don't get paid until a week from Friday. And I have bills. I can't spare any money until I work some overtime."

"Richard, don't pay one of your bills. The child has to have a couple of new dresses."

"I guess I could get a third job."

"You could get a better first job. Mom told me I shouldn't have married you that you'd never amount to anything. I should have listened to her. You'll never provide for us like a real man."

"Now, Agnes, don't be that way. I do the best I can."

"Well, the Taylors got new living room furniture and we still have the same we bought when we first got married. And Sheila's husband is taking her on a vacation to Florida. Richard, why can't we go somewhere?"

"Tomorrow I'll see about adding another job. School doesn't start till Monday. I've got the entire weekend."

After a pause Adeline said, "In scene two we have Richard's workplace with several desks arranged symmetrically with a water-cooler off to one side."

A female voice said, "What's the matter, Richard? You look tired. Can I get you a cup of water?"

"No. I'm just sleepy. I've taken another job as a night watchman. Last night I had to run off some kids who wanted to sling paint on the side of a building."

"Why do you need another job?"

"More money. Wait till you have kids. There isn't enough money in this world to satisfy all their wants."

"Not me. I'm not having kids."

"That's not what you said when you got married a few months ago. Nicole, what's that on your arm?"

"That's the reason I'm not having children."

"It looks like a cigarette burn. Has your husband been abusing you?"

"Richard, don't say anything. He's having a hard time right now at his job."

"Well. Nicole, I think you're in denial. I've heard some women lose their own identity when they come under the influence of an aggressive boyfriend or husband. Let's eat our lunch in the courtyard so I can tell you what to expect if you continue the relationship with no changes being made."

Adeline says, "At this point the actors go to their respective desks, the light dims with a weak spotlight focusing on a large wall clock. Richard puts a vase with a single red rose on Nicole's desk. The hands on the clock turn around the face to four-thirty the following afternoon.

Nicole is working at her desk. She now has a bandage on her chin. The telephone rings at Richard's desk."

"City water department. Richard Kelso speaking. May I help you?"

"Yes, ma'am. I remember your call."

"It's not turned on yet?"

"Yes, ma'am. I made out the work slip yesterday—right after you called."

"Yes, I know how important it is to have water."

"You know what. I go by your house on my way home every night. I'll pick up a wrench from the shop and be there in an hour."

"Yes, ma'am. We'll get it fixed today."

The pretty woman speaking Nicole's part stood and walked around the semi-circle of chairs till she was standing behind James. She paused and then reached down and ran her fingers through Richard's hair."

Adeline said, "Margo, we're only saying the lines."

"I know. But the audience might not understand what's happening unless they are privy to the undertones."

That night James dragged into his father's house. "Dad, you still got that typewriter?"

"Yeah, somewhere."

"Well, you need to find it. I got to type a bid to organize all the papers in the police department."

James' father started rummaging through the hall closet. From the top shelf, he lowered a small suitcase. "Here it is. In tip-top shape. It was your mother's, but she never used it much, not until she got that job at the newspaper then she had it serviced."

"Mom worked at the newspaper?"

"Yes. She wrote several letters to the editor and he came to the house one afternoon. I had heard he was a tyrant, but he minded his manners around your mother. He spent most of the afternoon trying to talk her into working for him. I was about to throw him out when your mother touched my arm saying she might give it a try. She started writing an article about the goings on in West Larimore. It was the focal point of the entire center section of the paper."

"Is there any other important information I don't know?"

"Did you know she was the moderator for those politicians when they came into town for a debate? She was in charge of the whole affair."

"Hell no. What did she know about politics?"

"Actually, quite a bit. That was what most of her letters to the editor were about. Did you know she was a Democrat—here in Indiana? Can you imagine? Told me while getting dressed for her first day on the job."

"My mother was a closet Democrat in a Republican stronghold. Dad, what's happening to the women?"

"Hard to say. Some think we should never have given in to their suffrage."

James set the typewriter on the kitchen table. He lifted the bar and inserted a sheet of paper against the circular platen and twisted a knob advancing the paper.

"Your mother always put in two sheets of paper."

"What for?"

"She told me the extra cushioning made the print more distinct."

James ripped out the single sheet of paper and inserted two. "You got any idea how a bid should be worded?"

"The insurance company made me get three when a hail storm tore up the roof. I'll go get them." When he returned, James was asleep with his head lying on the typewriter. Henry shook his son. "Boy, let me help you to bed."

James shook his head. "Naw, I got to type this bid. I told Patrick I'd bring it to him tomorrow morning."

"I'll do it for you. How much you asking?"

"Six thousand."

"Whew. That's a lot of money. Maybe I should wake you early in the morning."

CHAPTER 4

December 28, 1945

James handed over an envelope containing the bid he and his father had labored on all morning. Patrick unfolded the paper and looked closely at the bottom figure. He closed one eye and squinted the other half-closed while wrinkling his nose. Patrick said, "James, are you redoing our filing system or building an aircraft carrier?"

"I do exemplary work, Patrick. If you want a first-class job, you have to pay for the expertise. It will take me and an associate two months to finish the project. This is not an easy assignment."

"For this amount of money I'd expect all of the files to be linked together some way. And documentation available so we could keep it going long after you've skipped town with the city's money."

"Patrick, I broke it down into three projects. The employee personnel files, the case documents, and lumped everything else together as miscellaneous. I propose you let me do the personnel files first to see if you like my work and if you think it's worth the money I'm asking."

"And, if I don't?"

"You pay me half of that one project's itemized charge, so I can pay my associate, and I'll get a job digging ditches."

"Very well. I'll give it to the mayor this afternoon and get back to you with his determination."

Next door to Elisa's Gifts was a floral shop. James headed there with a determined attitude. He absolutely had to get the librarian on board.

"I would like a bouquet of red roses, please."

"Twelve or eighteen?"

"I think six will be plenty."

"Six?"

"Yeah, six. And some green foliage, some baby's breath—you know, with the white puffs, and a pretty vase."

"If you'll pick out a vase I'll put it together while you wait. Do you need a card? Will you need for me to deliver it?"

"No. Just put it together in this vase." James handed the clerk a green piece of pottery.

"It'll just take a minute."

While James waited, Adeline walked in and began looking at the accessories. She picked up several, appraised their values compared to the asking price, and replaced the items in their display location before spying James loitering around the checkout counter.

Holding out her hand, she said, "Sir, my name is Addy Moline. You did a fine job performing as Richard in our play. Do you have experience as an actor?"

"James Dandae, Miss Moline. Yes, I've done some acting—of sorts."

The clerk set down the bouquet of roses on the counter and wrapped the top in loose tissue paper. That will be three twenty-five, sir.

James handed the man a five dollar bill. To Addy, he nodded his head, pocketed the change, and said, "Good day, Miss Moline."

At the library, James went straight to the information desk and casually unfastened the tissue paper before placing the vase in front of an impressed librarian.

"How lovely. Are you planning on getting me to change my mind through bribery?"

"By whatever works, Sam."

"Bring me chocolate and we'll talk."

"Flowers aren't enough?"

"They're a good start. Have they given you the contract?"

"Not yet."

"See me tomorrow."

"Mr. Peterson, I'd like a moment of your time."

"What are you selling, sonny?"

"I'm not selling anything, Mr. Peterson. I'm James Dandae. I came to apologize for robbing you twenty years ago. I've brought your gun back and I need to know how much the silver dollars were worth."

"Your mother has already paid me for what you took. She got a job at the newspaper, and then came by every Friday for a year. Boy, you owe that woman a lot."

"I do for a fact. Do you want the gun? I don't need it anymore."

"Not really. I replaced it with a newer model and don't need two. I guess I could donate it to the police."

"No. Don't do that. If you don't want it, I'll give it to my father. And I want to tell you I am very sorry for the theft. I've changed my ways and plan on spending my life making amends for the misery I've caused. Thank you, sir, for listening to me."

After a light meal on the first floor of the Hotel Lexington, James took out his sheaf of papers and started reading the play. It was well written. Maybe, they would need him to say Richard's lines again. At a few minutes before four, he walked up a flight of stairs and saw the women congregated by the door to the ballroom.

To a slender brunette, James said, "May I watch the rehearsal again?"

"Certainly. But the man playing Richard will be reading his part this time."

"That's quite all right. I enjoyed performing but knew it was another man's lead."

"Sir, is Miss Parker with you?"

"No. I haven't talked to her since yesterday's performance."

Addy Moline walked over and said, "James, let me introduce you. Ladies, this is James Dandae. James, this is Margo. She plays Nicole and Michelle."

Margo was a tall slender brunette, an attractive woman in her early twenties. James shook hands all around but in a few minutes had forgotten all but the two names of Addy and Margo.

When they entered the ballroom Margo had linked her arm through his. She said, "James, my father mentioned you might be working on the mess at the police department."

"And your father is?"

"John Pauline, the mayor."

"Okay everybody take your seats. The audience will now be let in."

Agatha came through the door holding onto the arm of a stocky man in a three-piece suit. He reached into his vest and pulled out a pocket watch attached to a gold fob. After determining the time the man snapped it shut and put the watch into his pocket, helped Agatha to a seat, and walked onto the stage.

More people came in. This time at least twenty people would be watching the rehearsal. Agatha caught James' eye, raised her hand slightly, and wriggled four fingers. She had a big smile on her face.

"Ladies and gentlemen, this will be our second rehearsal. Yesterday we did not complete the play when our time ran out. So today we will continue. We've added a few props and the actors can remain seated or stand and use the props—whatever they feel comfortable with.

"Today, we have Reginald Howard playing Richard. We also want to express our appreciation to Mr. James Dandae for filling in yesterday for Mr. Howard.

"We start this afternoon's performance in the kitchen with Richard and Agnes."

After a pause the actor playing Agnes said, "So how goes it with your new job? I've noticed you haven't increased the grocery money."

One of the women sitting on stage nudged Reginald with her un-shoed foot.

"Uh . . . Oh yes, here it is. Uh . . . I don't have any extra money. You've saddled me with more bills. This third job has to pay them. Agnes, why did we need a new divan? I'm barely making ends meet. We can't be purchasing things we don't need."

"You stupid idiot. You have to have a place to put that big arse."

"Addy, do you think we could have this sentence reworded. I don't feel comfortable using vulgar words."

"Stick to the script for now."

"It was on sale. Richard, if you look at it like that I saved you money. Now I want that money to buy more groceries."

After a pause someone said, "Richard? Richard, it's your turn."

"Oh, I beg your pardon. Agnes, I don't think you know how money works."

"Yes I do. You bring it home and give it to me and I use it to run the house and to buy the things I need. What else is there to know?"

"For one thing you need to know how much is available."

"If you made more money there wouldn't be any problem. You need to go into your boss's office and tell him you need a raise. Tell him how hard you work. Lord knows how often you tell me. Richard, are you a man or a dog waiting for table scraps? Tell him if he doesn't give you a pay raise you're going to quit. See how he likes that."

"Agnes, maybe you should get a job. There are a lot of women in the workplace these days."

"You ignoramus. I can't work. Who'd take care of the house? You do what I tell you or I'll rap my rolling pin against your skull."

"Oh, all right. But you have to have them take the divan back."

"I will not. You work for the city, as a night watchman for the construction yard, and free-lance as a plumber. With all that income, you should have plenty to provide for me and your daughter—and give Mother a few dollars for her bills."

"Well, I don't. When I get up to go to work, you're still in bed. I have to make my own lunch and when I get home late at night, you say it's too late to cook my supper. On weekends, I work all day and night. Do you think Portia could bring me something to eat once in a while?"

"No. You should take it with you when you go after work on Friday. That poor girl is trying to figure out algebra and can't be bothered."

Addy walked to the front of the stage. "In the next scene we are in a woman's apartment. Richard is fixing her washing machine after working all day at the water department."

"Miss Holloway, you look awfully pretty this evening."

"That's very kind of you Mr. Kelso. I don't feel pretty. In fact, I don't remember anyone ever telling me that before."

"No one has ever said you look pretty?"

"My mother, when I was a child. But no, I can't think of anyone else."

"I think they would if you wore makeup. A woman is like a sign. A blank board never gets noticed. But one with lots of color and a pleasing picture attracts attention. Start off with a little blush and a soft pastel color for your eyelids. See how that works, then add mascara to your eyelashes and a conservative shade of lipstick. Try one thing at a time, ease into it."

"I would never have thought you were so knowledgeable about women's cosmetics."

"I'm not. I just know what I like and projected that onto you."

"Tell me what you like in women's clothes."

"Well, fashions vary by the season. Usually, the designers pick a particular woman's body part and design around that. Then the next season or years later if the previous style was a resounding success, they'll conceal the previous choice and pick another. Take the length of your skirts. Some years they're short exhibiting a long length of leg and a few years later they cover it up with hems to the floor. In those years, they may be showing a woman's cleavage."

"Mr. Kelso, what do you think about my cleavage?"

"Miss Holloway, in today's fashions the cleavage is concealed and the legs are covered. Women are wearing slinky tight-fitting skirts and high heels giving prominent display to their *derrieres*.

"Miss Holloway, hand me that wrench. I just about have it fixed."

"Richard, would you call me something other than Miss Holloway? It sounds so formal. And I feel like we have a closer connection than that between a woman and her plumber."

"I could call you Michelle."

"You can't think of something just between you and me?"

"Michelle, I'm a married man."

"Not happily married. No one could be happily married to that woman."

"How about I call you tiger. I think with a bit of effort you could break away from that conservative assessment you have of yourself and be the assertive beauty I see."

"Richard, I would prefer something soft and feminine."

"Michelle, when I look at you I see a beautiful princess."

"Addy, would a man actually talk like this? I'm afraid I'm going to be either sneered at or laughed off the stage."

"Okay. Let's take a break. We'll ask the audience what they think."

Addy walked again to the front of the ballroom floor, but this time with a glass of water. "Does anyone have a comment?"

"If I found my husband messing around with those women, a lack of income would be the least of his worries."

"According to the novel the play is based on, there are not any indications that the relationships Richard has with those women are physical in any way. He fulfills a psychological need and nothing more. Of course, there could be intimacy if Richard were so inclined. I mean the women would probably be for it."

Reginald Howard said, "Does anyone think the role between Richard and Agnes is believable? I would beat that woman and, if that didn't put her in her place, I'd show her the door."

"Mr. Dandae, would you give us your perspective?"

"Sure. Richard wants someone to love him. And all he has for comparative purposes is how he's treated by his wife. He would first like for his wife to treat him humanely, because if he left her for one of the other women, it could be that the new woman would become what the wife already is. So until he finds true love he keeps treading water, putting up with his wife, working as hard as he can, and helping the other women he comes into contact with overcome their problems.

"If one of those other women tells Richard they love him—and he believes them—at that point he will escape from the harpy that is his wife and smother the new woman with all the love she can handle."

CHAPTER 5

December 29, 1945

"James, Patrick called. He said, if you didn't mind tying up part of your Saturday, the mayor wants to talk with you. Can you meet with them at Pauline's Café for lunch? He said to be there at twelve-thirty. Son, you might be awarded that contract."

"Yeah, but it's one bugger of a job. Do you know where I can buy a box of chocolates?"

"You might try Elisa's Gifts on Main. They've got everything I have yet to find a need for."

"I know where it is. The woman who runs the place has a motor for a mouth and no governor. Say, if I were wearing ear muffs I might be able to make a statement."

"It wouldn't work. When people have a problem like that, they don't think they have a problem and everyone who makes mention of it is either mistaken or have their own problem. Did she accuse you of being a difficult person?"

"Yeah."

"I rest my case."

James made his way to see the talkative woman. "Ma'am, do you have chocolates?"

"Yes I do. I have rich, dark chocolate from Switzerland and Belgium."

"Do you sell by the pound or are they boxed?"

"Boxed."

"May I see them?"

"Certainly. Follow me. Are you James Dandae?"

"Guilty."

"I had two ladies talk about you this morning. They said you are quite intuitive about love. And they're disappointed you will not be portraying some character in an upcoming play. Mr. Dandae, what made them think you were knowledgeable in matters of the heart?"

"Huh?"

"Did you spout some wisdom, some intelligent approbation of the intimate art?"

"Uh."

"Really, Mr. Dandae. You can't make such a deep observation, such an important discernment, such a delectable reflection to my friends and come in here and act the problematic rascal to me."

"Ma'am?"

"Out with it, Mr. Dandae. Why do those women consider you the consummate elocutionist of the most important issue to the female gender?"

"I . . . I have no idea."

"How bad do you want those chocolates?"

"Pretty bad."

"I am the sole purveyor of quality chocolate in town. When you are ready to sit with me and tell me what I want to hear, then I'll give you the chocolates."

James scheduled his arrival at Pauline's Café at exactly twelve-thirty. Patrick met him at the cashier's station and escorted him to a corner table. A bald man in his fifties stood next to his chair and held out his hand.

"Mr. Dandae, I'm John Pauline, the mayor of West Larimore. Please, have a seat. Patrick has been telling me that his office is in disarray and he needs two new employees hired as records clerks."

"Mayor, sir, what Patrick needs is a self-service filing room that any responsible police officer can walk in and find what he wants on his own. A filing room so logically laid out that adding more records, as normal day-to-day activity requires, would be as simple as opening a desk drawer and raking off everything laying loose. If he had such an organized filing system, there would be no need for additional filing clerks."

"That's precisely what I told him. Mr. Dandae, I like the way you talk."

James was feeling pretty good when he strolled into the library. At the information desk, he found the woman he had come to talk with. "Sam, I've been offered the contract."

"That's wonderful. Do you have the chocolates?"

"Let's talk about that. The city is having a budget crisis. They can only afford to pay four thousand. I told them I would have to talk it over with my associate."

"Well, I'm sure you and your associate will be able to figure out a way to get the work done on the reduced amount."

"I'd really like to work with you."

"But there are no chocolates."

"The lady wouldn't sell me any unless I . . . unless I . . ."

"Yes. Unless you what?"

"Sam, show me where you have the biographies stashed."

At two o'clock James headed to Elisa's Gifts. He had to figure a way to get the woman to sell him chocolates. When he entered the store, a tiny bell announced his presence.

"Hello ma'am, I've come to talk to you about the chocolates."

"Just a minute." The lady went into the back room removed her apron, run her fingers through her hair, checked her appearance in the mirror, picked up a purse, and grabbed James by the arm on the way out. They stopped only long enough for the woman to turn over her open sign and lock the door."

"What about your store?"

"It can wait. Let's step into the Hotel Lexington and sit at one of their tables while you earn the chocolates."

James grabbed a handful of cellophane wrapped mints at the register and followed the woman and a waitress to a table. He pulled out a chair for the proprietor of Elsie's Gifts and sat down himself. Looking around the tiny restaurant, James realized there were no other men customers. No women customers either.

"I don't know where those women are coming from." James used his free hand to open the menu. "I have never been married. Never fallen in love. Never had anyone tell me they loved me, other than my mother. If I made a remark on love, you can be assured it was not from experience I spoke." James closed the menu and placed it back on the table. "Maybe it was the lack of experience or wishful thinking that made me speak up. We all hope one day to find someone to complete us.

"Plato, a Greek philosopher, suggested that humans were first formed with four legs, four arms, and two faces. Then the Greek God, Zeus decided humans were too proud and had them cut in half and dispersed throughout the land. Each new creature began searching for his other half, his soul-mate, to be complete again. I have not found my soul-mate, but I keep looking.

"There are several great love stories I suggest you research. The first is the love of Napoleon for Josephine and the second, Clara Schumann for her husband, Robert. Of course, I would be remiss if I left out maybe the greatest love of all time—the love between Elizabeth Barrett Browning and her husband and fellow poet, Robert Browning."

James piled the mints on the table in front of the woman. He picked one up and said, "One, I love." James set the mint to one side and picked up a second. "Two, I love." He added the second mint to the second pile. "Three, I cast away." James made a motion of throwing the mint, but the woman could not see the mint being hurled nor hear it crash when it landed. "Four, I love with all my heart. Five, I love, I say. Six, he loves me. Seven, he don't. Eight, he'll marry me. Nine, he won't. Ten, he would if he could, but he can't. Eleven, he comes. Twelve, he tarries. Thirteen, he's waiting. Fourteen, he marries." James now had all the mints in two piles.

"At this point the little girl—sometimes an adult woman—starts reciting the rhyme again until she has exhausted the original group of whatever it was she was using."

"And, Mr. Dandae, what does this have to do with your wisdom of love?"

"Only that women are entranced with the idea of love from a very early age. And it manifests itself in their psyches in different ways as they grow older. I think you want me to affirm your particular speculation. You need to know if it is true and not mere whimsy. And, if it is true, is it worthy of your time."

A waitress was standing directly behind James. "I hate to interrupt this wonderful dialog, but I was wondering if you've had a chance to look at the menu."

"So it's true. Mr. Dandae, you can see into a woman's heart."

The waitress smiled and nodded her head.

"Ma'am, I've already had lunch. Maybe you could choose one of their wonderful teas for us and possibly a confection of some sort."

When the waitress left with their order, the woman said, "Continue, Mr. Dandae."

James took a small collection of papers from his vest pocket and opened them. "Since I have never been in love I'll have to defer to the utterances of someone who is immersed in its clutches. This is a quote from a letter sent to Clara Baker by Robert Burdette in 1898.

"And when I have reasoned it all out, and set metes and bounds for your love that it may not pass, lo, a letter from Clara, and in one sweet, ardent, pure, Edenic page, her love overrides my boundaries as the sea sweeps over rocks and sands alike, crushes my barriers into dust out of which they were builded, overwhelms me with its beauty, bewilders me with its sweetness, charms me with its purity, and loses me in its great shoreless immensity."

"Mr. Dandae that is beautiful, but what does it mean?"

"It means that you can't put boundaries on love. That love—if love is true—is such a pervasive and expansive feeling that it can't be contained."

The woman rested her chin in her hands and gazed into the eyes of James. "Tell me more, Mr. Dandae. I need more."

"This quote is from a letter sent by Katherine Mansfield, a New Zealand-born writer, to John Middleton Murray in 1918.

"My love for you tonight is so deep and tender that it seems to be outside myself as well. I am fast shut up like a little lake in the embrace of big mountains. If you were to climb up the mountains, you would see me down below, deep and shining—and quite fathomless, my dear. You might drop your heart into me and you'd never hear it touch bottom. I love you . . . I love you . . . goodnight.

Oh, Bogey, what it is to love like this!"

"So what am I supposed to learn from this one?"

"That love can be thought of as a tangible state of mind. Did you recognize her imagery? First it was outside of her body, then it was a small lake surrounded by sheltering mountains, Then, even though it was small compared to the mountains, it was fathomless. And if Mr. Murray were to drop his heart into its depths it would never reach bottom."

"That is so beautiful."

"I have one more. Ninon de L'Enclos, a French courtesan during the reign of Louis XIV, wrote to Marquis de Sevigny in the late 1600s.

"Today a new sun rises for me; everything lives, everything is animated, everything seems to speak to me of my passion, everything invites me to cherish it. The fire consuming me gives to my heart, to all the faculties of my soul, a resilience, an activity which is diffused through all my affections. Since I loved you, my friends are dearer to me; I love myself more; . . . the sounds of my lute seem to me more moving, my voice more harmonious."

"So?"

"So, my good lady, you are correct. Being in love—even if it is just with the idea of love—makes you a happier woman, a woman more in tune with her life, a deeper more interesting woman to those she comes into contact with, and a woman completely satisfied with herself."

"Mr. Dandae, how many boxes of chocolate would you like?"

After escorting the woman back to her store, James walked the two blocks farther to the Library. "Sam, I have chocolates."

"Mr. Dandae, you'll have to control your enthusiasm and the volume of your speech. We are in a library after all."

"Yes, well let me give these to you before some woman comes and steals them away. You would not believe the effort I've had to make."

"Were they that expensive?"

"Expensive? No, they were free. I only had to convince a woman that love was just around the corner."

"Well, it appears to me, you could sell an annuity to a dying man, but let's talk about the project. You realize that the money they pay you is a matter of public record. There is no way you could tell me something I could not find the truth of for myself."

"Uh, no. I wasn't aware of that. The correct amount is five thousand. Your share calculates to two thousand."

"I want half—twenty-five hundred."

"My God, lady. I've done all the work. I've had to make the proposal. Sell it to the mayor. It's my neck on the line. I think forty percent is more than reasonable."

"You might be correct, but I'm holding all the cards."

"Damnit, give me back those chocolates."

"Mr. Dandae, you don't want to do that."

"You're right. Keep the blooming chocolates. Is there any way I can achieve a little manly dignity from our agreement?"

"Yes, if you look at the big picture. I propose we form a company with you as President. We'll each own half and you can use this first customer as a calling card to sell the same service to other police departments across the state. I'll supervise a clerk or two to do the actual work and we'll split the profit. This first one is only a stepping stone. James, you could become a wealthy man."

"I feel like I'm buying an iceberg floating south for the summer."

Sam opened the lid of the chocolates and reached in for a piece. She held out the box to James. "Let's celebrate the new arrangement with a delicious piece of Belgium chocolate."

James reached in with new energy. "Sam, I have to hand it to you. I thought I was the flim-flam artist, but I could take some pointers from you."

"Nonsense. We'll earn that five thousand and, from that small beginning, we'll parlay it into a business they'll talk of around conference tables from here to Denver. By the way, a young lady stormed in here this morning, and demanded I tell her who gave me the roses."

"Oh, no. Did she give you a name?"

"No. When I told her it was James Dandae, she did an about-face and marched out the door."

"What did she look like?"

"Very pretty. Flashing eyes. Pouty. I'm sorry I can't do any better than that, James. I was busy at the time."

James left Sam after talking her into taking a day off on Monday so the two of them could meet with Patrick. Sam would have to know the magnitude of the work and find out from Patrick what he thought were the important aspects of each case and how they should be linked.

He almost ran to the Hotel Lexington. On the second floor, people were milling around waiting to be admitted to the third rehearsal. Margo walked over and put her arm through his.

"James, what can we do? Reginald was offered the part weeks ago."

"I'm sorry. Don't you think he'll do a good job?"

"No. We're all in agreement that you would be a better choice. But there's nothing we can do. We've done several plays already and he's been in all of them. There's no way we want to make him mad. Addy thought about requiring him to wear stupid clothing. She thought he might tell her he wouldn't do it that she should ask someone else. Would you play the part if you had to wear stupid clothing?"

"Margo, I think he needs to act the part. He's earned it. If I can be of assistance by helping to make the stage props or filling in if he gets sick, I'll do it in a heartbeat. But I don't want to take the man's job."

"That's so big of you, James." Margo gave his arm an affectionate squeeze. She had a look of wonder on her face.

"I know, but that's the way I am."

James found himself a seat, while Margo made her way to the stage. And Agatha made her way through the door—again on the arm of Reginald Howard. James shook his head. What does she see in that dipstick?

Addy walked to the front of the stage and said, "Ladies and gentlemen. Take your seats. This is our third rehearsal and we'll pick up where we left off on the previous one. Make way for Mr. Howard.

"Please refrain from talking or exiting during the rehearsal. We will take occasional breaks and after the rehearsal we will stay to listen to your comments and to answer any questions you may have.

"The first scene in today's rehearsal is in the office. Nicole and Richard are talking about Nicole's black eye."

After a short pause, Nicole said, "What am I to do? I have to work. He doesn't get in enough hours when we have rainy weather to pay the bills. And the weeks when he can work full-time, he still takes off a day or two because he partied with the boys and doesn't feel like getting up. And, if I give him a hard time about it, he rants and raves until he's worked himself into a frenzy and lashes out like he did this morning."

"Nicole, it's only going to get worse. He doesn't think he has a problem. He thinks it's all your fault. You have to realize the man is sick—not physically but mentally. It'll just get worse until you've had enough. Hopefully, you'll come to that realization before he does any lasting damage—say break a leg or cause permanent damage by a punch to the stomach. You need to have an escape plan already made up."

"What do you mean? An escape plan?"

"Exactly. His aggression will escalate to the point he might do something . . . something we don't want to think about. If you pay attention to the intensity of his fits, you might be able to decide beforehand when it's time to leave. Have a plan. Take some clothes to a girl-friend's house, have an extra set of keys made for the car, a second makeup bag stashed somewhere. Put some money away—a little at a time so he won't suspect anything."

"Oh, I don't know, Richard. I love the man. I just need to back off and leave him alone when he gets that way."

"Nicole, you listen to me. It's not your fault. You are a beautiful woman. You deserve a good marriage, to a good man. The worst thing that can happen to you, besides being hurt physically, is if he beats down your self-esteem. You have to stand up for your rights. Find out from your friends if you can come to one of their houses if he gets out of hand, because, you'll need a place to stay. He'll come looking for you, so she needs to be a friend he doesn't know or one with a kick-butt husband."

"Richard, we better get back to work. It would be the worst of all possible events if I lost my job." Richard and Nicole left the water cooler and walked to their desks. Nicole grabbed Richard's hand. "Richard, thank you so much. You don't know how much you've helped me."

Addy spoke over the address system. "Here the lights dim and the hands on the clock move to five o'clock. The employees start putting their desks in order before leaving for the day. The telephone starts ringing on Richard's desk."

"City water department. Richard Kelso speaking. May I help you?"

"Hello, Agnes."

"Yes. I'll be coming straight home."

"How long will she be staying?"

"Okay. But tell me this, where will I be sleeping?"

"No. It's not all right. I'm not happy with that arrangement. You tell her we don't have an extra bed. And damnit, Agnes, she has her own house."

"I don't care. It's my home and I don't want to sleep on the divan."

"Oh, all right. Give me the list."

"Agnes, I can't afford all this."

"Okay, I'll do the best I can. Good-bye, Agnes."

"In our second scene, Richard makes it home with a sack of groceries. He comes in the kitchen door and finds his wife, his mother-in-law, and his daughter standing in front of the refrigerator with its door open." Addy sat down.

After a slight pause, Agnes said, "Richard, you idiot. What do you mean by eating all the food? I can't even make Mother a sandwich."

"I see hot dogs from here. And there's a container of tuna fish."

"Richard, use your head. You know momma doesn't eat anything but chicken."

"Here, I bought some at the store. Just take it and let me go to my chair. I've had a hard day."

"Well, whoop-de-do." Agnes slapped her thigh. "You've had a hard day. Don't you think one of us might have had a hard day? What gives you the right to sit down while we prepare your meal? Really, Richard, you lazy nincompoop."

"Agnes, I tried to warn you. You gave him the best years of your life and this is how he repays you: an empty refrigerator and sitting on his butt while you slave in the kitchen. Makes me want to take a rolling pin to him."

"Richard, someone by the name of Hazel called. She said her sink had backed up again. That you'd know who she is."

"Yes, I know her. Give me a couple of slices of bread, will you? I better go fix it."

"Watch your step when you get back. I won't have you waking Mother. You know what a light sleeper she is."

"In our third scene, Richard is sitting in a swing on a woman's front porch with a plate of food in his lap. A woman sits beside him."

"Hazel, you make the best rolls. So there wasn't anything wrong with your sink after all?"

"No. I just wanted to see your handsome face."

"And to tell me your son doesn't have time to come by for a visit, to send you a birthday card, or even to call."

"Yes, just like last year."

"Then let me tell you. Happy birthday, Hazel."

"Thank you, Richard."

"He's missing a wonderful meal, Hazel. Do you put vinegar in your peas? They taste tart. I like it."

"Richard, you are so easy to please. I never could satisfy my boy. Teddy would complain that I used too much salt or too little. The potatoes were too done. There weren't enough vegetables. It was always something. You, on the other hand, love everything I fix. I have pineapple upside-down cake for dessert."

"Hazel, if I didn't already have a family I'd move in with you. You could take care of me."

"I'd do it." Hazel took a napkin to dust a bread crumb from Richard's shirt. She said, "After you finish eating I thought we'd go inside and listen to the radio. Would you like to see my pictures?"

"Now, you know I can't stay gone for long. Agnes thinks I'm working."

"You are working—just not repairing a clogged sink. I'll pay you for your time."

"Hazel, I can't take your money for talking."

"Richard, when you go home your wife will be holding out her hand for the money. I have plenty. Just take it and make everybody happy. Besides if you don't take the money, I would feel like I was imposing and I so like our evenings together."

"But, I'm a married man."

"Oh, pooh on that. You don't love her. She certainly doesn't love you. And besides I don't want anything physical. I just need a little male companionship."

"Okay, let's go organize those pictures."

Addy walked to the front of the stage. "Ladies and gentlemen, does anyone have a comment?"

A lady behind Agatha raised her hand. "I think Nicole needs to start packing."

"I think she does. There are no scenes of her in this act, but she eventually gets fed up with the abuse and leaves with her clothes."

"No, I mean packing a gun. I'm from Texas and most of us tote a gun of some sort. The men have rifles on the rear window racks of their trucks. We women have ours in large purses. Mine's loaded. I can whip it out and have it cocked and aimed in less than eight seconds. If Nicole's husband knew his wife was carrying a gun, he might think twice about pulling any of those shenanigans. He might get his head blown off."

"You, sir. You have your hand up? You have a question or a comment?"

"Yes, I do. Is there any action in this thing?"

"Addy, I'll answer that." Reginald walked to the front to stand beside his director. "No, there is not one bit of action. I have suggested that if they would let me take a swing at Agnes or spank Portia I'd pony up a meal for the entire company after our first performance. So far, no one has taken me seriously."

Agatha raised her hand. "Mr. Howard, do you think taking a swing at Agnes or spanking Portia would be the proper action for a man every woman, other than his family on stage, loves, and every woman in the audience is comparing her husband to?"

"I don't think any woman should be allowed to talk to her husband the way Agnes does to Richard. A thrashing would do her good."

Another woman raised her hand. "I'd like to hear what Mr. Dandae has to say."

James looked around. Every person in the audience and on stage was looking straight at him. "Well . . . I . . . uh . . . I think Richard is a gentleman. He could resort to roughing up his wife, but it would not be true to his character. Richard is a mild-mannered man who wants his marriage to work out. When his wife makes things unbearable, he resorts to additional work.

"It's the women who seek him. He exhibits what they want to see in their husbands or boyfriends—a kind, considerate, passionate, caring man who would not harm another individual even if his own happiness were at stake. But if he simply walks out, then he's not really hurting his wife. He's just giving her what she had been saying she wanted. The problem is his wife was loving and considerate before they got married, and he is not so sure that these other women wouldn't turnout the same way. He does know Agnes does not love him now, but no one else has intimated that they love him either. So he puts up with his wife's belligerence and keeps looking for that one woman who will willingly express her love for him—the love he's looking for."

"Bravo, Mr. Dandae."

CHAPTER 6

December 30, 1945

"James, would you like to go to church with me?"

"Uh . . . sure, Dad. How long have I got before we have to leave?"

"About an hour."

Swinging his feet out from under the covers, James sat up and rubbed his eyes. "Will Agatha be there?"

"She was last week. Do you see something in her that interests you?"

"Yeah."

"She sure is pretty, but I want to give you a word of caution. That woman is a good person but a tempest in a teapot. Whoever marries her will have a challenge. She doesn't let anyone tell her what to do, to set the agenda, or to regulate her time. She'll have to be handled with kid gloves, until she figures out that marriage is a team effort, and individualism impedes progress. You might be just the person for her. But, more aptly, she might be just the person for you."

"What do you mean by that?"

"Well James, you've always been a man no one could tell what to do. You were a rebel. And that would have been all right if you'd had a grown up attitude. But a man with a wild streak, one who doesn't take direction from his elders, and with an adolescent view of things will always be in trouble. Being shackled to a woman like Agatha would either make him or break him. I think she'd be good for you. Give you the guidance no one else was able to."

"I was a handful, wasn't I?"

"Always."

James spent the morning listening to a powerful sermon about Paul getting his churches to stick to the path. Agatha did not show and he didn't know anyone in the congregation so, after he and his dad had a meal at Pauline's Café, James asked his father for Jacqueline's address in Lindale.

It had been snowing for several hours and the road to Lindale was treacherous—especially crossing the bridges. Lindale was about half the size of West Larimore. It was built near a famous river crossing with residential areas extending out in three directions from the small downtown area. Finding the house wasn't hard but James retreated back to town anyway. He had decided he should call first.

"Hello, is this Jackie?"

"Yes, who's calling?"

"It's James Dandae, Jackie."

"Jimmy? I don't believe it. After all these years."

"It's good to hear your voice, Jackie."

"Jimmy, where are you calling from?"

"A small cafe downtown called the Lindale Steakhouse. Do you think we could meet?"

"Yes, I guess there's no way around it. You stay where you are. I'll be there in fifteen minutes."

James picked up a local newspaper and followed a waitress to a booth. "I'm waiting for someone, so I'll order after she arrives. In the meantime, would you bring a cup of black coffee?"

James read the newspaper. When he was halfway through the want ads, his high school sweetheart approached. James stood and reached out to hug the stranger he once knew.

She pulled back. "No, Jim. Don't touch me. There's no way you can leave for twenty years and finally return to pick up where you left off."

"I understand. Let me help you with your coat. You look marvelous."

"I do not. I've put on fifty pounds. You, on the other hand, look emaciated. You smoke or drink?"

"Not for the last few years. Jackie, tell me about you. When I left, you thought you were pregnant. Did you have the baby?"

"Yes. Even after it's no good father ran off. I had to move here to start over."

"Dad thinks you've become a teacher. Did you go to college?"

"I wanted to but that was out of the question. My family helped me until I could get a job. I worked at the hospital—eventually becoming a licensed nurse. For the past ten years I've worked as the school nurse so I could be around my boy."

"Our boy."

"No, my boy. You gave up your parental right when you cut and ran."

"Jackie, I've changed."

"Too late. I'm seeing someone. He loves me and Michael looks up to him as the father you never were."

"I completely understand. Would it be possible for me to meet Michael? You wouldn't have to tell him I was his father. I could be a friend you haven't seen for a long time."

"I'll have to think about it. A slip of the tongue could cause a lot of problems. I'd have to feel comfortable you're not trying to pull something over on me. Jimmy, I know you. You couldn't have changed that much."

"I see. Well, how about me giving you an address and a telephone number. Jackie, I really would like to see Michael—even if it's from a distance."

"Jim, Michael is grown up. The boy will soon be twenty years old. Still, I'm not sure I have the right to keep you from him. He might should be afforded the opportunity to meet his real father, the scoundrel who messed up his mother's life. If I decide to let you see him, I'll call. How long will you be here?"

"I'm not going anywhere. I've come back to take care of Dad."

Jackie stood from her chair and grabbed her coat. "We'll see."

James traveled back to West Larimore with a depressed attitude. He pulled the black Ford into his father's drive and sat for a few minutes wondering if it was all worth it. Maybe he should shuck this town and go back to the lifestyle he had once lived. The one where he was running from the law, robbing banks, and shooting people. No, that was not going to happen. James went into his house. He wanted to spend some quality time with the one individual who knew how he really was and loved him anyway. The only one that was that way and still alive.

"Dad, you want to play some Gin Rummy?"

"That might be fun." James' dad went looking for the cards. From the bedroom he called out, "James, a woman called. She left her number—and it wasn't Agatha. I wrote it down by the telephone."

James picked up the receiver and dialed the number.

A woman answered, "Pauline's residence."

"Hello. My name is James Dandae. I received a telephone call from this number. Pardon me, is this the mayor's house?"

"Yes it is, let me get him for you."

"Hello, Mr. Dandae. I think it was my daughter who was calling. I'll give the telephone to her. Are you going to be able to start the project on Monday?"

"Yes, sir."

"Good. Here she is."

"James, this is Margo. I called to invite you to a New Year's Eve party. Everyone's going to be there. Several have asked me to call you."

"Who will be there I know?"

"All the members of the cast, your friend Patrick and his wife, Cynthia. Reginald is bringing Agatha Parker. There are some others, but they're friends of my parents."

"Do I need to bring a date?"

"No, James. You'll be with me."

CHAPTER 7

December 31, 1945

On Monday morning, the 31st of December, 1945, James was up early. At eight, he arrived at the West Larimore Bakery, which happened to be across the street from police headquarters. Patrick had requested that James start his first day at nine so the normal shift change would already have been accomplished and everyone supposed to be there would be clocked in and at their desk. Evidently Patrick had a regular routine in starting his day and wanted James to arrive after he had finished with it.

Sam was sitting at a table with her chair facing the front door. She was smartly dressed. James felt he should have worked harder on his shoes and adjusted his tie before sitting at Sam's table. He didn't want anyone to think Sam was the boss.

"Good morning, Sam. Are you ready for our first day?"

"I am. Are you?"

"I'm worried I might have cut a bigger slice than I can eat."

"Don't be. This is my bailiwick. You do the selling and I'll get it done. That was our deal. Do you think a stiff shot of black coffee might be in order?"

"I do. Do you know anyone in city government?"

"No."

"How long have you lived here?"

"Two weeks."

"Only two weeks? You blew into town a week before Christmas? Where did you live before coming to West Larimore?"

"I'd rather not say."

"Uh, Sam? We got a problem?"

"Maybe a tiny one."

"I suppose you had a job you left. Will you tell me what you did?"

"I'm sorry, James. I can't."

"Good grief. You're an ax murderer!"

"No, I can tell you, I've never killed anyone, but we'll have to drop it at that."

James took a huge drink of coffee before realizing how hot it was. He choked, grabbed his throat, and downed an entire glass of water. When the pain subsided, James wiped his eyes with a napkin and asked, "Will your name . . . uh . . . will your name show up on one of the case files?"

"I don't think so. They're not linked nationwide are they?"

"We'll find out . . ." James looked at his watch, "in about thirty minutes."

For the next fifteen minutes James and Sam orchestrated their efforts: the questions they would ask, the data they would need, and the information about themselves they would give up. At five minutes till nine they were escorted into Patrick's office.

"Patrick, let me introduce you to my associate Samantha Crocker. Sam, this is West Larimore's chief of police, Patrick York."

"James, your associate is our new librarian?"

"Yeah, I didn't think I would need her expertise anymore, so I told her to find another job. And since this one will only be for a couple of months I'll be doing most of the work with Sam helping after her day at the library is over."

Patrick turned toward Sam. "Miss Crocker, is the library closed?"

"No, sir. I have a high school student as an assistant. Since school is out till after the first, she offered to work for me today."

"I see. Okay, let me show you around."

For the next hour, Patrick answered a few questions. He also showed James and Sam the file room, a second room filled with stacks of paper and boxes of forms, and a caged area where the evidence from previous trials was kept. He showed them the break room and where the bathrooms were located, and then he left to let them plan their strategy.

"Sam, you should have told me you were a Nazi. I've heard your friends are leaving Germany in droves."

"I'm not a Nazi. Besides the only people coming to America from Germany, are scientists. Most of the ones escaping on their own are going to South America."

"All right. Where do you want to start?"

"Let's look at the case files. What facts are so important by themselves that they need to be cross-referenced?"

James picked up a thick folder. "Here's one." He opened the cover. "We got the crime, the perpetrator, the witnesses, the evidence, the trial, the verdict, and the sentence."

After a moment's hesitation Sam said, "James, we got more than that. There's the list of possible suspects, the names of the people interviewed, the arresting officers, the officers of the court, the members of the jury, and the presiding judge. And that's just for the people involved. There are lots of notes taken by those investigating the crime. Those notes include the alibis, leads that didn't pan out, extraneous material not germane to the case, and pictures of the crime scene. But what we want to know is, of all that, what portion do we need to list in secondary locations."

"I see. Well, I think I see. The most important names to keep are probably the suspects, the person indicted, the investigating officers, the arresting officers, the attorneys, the jury, and the Judge."

"Good. Now make columns with those eight categories listed at the top and start entering names. Wait a minute. Actually we have one other thing to do first. And that is to decide what labeling conventions we need to use in designating each case file. So let's sort through and place every case in stacks according to the crime committed. Then we'll order them chronologically by date of trial—or do you think the more important date is the date of the crime?"

"I don't know. Maybe the most important date is when it is determined that a crime has been committed and assigned to a detective. Sam, this might be another question for Patrick."

For the remainder of the day Sam and James worked to sort the cases into stacks. Sam was the methodical one with James offering advice but leaving the final decision on everything to Sam. Patrick checked on them off and on throughout the morning. At lunch, they walked to Pauline's Café. Sam and James were so engrossed with their work that they didn't notice the stares they received from some of the other patrons. During the meal, James excused himself to call his dad.

When four p.m. rolled around, James stood up from his chair in the middle of two stacks of cases: one for vandalism and the second for petty larceny. "Sam, it's New Year's Eve and I have a date. Let's call it a day so I have time to get properly dressed."

"You going out with the woman who wanted to know about the roses?"

"Uh . . . probably not. If that woman is who I think she is, then she's being escorted to the party on the arm of the town jerk."

"James, I haven't got a party to attend, so I'll work for a few more hours. When you come in on Wednesday morning, I'll have all the cases sorted. You'll need to start entering the names we talked about on a master list. One page of eight columns per case. Stick each page under the case's front cover."

"You got it."

"James, you're altogether a different man than the one who ran away from his problems twenty years ago. I don't ever remember you shining your shoes nor wearing a suit. By the way, the cleaners got the mud off your cuffs. But there weren't any loud ties at Hanson's Department store. Well, not two to give me a choice. They had one that was burnt orange with bright yellow silk threads running through. I think it's sufficiently loud.

"Son, you going to be wearing a fake nose?"

"No, Dad. I'll forego the nose. I think the tie will do the trick all by itself."

"So how are you going to exchange the mayor's daughter with Agatha? Boy, I wish they'd asked me. Heck, I'd serve the eggnog if I could be there to watch."

"Did you get the chocolates?"

"Yeah, but I had to promise the woman you'd come by and talk with her. Son, that woman had stars in her eyes. What did you tell her? And how come she didn't want me to pay for the candy?"

"Dad, you doing anything tonight?"

"Going to the senior center for bingo."

"Okay, don't wait up for me. I won't be home until after midnight."

"Me neither."

James had to park five houses past the mayor's. When he reached for the door, he confronted a sign that said to enter and to immediately put on a mask and a hat. There was also a table with name tags. On the edge of that table a second sign said to pin the tag on your shirt or blouse, with the picture side showing. James looked on the reverse side of his name tag and saw the picture of a fox. He proudly pinned the picture to his shirt, adjusted a black silk mask, and rakishly cocked a red and white striped hat. At the end of the foyer, James came to a third sign that said the masks and hats had to be worn until midnight—Eastern Time. And that his date until then would be the person who displayed a picture most nearly matching or completing his.

James walked into a large room at the end of the foyer. Furniture had been pushed against the wall and quarantined by green ropes leaving a vast expanse of shining hardwood floor. Small groups of people littered the area. Uniformed servants passed through handing out drinks and tidbits of food. In a corner, a woman plinked piano keys while a man standing beside her strummed a guitar.

Several women came by to see James' picture. Guests masked their voices as well as their faces, with each individual trying to determine the identity of the other guests without letting his or her identity be compromised. James needed to find Agatha. What suitable picture would go with a fox?

"Monsieur Fox, do you think a girl on a bicycle might be complimentary?"

"Not really, but you are the closest so far. May I get you a drink?"

"That would be lovely, Monsieur Fox, but I already have one."

"I don't," chimed in another woman arriving on the scene.

"Mademoiselle, you are a peacock. Do foxes eat peacocks?"

"Quite possibly. I think I would be delectable to the right fox."

"Oh my, here comes Dudley Do-Right. Dudley, are you looking for poor little Nelle?"

"I might. You are aware, of course, that it is the male peacock that sports the wild array of feathers."

"Oh dear, I'm mis-cast."

"Monsieur Fox, do you dance?"

"Not very well—but I give it my best effort. Are you Gretel?"

"Yes and Hansel has yet to show. So I'm thinking about laying a trap for a fox."

"Hmmm." James continued with, "Actually, I think I see the match for the fox. Little Bo Peep is standing beside the piano. Excuse me."

"Don't go, Mr. Fox."

"But I must." James started for the piano, but a large ram arrived first. James paused. A hand reached out and lightly touched his arm. A woman with the picture of a lost lamb said, "I think you would be with me if you were disguised in a wool mantle."

"If I could find Crayons I think that might be accomplished."

Over a loudspeaker a voice said, "Gentlemen, please take the hand of the lady standing nearest and bring her over for our first dance. Music if you please." Instantly the piano and guitar started playing a slow waltz.

"I am such a lucky lady."

"I was about to say the same about me."

"So, Monsieur Fox, am I in great danger?"

To the Little Lost Lamb, Monsieur Fox said, "Not in the least, my dear. Will you be missed if, indeed, you are lost?"

"I'm so afraid, Monsieur Fox. Hold me close."

At the end of the dance Little Red Riding Hood said, "So the terrible bad wolf has finally arrived."

"Uh . . . no. I'm a fox."

"You look like a wolf to me."

A farmer stepped in the midst of the small crowd that had gathered around the Little Lost Lamb and Monsieur Fox. "Excuse me, but I've been looking for you." He held out his hand, "Miss Lamb, would you dance with your farmer?"

Another woman walked up. "I'm the Princess. Has anyone seen the Toad?"

Little Red Riding Hood said, "I think you mean the Frog."

"Whatever. Being royalty, I get to choose whomever I please. And right now I choose Monsieur Wolf."

"He's a fox."

"Then I choose Monsieur Fox."

After dancing with the Princess, James found himself close to Little Bo Peep. While the Princess was helping herself to another glass of punch James slipped away. "Little Bo Peep, I'm not sure I remember your nursery rhyme. Does a nasty old fox play a part?"

"Possibly. Are you sure you're not a sly old fox?"

"If it would get me a dance with Little Bo Peep, I'd be the man in the moon."

"Oh, no. You don't want to be him. I danced with him earlier and we kept bumping into people. He's now going around the room looking for a jumping cow."

"Little Bo Peep, are you having a good time?"

"I'm having a wonderful time. A few minutes ago I saw a man with a picture of a wash tub. Who do you think he was looking for?"

"Winkin, Blinkin, and Nod?"

"Probably. Monsieur Fox, you are so smart. But why would three women want to share one man?"

"I don't know. They'd have to be awfully liberal minded. But then maybe the man was worth it. Or the women were already committed and only wanted a discrete dalliance. And sometimes people have to pool their money if the item's price is beyond their means."

"Really, Monsieur Fox. That would be opening Pandora's box."

"Shall we dance, Little Bo Peep, I'd like to see if I can come up with a more plausible answer—or better yet, refute the ones I've already offered. Come to think of it Winkin, Blinkin, and Nod were three men so the person in the tub should have been a woman. There must be someone else the tub was meant for—maybe, a washerwoman."

During the evening James managed to dance with Little Bo Peep three times, Little Red Riding Hood twice, the Little Lost Lamb three times, and several others a single time. When it was eleven o'clock the lights went out and James kissed Little Red Riding Hood. It was a good kiss with Little Red Riding Hood sliding her hand inside his shirt to feel smooth albeit somewhat hairy skin. When the kiss ended, James stepped away in the dark. He left Little Red Riding Hood groping for her wolf.

James' sense of direction allowed him to steer toward the piano. Quietly he whispered, "Little Bo Peep, where are you?"

From a short distance he heard, "Stay put."

In the background James heard feet shuffling, women giggling, lips smacking, and one loud slap. Then a small hand reached into his. "I am here."

"Men, before we turn the lights back on, please un-pin your pictures, now fold them in half and put them in your pocket. Next remove your hats and masks. Now gentlemen—be patient ladies—we need to shuffle the deck. Men, be so kind as to take three steps to your left and two steps back. Please go slow. If you move slow and bump into someone, no one will get hurt. Just feel your way around. Please be careful of what you grab to guide your way. Now turn in three circles.

"Okay, now you women remove your masks. You'll need to store them in those velvet bags you were given when you arrived. Now the hats. Okay, it's time to remove your pictures and fold them. Now slowly take three steps sideways in either direction and two steps forward or backward. Be careful. Ladies, turn around three times.

"Okay, is everyone set? When the lights come on everyone toss your hats and the men's masks high to the ceiling."

With the lights came pandemonium. The men thought they knew who they danced with, who they talked to, who they held hands with, who they kissed, but when the lights came on every woman in the house was wearing a white blouse and black skirt.

"I'll be dad-burned. I didn't notice you ladies were dressed alike."

"Whoa. I have to admit I didn't see that coming."

"Yeah, it must have been those outrageous hats and . . ."

"And the flamboyant masks. We had simple masks, but you ladies were wearing masks with feathers and ribbons and tiny bells."

"And they were much larger. Your masks covered the entire face."

Addy said, "So now they're paying attention?"

"I told you they wouldn't know the difference," said Margo.

Cynthia poked Patrick in the ribs. "Now do you understand why I wanted to meet you here? Do you realize we did not dance? Not one time."

"No, honey. I thought we danced almost every dance. Wasn't that you, I kissed?"

"Music, please. Ladies and gentlemen, there is still forty-five minutes until midnight in Indiana. Find your dates. Please throw the folded pictures in the trash receptacles."

James looked around the room. It was a conspiracy. The ladies were in cahoots. All probably arriving earlier and separate from their male escorts, spending the afternoon figuring out ways to deceive the men, and now orchestrating a grand scheme of hiding their earlier identities.

Margo gave her bag to one of the servants. She said, "Monsieur Fox, did you save a dance for me?"

"Lady, I have been dancing with you all night."

"You think?"

As they danced James whispered in Margo's ear, "I'll tell you about my picture if you'll tell me about yours."

"You need to do better than that. I already know who you were."

"I'll give you three wishes."

"Anything I want?"

"Anything within reason."

"Let's shake on it."

"Maybe, I should reconsider."

"James, I only want one wish tonight."

"Okay, I'll shake. What is it you want tonight?"

"I want you to kiss me in the garden at midnight."

"I'd do that anyway."

"Yes, but Monsieur Fox, for the next forty-five minutes I now don't have to fret that it might not happen. I can be giddy with anticipation."

"Tell me, Margo. Which one were you?"

"After the kiss, Mr. Fox. After the kiss."

A few minutes later Agatha walked over and stood beside Margo. A servant took Agatha's bag. "Jim, that is a peculiar tie."

"It was Margo's idea. She asked if I would consider wearing stupid clothing."

"And no man can turn down a dare."

"Or a call to arms."

"I wouldn't call it stupid. More like making a statement."

"I know. I wanted to stand out. No more mister conservative for me. You ditch Reginald?"

"Not yet. He's hovering near the punch bowl trying to determine if we danced and who was the woman he kissed."

James added, "And which woman slapped him?"

"Probably the same one."

"Agatha, did you and I dance?" asked James.

"If I wouldn't tell Mr. Howard, do you think I would tell you?" Agatha turned toward Margo. "Margo, I am impressed with your party. And we all think that was a wonderful idea you had about the masks—and the pictures."

James took three drinks from a passing servant. He handed one to Agatha then turned to Margo. "Was it your idea as well for the women to dress alike?" He held out a small cup of sparkling punch.

Margo's face turned bright pink. She looked down. Obviously she enjoyed the feminine accolade but was also embarrassed by her denigration of the male sense of perception. "I was only worried by your ability to see things as they really are. That's why I allowed all those women to fawn all over you. I was hoping they would distract you enough that you wouldn't give the game away."

"Margo, you are a real treasure. May I have this dance?"

"Wouldn't you rather dance with Agatha?"

"No, Margo. At this moment, there is not another woman in this world I'd rather dance with than you."

After the dance James and Margo returned to Agatha. Reginald was standing beside her. To Agatha, Reginald said, "My dear, surely I danced with you?"

"I'm sorry, Reggie. As I have already said, I will not be forthcoming with that information."

"Will you tell me why you slapped me?"

"No."

"Then you did slap me?"

"No. I will not tell you why I slapped you, if I actually did."

"Mr. Howard what did you do or say to get slapped by Agatha or some other woman?" asked Margo.

"Uh . . . I'm sure I don't know." Reginald Howard turned back to Agatha. "Would you care to dance, Miss Parker?"

"I have already promised this dance to Mr. Dandae." Agatha reached for James' hand and led him to the dance floor.

"Agatha, sometimes you are not the nicest woman around."

"Jim, are you comparing me to that simpering, Miss Goody Two-Shoes?"

"Now, that wasn't called for. Margo has never said anything but to express her admiration for you."

"Then you must forgive my caustic remark. I have nothing against Miss Pauline. I just didn't care for her being escorted to the party by the man I'd planned on replacing Reginald Howard with."

"Agatha, I'm not a sack of potatoes."

"Indeed, Jim, you are so much more. You are a fine gentleman in total command of his emotions, never saying what had not been intended, never finding himself in a compromising situation. Jim Dandae, I have not known you for very long but I feel comfortable in your presence, and I think there might be a connection between you and I that I can't quite put my finger on. Do you feel the same way?"

"Agatha, you have caught me off-guard. I don't know what to say, but tonight I am Margo's date and will conduct myself accordingly."

"I can wait."

James and Agatha returned to two agitated individuals. Margo had no desire to be communicative with the dim-witted Reginald Howard, nor did she want to lose her date to the flirtatious Agatha. And Reginald could not fathom why Agatha was so combative. What had he done to be treated with so little respect? He was also unaware that Margo harbored for him the same contempt. When James and Agatha returned, the two they had left still stood on the exact spots as when they had left to enter the dance floor.

"James, let me show you around. You've been here four hours and have yet to see my father or meet my mother."

"That would be delightful, Margo." To Agatha and Reginald, James said, "Would you please excuse us?"

Margo placed her arm through James' and led him away. She said, "I think they're having a slight disagreement. Let's not let their moods spoil our evening."

Margo took James to a double French door. Before James could reach around her for the door handle, she opened it a few inches and slipped through. James followed and closed the door behind him.

A cold stillness greeted the couple. Undefiled snow lay at their feet like a giant sheet spread over the lawn. A series of standing torches emitted flickering flames to light a curved garden path. Margo shivered. "I should have brought a coat."

James removed his jacket and placed it over Margo's shoulders. This is beautiful. Do you have a gardener?"

"Yes."

"And such a large lot. It didn't look this big from the entrance."

"Our house is built on the outside curve of a circle. The property lines skew out giving much more expanse toward the rear than the small area by the street. There is a swimming pool and cabana to the right with the garden taking up everything else."

"Are you taking me anywhere specific?"

"No. the path meanders around the garden and returns to the other side of the patio."

"What's that building? It doesn't look like a cabana."

"It's not. That's the garden shed where Antonio keeps his tools."

"Margo, it must be midnight. I hear the band playing *Auld Lang Syne.*"

Margo stopped and turned to James. He put one arm around her and a hand to the side of her face. James lowered his head and touched his lips to hers. It was a passionate kiss but not one of long duration.

"Margo, I don't have much experience kissing a woman. In fact, I am not the man I seem to be."

"Nonsense, I know exactly what kind of man you are. If you've done things in the past you're not proud of, that is of no importance to me. I am only interested in the man you are at this moment, and I know that man.

"As for not having much experience kissing a woman, I find that to be a marvelous advantage. James, let me show you how a woman wants to be kissed.

"By the way I was the Little Lost Lamb."

"Call me Jim."

CHAPTER 8

January 1, 1946

New Year's Day was a lazy affair for the Dandaes. James and his father slept in after their exciting merriment from the evening before. At eleven, James threw back his covers, sit-up, and pivoted his feet to the floor. After an expansive yawn, he stood on the wool rug beside his bed. With a bare toe James felt the cool wood floor beside the rug. Shivers ran through his body. He calculated how many steps to cross the glacier his bed was now perched atop. Four long strides to the hall runner. One more going from the hallway into the bathroom before landing on the mat.

In the hallway, James found his dad's door half open. He said, "Dad, are you awake? Dad?"

"I am now. What is it?"

"How come the house is so cold?"

"Because last night someone spiked the eggnog. And I toasted the New Year with two glasses of champagne. When I got home, I felt hot and in need of fresh air, so I opened a few windows. And when the furnace came on I turned it off."

"Could you turn it back on?"

"Yeah, will you bring me my house shoes? The floor is like ice."

"Not for a few minutes. I'm stepping into the shower. You didn't turn off the hot water, did you?"

"Well no. Do you think I'm a misogynist?"

"Dad, that's a man who hates women."

"What's the word for hating yourself?"

"Weird."

"Okay. Do you think I'm weird?"

"A little. Pull up your covers. When I get out of the shower, I'll bring your shoes."

In an hour James had shaved, showered, dressed, shut the windows, turned on the furnace, and delivered house shoes to his father. "So what are we going to do about lunch, Dad?"

"I was hoping one of your lady friends would invite you to their house. Then when you told her you couldn't leave your old man alone, she'd invite me too."

"How about one of your lady friends?"

Henry Dandae thought for a moment. "Son, let your old man show you something about female psychology." James' dad walked to the telephone and dialed. "Hello, Ruth. Have you got plans for lunch? No? Well, why don't you come over here and let me fix you something?

"Uh . . . sauerkraut and sausage. Uh . . . no, just the sauerkraut and sausage. I could add oatmeal and toast.

"Whenever you want?" James' father hung up the telephone. "James, let that be a lesson to you. No mortal man can fathom the depths of the female mind."

"Dad, I think I'll be going into town to eat. Do you want to go with me?"

"No. Ruth is coming over for sauerkraut and sausage."

At the Hotel Lexington, James had the desk clerk ring Agatha's room. "Good morning, Agatha. May I take you to lunch?"

After a slight pause James said, "Downstairs. Okay, fifteen minutes." He gave the desk clerk the telephone and walked to a huge fireplace with a seating area. James hung his jacket on a hall tree before falling into a large leather chair and stretching his feet toward the fire. From a side table, he grabbed a newspaper and started reading the local news.

When Agatha arrived, James had fallen asleep. "Wake up, Jim. We have to go to Pauline's Café. They're only serving sandwiches here and I want a meal."

In James' automobile, the heater spewed warm air on their feet. Agatha removed her muffler. She said, "After last night I was worried I might not hear from you again."

"You were? Why's that?"

"It looked like you and Margo were having such a good time that the two of you had become a couple."

"Margo is a good woman. And I enjoyed her company but I'm not tied to any woman. Not yet. Besides she's not much more than an adolescent."

"She's two years younger than me. Do you think of me as an adolescent?" Agatha opened her purse and took out a make-up mirror and tube of lipstick. After re-applying, she blotted the lipstick on a tissue and stuffed it under her seat back to be found at a later time, most likely, by another woman.

"You, an adolescent? Certainly not. You're the woman I fantasized about when I was twelve."

"Jim, you are too funny." Agatha paused for a moment then continued with, "You must realize that tomorrow I'll be leaving. Seth will be driving me to the next town. The men handling the tent will follow in a day or so. Our next service will be a week from tomorrow, in Lindale."

"So soon?"

"Yes, I know. It was hardly long enough to get to know someone. Here we are. Let's go inside and drink something warm to toast our friendship."

James and Agatha followed a middle-aged waitress to a table beside an earthen fireplace. Fire crackled and shot sparks against a wire mesh screen. James took off his jacket and placed it over the back of an empty chair. The restaurant was about half full.

"I thought there would be standing room only."

"Jim, New Year's Day is for families. I think most people in Indiana are gathered in large family units, eating huge meals, with their radios tuned to football."

"Agatha, we haven't had time to get to know each other. And I got off to a bad start. How about you post-phoning your next service for a week and let me show you how much of a gentleman I can be?"

Agatha reached across the table and placed her hand on top of James' hand. "I can't. Seth has already made arrangements. But you could join us. Take a little time off and travel with us. You could help with the tent and . . ."

"And have you had a chance to look at the menu we have for today?" Margo abruptly set two glasses of water on the table spilling the top third of each on the table cloth.

Agatha and James looked into the face of a woman not happy—not happy at all. Agatha snatched her hand away from James' and picked up the menu.

"We have turkey or ham and assorted vegetables."

James stammered, "Margo, you . . . you work at Pauline's Café?"

"Twice a year. On the Friday after Thanksgiving and New Year's Day, Dad cooks while Mom and I wait tables. We give the full-time employees those two days off. So what can I bring you?"

James said, "I'll have the ham and whatever vegetables you have. And iced tea to drink."

"And you, ma'am?"

"I'm sorry, Margo."

"Don't be. I'm a big girl. I can take care of myself."

"Well, then, I'll have the turkey and a cup of coffee."

Margo stomped off in a huff. Agatha unfolded her napkin and placed it in her lap. James could see Margo was visibly upset. Agatha said, "Margo's father owns the restaurant, but I had no idea he or any of his family would be working in it today. I think Margo will be all right after she's had a chance to collect her wits."

"I don't. I think I need to sit in another chair. One where I can have my back against a wall and can see all avenues of approach. You know, Wyatt Earp was killed by a gunshot in his back the very first time he sat in a saloon facing away from the door."

"Another example of your wit."

"Agatha, I'd take you up on your offer but I've started a project for the city. It'll take two months to complete. Where will you be in two months?"

"Somewhere in Missouri, I suppose. Give me your address and I'll write."

After James added his name and address to the bottom of a list Agatha had been collecting he asked, "Did we kiss last night?"

"Why do you want to know?"

"I kissed three women last night; I was hoping you were one. I think you were Little Bo Peep."

"Yes, that was me. I see you are more perceptive than the other men. The women think it was a hoot. Some of them orchestrated a bit of strategy so they would be near someone at midnight on whom they'd dreamed about for years. I haven't heard any of the other men making accurate guesses. Reggie spent most of the evening with Addy Moline."

Margo brought iced tea for James and an empty coffee cup for Agatha. She set both on the table and started pouring coffee. "Your food will be out in a few more minutes. Everything's a bit slower than usual." Margo must not have been paying attention because she overfilled the cup losing a good portion. "Oh. I'm so sorry. I'll be right back with a clean table cloth."

James and Agatha looked at each other with stifled grins. Margo reappeared. She picked up the sugar and salt and pepper shakers and grabbed the soiled tablecloth. James snatched his silverware while Agatha held hers in one hand and her teeming cup of coffee in the other. Margo yanked the tablecloth from the table sending James' iced tea into his lap. He jumped to his feet while grabbing his glass—now almost empty. He placed the iced tea glass and wet napkin into the tote. Under his breath he said, "I should have expected that."

Margo acted like nothing happened. She wadded up the wet tablecloth and tossed it into a gray tote before unfolding and spreading out a clean cloth.

"James, I'll get you a towel."

"Honey, do you need any help?" The middle-aged waitress stood next to Margo.

"Mom, this is James Dandae and you know Agatha. James, this is my mother, Jane Pauline."

James was still standing. He held out his hand. "Pleased to meet you, Mrs. Pauline."

Before shaking James' hand Margo's mother smiled and gave Margo a towel. "My pleasure, Mr. Dandae." She then picked up the tote and said "Honey, I'll take this to the kitchen for you. Do you need anything else?"

"No, Mom. I'll be all right."

The rest of the meal James spent eating, making small talk with the woman he wanted to impress, and keeping a wary eye for the bottled fury he had kissed the night before in a garden at midnight.

"Uh . . . Miss . . . Uh, Margo. I'd like two plates just like mine to go."

"Sure. You got a date with another woman after you take Agatha back to the Hotel Lexington?"

"Uh . . . no."

"The woman you gave roses?"

"Roses?"

"Or maybe she's the woman given the Belgium chocolate?"

"Margo, I can see I have a lot of explaining to do."

Agatha was on her feet. "You sure do, buster."

"The food is for my dad and some woman named Ruth for whom he's trying to prepare a meal. The roses and chocolates were a bribe for the woman helping me organize the records at the police department."

"And the woman in Lindale?"

"This is getting completely out of hand. I have no intention of explaining every time I open a door or say something nice to a member of the fairer sex."

Agatha turned and walked toward the door. Margo glared at James then stomped off. James wondered how Margo got her information. There must be a whole network of informers keeping up with his activities and reporting back to command central.

In a few minutes, Margo brought two plates wrapped in foil and placed in a sack. James thanked her, paid his bill, left a hefty tip, and went looking for Agatha. He spent several minutes waiting outside the ladies' room before Margo's mother told him Agatha had taken a taxi.

When James got home, he expected to see a visiting car in the driveway. He found his dad sitting alone at the kitchen table. Two plates of sauerkraut and sausage and two glasses of water lay on the table undisturbed.

"Dad, your meal not go so well?"

"No, son. How about yours?"

"A complete mess."

CHAPTER 9

January 2, 1946

At eight in the morning, James sat in a room full of stacked folders. There was no place for him to position his feet. A narrow walkway stretched from the door through the stacks to his desk. Eight shorter stacks arranged in two rows of four graced his desktop. He looked around. What had he gotten himself in for? Each folder was held tight by a rubber band and each stack labeled with a crime designation. James looked through the stack directly in front of his chair. The slip of paper said this stack was for armed robbery. One hundred thirty-two cases arranged chronologically. James removed the rubber band from the case lying on top of the stack. It was dated November, 1945.

For the greater part of the day, James listed the data in the folders on a columnar pad. At two-fifteen, James quit working on the stack beside his chair, leaving the remaining three-foot pile for later, and resumed with the stack he had earlier left on his desk.

Sam arrived. "James, I think we ought to give each case a name and a numerical designation. Let's use an acronym for the crime, a dash, the name of the person or place that the offense was perpetrated upon, and the date in parenthesis. For instance, a crime of manslaughter, with a Mrs. Whittaker killed, happening in March of last year would be MS – Whittaker (Mar 45). What do you think?"

"Sam, I'm glad you're here. And I'm glad that you're in charge of the details, but right now my hand aches from writing page after page of names, and I couldn't care less about improving on something you've come up with. I do have a comment to make on these names. Supposing we got rubber stamps for the names of the three judges, the six prosecuting attorneys, and the fifteen private-sector lawyers."

"The sheets are just for us. Why don't you abbreviate? And if you'd use a fountain pen instead of that ballpoint your hand wouldn't cramp so bad. You ever wonder why stenographers always use fountain pens?"

"Not lately."

"Because with a ball-point you have to press down hard enough for the tip to recede letting the ink flow out around it. And you have to have a firm grip on the case to exert enough downward pressure. With a fountain pen, the weight of the pen is sufficient to get the ink flowing. James, start using a fountain pen, your hand will thank you."

"Will you give this list of supplies we need, including a new fountain pen, to Patrick?"

"Sure. Would you mind if I left for a couple of hours? I've been attending rehearsals for an upcoming play. There was a time when I might have been chosen as a substitute for one of the parts. But now I've offended my main thespian supporter and the offer's probably been rescinded."

"Go ahead. If you finish early, you might stop back by. I plan on working until seven or so."

"Good afternoon, Miss Moline. Am I allowed in?"

"Certainly, Mr. Dandae. Unless you've done something you need to be chastised for. Is there anything you need to come clean about?"

"Are you the one who told Margo about the roses?"

"Really, James. May I call you Jim? I may have made a casual remark about those beautiful red roses."

"Just how much do you know about me?"

"A great deal it seems. You've made quite an impression on several of my friends. And you know how women pool their resources. No one knows much about the woman in Lindale, but everything else has been discussed thoroughly. Are you thinking about taking Agatha up on her suggestion?"

"Do I need to clear that with anyone?"

"Jim, you are such a charming man. Everyone is excited you've come home after being gone for twenty years. We're now trying to decide where you've been and what you were up to. Would you mind talking to us about it? We've already made a list of questions and divvied them up around town. Several people have offered to help."

"What question did you take?"

"Would you answer truthfully if I promised not to make it public—just to a few women?"

"Ask the question and I'll decide."

"Fair enough. James . . . uh, Jim, did you ever go by the name of Merle?"

"Good Lord. You ladies need to get a life—and leave mine alone."

"But, Jim, yours is so interesting."

"Ladies and gentlemen we have allowed an audience for these opening rehearsals to generate enthusiasm for our upcoming year. Our first play—the one we've been rehearsing—is entitled *Tell Me I'm Pretty One Last Time* and will open on Valentine's Day—seven weeks from today. There will be eight plays this year. So please support your local theater and buy season tickets. This rehearsal completes the story and, as always, we will take comments and observations at the end. This is also the last rehearsal available for public viewing prior to the opening performance. There are a few props and some of the actors will be in costume. Please do not talk during the performance and the Hotel Lexington does not allow public consumption of food or beverages outside of their café. So now, sit back and enjoy.

"Lights, please."

When the lights came on, the scene was the water department with Nicole standing beside Richard at the water cooler.

"Richard, I just want to thank you so much for your advice. I left my abusive husband last night. He begged me to stay—said he'd do better, he'd quit drinking. I told him I'd heard all that before and there was nothing he could say that would make me change my mind. Then my dad showed up and helped me load all my things. I'm going to stay with my parents for a few months before I find a place of my own. And, Richard, that's not all. I start counseling tonight."

"Do you think he will retaliate?"

"No. I took out a restraining order. And he's afraid of my father—a retired deputy sheriff who would tear his head off with the slightest provocation."

"Nicole, I'm happy for you."

"Richard, I never could have stood up to him without your help." Nicole put both arms around Richard and kissed him hard on the lips. "I know that was improper but I had to do it. Richard, you're my hero."

Addy Moline walked to the front of the stage. "In the next scene we are in Richard's small townhouse."

"Richard, I need money for Portia's dance lessons. And she has to buy new shoes. She left her old ones in Jack's car and now they can't find but one."

"Why was she taking off her shoes in that deadbeat's car?"

"Not her school shoes. The dancing shoes."

"It doesn't matter. We're barely making ends meet and I can't spare extra money. I can give you money for the lessons, but she'll have to find that shoe or dance in her socks. You can't get blood out of a turnip."

"Turnip? Turnip, you say? Just you listen to me you knucklehead. Portia is your only child. If she wants new dancing shoes then, she's going to get new dancing shoes. In fact, I've already bought them."

"You did? What did you pay for them with?"

"I pawned your father's gold watch."

"Oh, no. Agnes, that's the only thing I have in this world of any value. The train gave Dad that watch when he retired. He handed it to me from his deathbed and made me swear to think of him every time I looked at it."

"And when was the last time you looked at it?"

"It's been over a year. I had to quit wearing it when you pawned the gold fob. I was afraid I'd lose it. We have to get it back."

"Probably too late now. I took it in last week and spent most of the money on me. There was just enough left to buy the shoes. Are you going to talk to your boss about a pay raise? You don't make enough money to keep us in food and clothes. You bozo, we're penniless."

Portia came onto stage by hurrying through a door. She said, "Dad, I got just a minute. Give me some money. Jack's car is empty and I told him I'd help with gas money."

Richard pulled out his billfold, opened it up, turned it over, and shook. A single coin fell to the floor. "Take it. It's all I've got."

"Dad, you are an embarrassment."

"In our next scene Richard is back at Michelle's apartment." Addy walked into the dark of the stage with the spotlight now shining on Richard and Michelle.

"Princess, what can I do for you tonight? Your washing machine running okay?"

"Richard, tell me I'm pretty one last time."

"Last time? Are you going somewhere?"

"Yes. My mother is dying. I'm going to Chicago to be with her. In not so many weeks, I'll be coming back for you, Richard. I love you."

"You love me?"

"Yes, Richard. And I want to shower you with that love, to take care of you, to give you everything you've been missing. Agnes doesn't love you. You're just a meal ticket for her. You and I were meant for each other. Have you not wondered why my appliances breakdown on a regular basis? Why my drain is so easily clogged. I need you Richard. I need for you to put your arms around me and tell me you love me too." Michelle took the toolbox out of Richard's hand and placed it on the table. She put her hands around Richard's head and kissed him on the lips. It was a passionate kiss. A kiss from a woman who finally had worked up enough courage to bare her heart. A long kiss from a woman hungry for Richard's love. A wet kiss. A lingering kiss. She went from his lips to his eyelids to his neck. Richard kissed her back. He encircled her with his arms. They swayed.

"Princess, you are twenty years younger than me. How could you love an old, broken-down plumber. I don't have an education. I don't have money. There is no way I could provide for you."

"Richard, you're a good man with a big heart. I have enough money for both of us. You'll never have to work again. And I promise you that I will always love you and treat you with respect. You don't have to worry about me. I'll never be the vile person Agnes has become. You and me, Richard. We are one."

"Princess, no one has ever said they loved me. Those are the words I've been searching for my whole life. But more than the words I've been searching for the love the words signify. Tell me again you love me."

"I love you."

"Princess, I loved you from the time when I first fixed your washing machine—the night I told you how pretty you were. When you come back, I'll be ready."

The stage light dims to darkness.

In a moment, the stage is still dark but now a spotlight shines down on a single church pew. "Ladies and Gentlemen the last scene is in the church."

Agnes is sitting between Portia and her mother. Women are openly weeping in the background. Over the loudspeaker comes a solemn voice.

"Richard was a hard-working man. He spent his days at the water department and his evenings repairing appliances and whatever else the good women of our town needed to be repaired. On weekends, Richard safe-guarded other peoples' possessions."

Here, in the dialog, a loud chorus of wailing came from all corners of the room. Agnes, her mother, and Portia stare around the church in disbelief.

"I have been told that Richard was much more than an appliance repairman. He helped people fix their lives. And he was generous. He was generous with his time. That's for sure. But he was also generous with his money. Hardly any month went by that Richard did not pay the water bill for someone financially unable to do so themselves.

"Richard was not a wealthy man. He worked three jobs to make ends meet. But what he gave Agnes was more than money. He was the foundation of her world. Agnes told me that on his last night he left to repair a woman's washing machine. He didn't even have time to eat his evening meal. He picked up his toolbox and left with two slices of stale bread saying how tired he was. When he came home several hours later, there was a smile on his face and a gleam in his eye. Richard was a man proud of his work. He was a man who lived for the feeling he got from helping someone in need. Agnes said he was ecstatic. He shook her awake saying he had something important to tell her. She said he was bouncing off the wall like he had won the lottery. But before he could get it out he grabbed his chest and keeled over at the foot of the bed. Our town has lost a wonderful man."

Loud weeping filled the sanctuary.

"Humanity has lost a wonderful man."

A funeral dirge started and morphed into silence.

"Mom, what are all these women in here for? See all those standing in the back. There's not enough room on the pews for them to sit. And why are they crying?"

"Agnes, there are more than a hundred women in here crying over your lamebrain husband's death."

"I know. Before we came inside the church, two women asked what it was like to live with Richard—to have him around every day? They asked me what my nights were like? If I was looking forward to a normal life, to getting some sleep for a change? They wanted to know if I would I miss the fun?"

Portia said, "Mom, I don't understand. If your life after Dad will be normal, then life with Dad must have not been normal. Is that the fun they're talking about—life with Dad?"

"Yes, something like that. I think they were envious of me having him all to myself." Agnes turned to her mother. "Mom, do you think Richard has had affairs with all these women?"

"Dad?" asked Portia

"That ignoramus?" asked Portia's grandmother.

Agnes lowered her head. "Well, he couldn't have paid all their water bills."

The lights slowly faded to complete darkness. Then people started clapping. There were a few whistles and stomping of feet. When the lights came back on, Addy Moline was at the front of the stage and the other actors were bringing chairs to sit beside her and answer questions.

"Are there any questions?"

"Yes ma'am. I'd like to know if the author has written any other books. If he has, are they in our library?"

"We don't know yet. The author is Agatha Parker's friend and lives in Dancing Deer, Arkansas. She told us she and the author have written to each other for several years. In her last letter, she asked him to turn his novel into a theatrical play but so far she has not received a reply. She's now sent him a copy of her effort and asked his permission for us to stage it. Our mayor has offered to write a follow-up letter—in case the two Agatha sent got lost."

"The lady on the second row. You have a question?"

"Are there any men in this world like Richard? All the men in my life have been skunks."

"Reginald, would you care to comment on this?"

"Certainly. No, there are no men like Richard in this world. He is a composite of what the author thinks women want in a man. A real man would not have put up with the badgering he received from his abusive wife, his lame-brain daughter, and the real stinkeroo—his mother-in-law."

"Miss Moline, would you ask Mr. Dandae if he thinks there are men like Richard."

"Yes, I will. Mr. Dandae, the women want to know your opinion."

"I was afraid of that. My opinion is not completely thought out on the subject, but I can give you an indication of my current reflection.

"Men are reactionary. We analyze our circumstances and adjust our behavior accordingly. If a woman wants a compassionate, loving man in her life then she needs to put him in a situation brimming full of compassion and love. Give him what she wants to receive. I think she'll find love begets love. A passionate woman who goes out of her way to make the man in her life thank the good Lord for giving him the one woman who could make him happy will be the man that woman deserves. A worthy woman will reap the benefits of the seed she sows."

"Mr. Dandae, do you offer counseling?"

"Uh . . . no. I am only a man who observes."

"Thank you, Mr. Dandae. If there are no other questions then the play will . . ."

"Addy, I have a question. If the author does not give you his approval will you still put on the play?"

"I hope it doesn't come to that. I suppose it will depend on what the mayor decides."

"Give us the man's name and address. We'll mount a campaign. I'm sure several fans would send a letter begging for his acquiescence."

"I'll mention it to the mayor."

CHAPTER 10

January 4, 1946

Gladys spooned peaches into Edwin's open mouth. After each portion, she used the corner of a napkin to wipe off the small amount that trickled down his chin. "Edwin, Issie called. She said she would be a few minutes late. Her cat got out and she's combing the neighborhood.

"Poor thing. Issie had her claws removed to protect the furniture and now the other cats are mean to it. Issie should have gotten the kitty a scratching post. Anyway, I have to go to work so Laurie will be with you until Issie gets here.

"Laurie . . . Laurie, are you in the kitchen? Oh, there you are. Edwin has just eaten his breakfast. He'll be okay until Issie gets here. Would you mind reading to our guy? He'll help you pick out a book."

"Gladys, what if Issie doesn't come?"

"Give me a call—or you can call Issie yourself. Her number is . . . oh, you know where the numbers are. I have to go. I'll try to be home early. Toodle loo, kids."

Gladys was backing out of the driveway when the telephone rang. "Hello.

"No, ma'am. She just left.

"No, ma'am. Mrs. Stanky has not said anything about Edwin having a post office box. Has she ever picked up his mail?

"Then you need to send it because we don't know where the key is."

After hanging up the telephone Laurie pushed Edwin into the living room and positioned his wheelchair in front of the windows facing the street. "Edwin, you have mail."

Laurie walked to a bookcase. She pulled out a glass door, rocked it up, and shoved it back in above a shelf of books. "Let's see, we've finished *The Red Badge of Courage* so it's time to start a new one. Do you have a preference? No? Okay let me choose one I'll like. What's this book by John Milton? Is it all right if we read *Paradise Lost*? I'm going to fix some toast and a glass of milk. Yell if you see Clarence bringing the mail. I'm sorry Edwin. I wasn't making fun of you. I know you can't talk. He'll ring the bell anyway. Who do you think is sending you mail? And why did it go to a post office box instead of being delivered like normal?"

Issie came while Laurie was in the kitchen. Edwin saw her pull into their driveway. He tried to call to Laurie, but it was just heavy breathing. He could barely open his mouth. It had been a little over two weeks since he was shot by the bank robber. And there was the operation right before Christmas when the doctor removed the bullet from his chest. He didn't remember the operation. All he could remember was being handcuffed through the metal fire escape ladder to the guy from the bank. He yelled at the man with a gun saying that he knew who he was and he'd be coming after him if it was the last thing he did. It almost was. The man pointed his gun and pulled the trigger. Edwin remembered seeing the blast from the gun and feeling an immediate thump against his chest. He saw blood spurting out like a fountain. Then he grew faint and the next thing he knew he was lying in a hospital bed. Gladys was kissing his face. She was so happy, saying things like 'Honey, everything's going to be all right,' 'Eddie you're awake,' 'Thank you Lord . . . thank you,' and 'Laurie, come quick Edwin's come out of his coma.'

Yesterday, Gladys said the Calhoun brothers had finished remodeling their home and the doctor was releasing him. The bank was even paying for someone to take care of him while Gladys worked.

Issie came in the front door without knocking. "Good morning, Mr. Stanky. Are you ready for your bath? Let's see, I didn't shave you yesterday, so we'll do that today."

Laurie held a piece of toast in her hand. "I haven't done anything with Edwin this morning. You'll need to brush his teeth before he gets that shave. But Gladys has already given him his medicine and a little breakfast."

Laurie took the book she had retrieved from the bookcase to Edwin's recliner. Since Edwin now spent his days in a wheelchair, Laurie had taken over the green corduroy recliner. She opened the book. When Issie started pushing Edwin to the bathroom, Laurie said, "I'll just glance through a few pages. We'll get started from the beginning when Issie finishes."

Edwin was sitting in a giant bucket of heated water when he heard the doorbell ring. It must be his mail.

A few moments later Laurie spoke through the bathroom door. "Edwin, you received two letters: one from a woman named Agatha Parker and the second from the Mayor of West Larimore, Indiana. There's also a package from Agatha Parker, two *Grit* Newspapers, and a magazine called *American Writers Gazette*. Hurry up. I can't wait to open them up. I've never gotten a letter myself. This is exciting."

When Issie wheeled Edwin into the living room by the front window, Laurie said, "Which one first, Edwin?"

"The letter from Agatha Parker? I agree."

"I didn't hear him say the letter from Agatha Parker. Young lady, you're making that up. What if he really wants you to open the package first?"

"No, Issie. He wants the letter from Agatha first. Edwin and I communicate by telepathy. We both concentrate real hard and I get what he wants. For instance, right now he wants you to be quiet so I can read him this letter."

Laurie held the letter to her nose. "Edwin, this has been sprinkled with perfume. Are you sure you want me to open it in front of Issie? What if it's from one of your old girlfriends? Issie will have to tell Gladys and you'll be in hot water—and it won't be bath water. Okay, if that's what you want." Laurie turned to Issie. "He said you wouldn't tell anyone without asking his permission first.

"This letter is old. It's dated back in November of last year. It says:

Dear Edwin:

We had a large crowd at Saturday night's service. Over a hundred in attendance and fifteen came forward to renew their dedication to the Lord. I think I am finally making headway. Sometimes people say they have heard of my evangelism. So after a very productive service, Seth brought me the mail and it included your novel.

Our next service was four days later, so I had time to read it. I must say, you are quite the romantic. I am so impressed with your story. Is it fact or fiction? I've heard that most first stories include a lot of biographical detail. But I can't imagine you living with a woman like Agnes. And it would have been a better read with a happier ending. Why did Richard have to die?

I told Seth to include Dancing Deer on our itinerary. No word from him yet on when that will be.

Do you think you could make it into a play? I have friends in West Larimore, Indiana, who put on plays. They are not professional or anything. And all of the money they raise goes into the city's budget to provide food and housing for the poor. Most small towns don't even try to help the disadvantaged and West Larimore sets aside a substantial amount each year.

Please let me know about the play. Seth says we are set to visit West Larimore on the fifteenth of next month.

Yours in Christ,
Agatha Parker

"Edwin, you've written a book? Where is it? Can I read it?"

"Young lady, if you and Mr. Stanky can communicate telepathically then he should be able to tell you where the book is."

"Maybe it's in the package. It's also from Agatha Parker. Edwin wants me to open it next. All right, Edwin. Issie is just a bit skeptical about our ability to communicate."

Laurie tore open the package. She held up a thick group of papers tied together with string. It says on the front it's *Tell Me I'm Pretty One Last Time*, a play in four acts adapted by Agatha Parker from a novel of the same name by Edwin Stanky.

"Edwin, it's not the novel but her play. Wait a minute. Here's a note."

Dear Mr. Stanky:

I couldn't wait any longer for you to pen the play so I thought I'd try my hand. I think it turned out remarkably well. Although I don't have your lyrical style, I did try to produce it, to the best of my ability, like I thought you'd write it.

I have supplied my effort to the actors in West Larimore. They would like your permission to perform it in February. If you need payment for your royalty rights, they have paid up to a hundred dollars before to the owners of other copyrighted plays. I'm sure they would do the same for you. As for my efforts I will not require payment. Just being able to put my name beside yours is sufficient for me.

Yours in Christ,
Agatha Parker

"Edwin, do you want me to read the play or the letter from the Mayor of West Larimore?"

Issie rolled her eyes. Edwin and Laurie could tell that Issie did not believe Laurie could pick up Edwin's thoughts. "Okay, it's the mayor's letter then."

Dear Mr. Stanky:

Although I have not read your novel nor Miss Parker's adaptation of it for the stage, I have received several requests for your name and address. It seems other people have observed the actors reading their lines and want to make sure the play gets produced. My daughter is one of those people, and she can be very persuasive.

Miss Parker was here for the first three rehearsals but has now continued her tour of towns in the midwest. We expect her back for the premiere performance on February 14, 1946.

If you would give us your permission to perform the play, the city council has authorized me to send you two round-trip train tickets, reimbursement for your food, and two nights lodging at our finest hotel.

Mr. Stanky, on Valentine's Day the town is yours. Bring your missus, girl-friend, or suitable companion—as the case may be. Enjoy our famous Indiana hospitality and meet the constituents of your new fan base.

Please be prepared to answer questions. I understand that your novel, or Miss Parker's adaption, has struck a chord with quite a few of West Larimore's women. And, if you are not married—there are a number of those women who think you were meant for them.

Thank you, Mr. Stanky, and please reply as soon as possible. The date of the performance draws nigh.

John Pauline
Mayor of West Larimore, Indiana

"Edwin, are you a romantic? Does Gladys know? School starts back on Monday. Can I tell my friends that you wrote a novel? Edwin, can I?" Laurie went to the wheelchair and held Edwin's hand. "No? I won't say anything then."

"Are you going to read the play?"

"Edwin doesn't want me to tell anyone about the book and he's trying to decide if I can read the play to you. He said he might want to keep the story just between the two of us."

"Now listen here, young lady. Mr. Stanky is not talking to you. You're making that up. And besides, if Mr. Stanky doesn't want anyone to know about the novel or the story, then . . . I can keep a secret."

"Like the time I dropped his medicine through the floor grate of the furnace. Like that time?" Laurie and Issie were now involved in a staring contest. Neither blinked waiting on the other to give in.

"What? Well, I don't want to." Laurie picked up the play. "He said for me to apologize to you and to read the dadgum play."

CHAPTER 11

January 9, 1946

"Sam, your supplies came. The box said they were from a library supply store."

"Good. How fast do you type?"

"Twenty words per minute with fewer than ten mistakes."

"Then, Mr. Over-achiever, you better keep on entering the data in those columns."

"Sam, I'm getting tired of this. I work all day on these columns and you get here in the afternoon and we work together till late at night. Do you have a social life?"

"No."

"Me neither. Not anymore."

"I know, James, but we've started to make a dent in the stacks of cases. And we have a plan. We just have to keep at it."

"Sam, you could have been a high school football coach. I can see it now. It's half-time. The most important game of the year—your homecoming game. Your team is playing its arch enemy—the school down the road. Your kids are losing twenty-four to nothing. The only drive they were able to sustain ended in an intercepted pass close to the other school's end zone. Your boys are gathered around you in the locker room waiting to hear how you plan on pulling off the big comeback. While walking back and forth in front of the blackboard here's what you say.

"'Boys, we came into this knowing how big and how fast they were. They've won all their games and we've lost all ours but that doesn't matter because we have the plan. We were going to use their speed against them. Our game plan was to use a ton of misdirection plays. With the guards and linemen moving one direction and, trying to keep them from running all over us, we'd hand off to our fastest running back racing in the other direction.

"'Then, with our running game finally established, we had planned on letting our freshman quarterback—the boy with the golden arm—throw a few short passes to the tight ends and a few screen plays to someone running out of our backfield. Then an occasional long bomb to a wide receiver to keep them honest.

"'And you guys on defense. You're tired. They've held the ball twice as long as us. You're walking around with your hands on your hips, wheezing for air. You got to stand firm. I know their guys are bigger than you. And all they have to do is keep you from getting through their line. But you got to figure some way to put pressure on their quarterback. In the second half, we're going to send in the linebackers on passing situations giving their wide receivers man-to-man coverage.

"'I know it's tough, men, but we've already started to make a dent in their armor. And we have the plan. We just have to keep at it.'"

"James, you are too funny. Have you been to many football games?"

"Hell no. I've been entering data into eight columns for each of these cases. My hand has developed arthritis, my eyes won't focus, and my stomach thinks I'm not giving him any respect."

From the hallway came, "Then how about a break for supper?"

Sam and James looked toward the door. "Hello, Margo. I didn't hear you come in. You been here long?"

"Long enough to hear about the plan. I waited in the hall. I have pot roast with boiled onions, potatoes, and carrots set up in the break-room. How about taking a short break?"

"Is there enough for me too?" asked Sam.

"There's plenty for everyone. I've already prepared a plate for the night dispatcher."

"Margo, this is Samantha Crocker. Sam meet Margo Pauline."

Sam walked to Margo and extended her hand. "Is there anything I can do to help?"

"No, I've got it covered."

At the meal, Sam asked Margo how the play was coming.

"Just fine. We finally heard from the author. Would you like me to read his letter? It's actually from a young girl writing for him. Dad has supplied a copy to the newspaper. They're going to print it in Sunday's paper."

Margo pulled out a piece of paper from her purse and started reading.

"Dear Mr. Pauline:

I am Laurie. I help take care of Mr. Stanky. He was shot by a bank robber three days before Christmas and barely escaped death. Right now, he sits in a wheelchair unable to take care of himself or even to talk.

I read him your letter and the two from Agatha Parker. And I've read him the play Miss Parker adapted from his novel. He thought it was good. We all did. He told me that he had no objection to you including its production in West Larimore's 1946 scheduled performances, but any future production would have to be authorized through a similar transaction.

The doctor has given Mr. Stanky permission to travel to your town for the play, but so far, we can't decide who gets to come with him. There is his wife, Gladys, who has taken a job for the first time in her life, his caretaker, Issie, and me, his adopted daughter.

Also, we can't find a copy of Mr. Stanky's novel. He knows where it is but won't tell us. Of course, Mr. Stanky can't talk but he and I communicate telepathically.

He told me to tell you the novel is entirely fiction. There is nothing in his personal life portrayed in the book whatsoever.

Thank you, Mr. Pauline, for your communication. You may use this letter as your authorization to perform the play during the months of February and March of 1946 in West Larimore, Indiana.

Laurie Stansberry for Edwin Stanky."

Sam said, "And how old do you think Laurie Stansberry is? She sounds like a Gypsy legal secretary to me."

"I don't know. Dad gave the letter to Mr. Thornton at the newspaper. He thinks there may be a story involved. Jim, I told him you had been in Dancing Deer. I think Mr. Thornton's planning on asking you some questions."

"And you knew I've been to Dancing Deer? Exactly how did you come across that information?"

"Now, Jim, don't get testy. You're a hot topic. There's a whole pile of information being dredged up on you."

"Should I think about leaving town?"

"It depends. Someone's trying to locate a man by the name of Lenny. You might hold off on running until he surfaces."

"Damn." James took a handkerchief to wipe the back of his neck.

"Jim, I'm sorry. I didn't come here to upset you. Are you feeling okay?"

"Who's the ringleader in this feminine gumshoe operation?"

"I can't tell you that, Jim. You know—confidentiality of sources. No one would divulge information if they thought we couldn't keep their name secret. Are you actually worried? Some of my cohorts believe you've left a string of desperate women—each one waiting on you to come back. And getting to the truth of that is what drives the grist mill."

"Such colorful metaphors. Miss Pauline, you should consider writing a novel," said Sam.

"If I come up with many more entanglements for our friend here or if half of the ones we're researching happen to be true, I just might. I'll name it *Jim Dandy, The Man Your Mother Warned You About*."

James stuffed the wadded up handkerchief into his back pocket. "Do you know anything about this bank robbery?"

"No. But that's why Dad is giving the letter to Mr. Thornton. He wants to know. We all do. What did Mr. Stanky do to get shot? How much money did the robber make off with? What kind of car was he driving? Who were his accomplices? Did it happen inside the bank? Did he get money from the vault or the tellers? What does the FBI have to say? You know bank robberies now come under their jurisdiction."

"No. I didn't know that."

"Yep. Tried at the federal level. Stiff prison terms."

"Let's talk about happier events. Margo, I have something for you in the backseat of my car. I've been carrying it around since the New Year's Eve Party."

"Why didn't you give it to me then?"

"After we kissed in the garden, my mind went blank."

"Are you going to give it to me now? You know I still have two wishes."

"Yeah. But you don't want to waste such a hot commodity."

"Jim, I was pretty mad at you for taking Agatha to lunch right after our date so I asked around to see if any of the girls might be interested in two white elephants. I got three offers."

"Should I give your box of Belgian chocolates to one of those offering to take me off your hands?"

"Uh . . . no. I can take care of the chocolates."

Sam stood beside her empty paper plate. "Miss Pauline, that was a delicious meal. Did you prepare it yourself?"

"No. I had someone at the restaurant put it together for me. It was one of Dad's original recipes. When we started the restaurant, he had a collection of recipes he thought were good enough to build a reputation on. He invested every dollar we could scrape together to get it going. That was fifteen years ago. Now a lot of people consider Pauline's Café to be one of the finest in the state. Do you not want any of his bread pudding? It's my favorite."

"You've talked me into it," said Sam.

"I'd like some." James shoved his plate toward Margo.

CHAPTER 12
January 14, 1946

Gladys was not a popular person—at least not in her own house. "I think it's a bad idea." That's all she had said. Now everyone shunned her. Issie didn't have anything nice to say. Laurie hid out in her room. Edwin—well, no one knew his take on the situation.

Edwin watches her cross the room. No emotion showing with him. Gladys wonders what he's thinking. She imagines he thinks she's overstepped her position—exactly like what everyone else thinks.

It would have been an easy decision if the letter from the *West Larimore Courier* hadn't arrived asking for more information about Edwin. Like a good wife, Gladys had responded. She was proud of Edwin for standing up to the bank robber. In retrospect, it was a bad decision for Edwin, but he showed unflinching courage. How was he to know the man was morally corrupt? Now Edwin, and everyone connected with Edwin, was suffering.

Maybe they needed something to lift their spirits. Maybe she should give in, and say they would now accept the tickets to the play and travel to Indiana. Edwin's letter giving his permission to produce the play was soon followed by him receiving a copy of the newspaper article they had printed about Edwin's adventure resulting in life-threatening surgery. In an attached note someone had hand-written that for the two additional passengers the newspaper would spring for the extra train tickets, food, and lodging. And when she had replied—over the doctor's permission—that Edwin was still too weak to travel, there had been an avalanche of mail begging her to reconsider. One packet of letters came wrapped in a ribbon. They were from a fifth-grade class.

Gladys walked to Edwin's wheelchair. "Eddie, you really want to see the play, don't you?"

His eyes shot left. "All right, I give in. We'll all go to Indiana. I guess if we don't go see the play, we'll never know about the book you wrote. Laurie has torn the house apart looking for it. Issie has even helped. If you can actually communicate with that girl why haven't you told her where it is? She thinks you don't want anyone to read it. Is there something in the book you're embarrassed about?"

Gladys pulled up a chair beside Edwin and watched the people pass by on the sidewalk. Edwin was now able to turn his head as he watched. In a few minutes, she got up to see how Issie was coming on supper. Maybe there was something she could do to help.

Gladys was taking the cornbread out of the oven when Laurie came charging into the kitchen. "Gladys, Edwin's trying to tell me something. I think he's coming clean about the book."

"Edwin's trying to tell you that I've given in. We're all going to Indiana."

"Fantastic. Gladys, you won't have to do anything. Issie and I will handle Edwin by ourselves. You and Edwin can consider this a vacation. This is wonderful. Isn't that so, Issie?"

"Yes, ma'am. You deserve some time off. Mrs. Stanky, Laurie and I will see that Mr. Stanky is well-taken care of. I've never been to Indiana. My, my. I've never been out of Arkansas."

"Young lady, do you want to write the paper to tell them we'll be there after all? You might also mention that Edwin is happily married and those women the mayor was talking about need not apply for my job."

"I'd be happy to."

CHAPTER 13

January 13, 1946

"What? No, I'm up. Hello, . . . Jackie?"

"I've talked it over with Theo. He says you need to meet Michael. That I have no right to keep you away from your son. So how about I meet you half-way? We'll just say you're a friend from school. If there's no problem, we'll eventually tell Michael the truth but not at first. Are those terms you can live with?"

"Yes. I'll do whatever you say."

"Come over today for lunch. Theo will be here."

James got the directions and went back to bed. He had to think this through. Sometimes a man is only given one chance. He didn't want to screw up his first meeting with his son. James interlocked his fingers behind his head and stared at the ceiling.

At nine, James was still staring at the ceiling. But he had memorized answers to every question he thought he might be asked. He fixed coffee in a new percolator. And, after sitting down, stole a piece of toast from his dad's plate.

"You don't mind if I have a cup of coffee do you?"

"Good heavens no. I like the aroma. Sometimes I go into town and eat breakfast. Oatmeal gets old and I go to Pauline's Café about every other week. They grind their own beans." Henry Dandae paused. He dropped a scoop of butter into his bowl. "You know though, I must go there to talk to someone, because I order oatmeal and toast and I wouldn't do that if I was trying to add variety to my diet. Then you showed up and I haven't been back—or felt the need to go. You want to play some gin after we eat?"

"I can't this morning, Dad. Jackie called and I'm going to meet my son today. His name is Michael."

"You think I could meet the boy some day?"

"Sure, Dad. We'll play gin when I get back."

James sat in the car a few minutes before walking to Jackie's front door. He was greeted by a muscular, bald, black man. "You must be James. I'm Theo, Mr. Dandae, Theo Jackson." Theo's hand enveloped the one James extended. The two walked into the living room. "Have a seat Mr. Dandae. Michael has gone to pick up his girlfriend. Can I get you something to drink?"

"That would be great. Do you have anything warm? I'm still trying to get a handle on this weather."

"Jackie's got coffee and hot chocolate."

In a moment, Jackie entered the room with a tray. "James, how do you drink your coffee?"

"Black."

Jackie poured two cups. She gave Theo the first and sat James' cup on a coaster beside his chair. "You might should let that cool a bit."

"What can you tell me about Michael?"

"He's a normal boy. Got through high school with decent grades. Played all the sports. Wants a car real bad. Works for Theo at the garage. And has a girlfriend named Betty. They'll be here any minute."

"Is he a mechanic?"

Theo said, "Yeah, most of my business is on diesels but I get a few cars. Michael works on them. He's a fast learner. At first I had him doing oil changes, and then he did a few brake jobs. We had an old engine we had replaced so I had him take it apart. He came to me one afternoon saying it had a cracked block. Together we machined the cylinders and inserted new sleeves. It's a project. He's used what he's learned to take over the car repairs—and a few tractors."

When Michael arrived, he introduced his girlfriend but was not interested in talking with one of his mother's old friends from eons ago. He and Betty adjusted the radio and sat close by listening to Cab Calloway's band play their current hit. At the meal James and Jackie made small talk about their school days and James went into great detail on his fabricated story of why he left and what he did during the twenty years he had been gone. Things were ho-hum until he asked Betty if she would be making Michael bring her to West Larimore to see the play on Valentine's Day.

"I might. What's it about?"

"True love. How a man, who lives with a despicable wife, looks for love in his relationships with other women and how his wife realizes what she had when she no longer has it."

Michael squinted one eye and wrinkled his nose at the same time. Jackie said, "Now son, it's Valentine's Day. You can put up with a love story for that one day. Maybe we could double-date. I think Theo's planning on taking me."

"I am?"

"Yes, I think you are."

James said, "Its first performance is on Valentine's Day and that'll be a weeknight. But I think they have several more slated on the weekends. With the drive, it might be more convenient to come on a Saturday night."

"Or a Sunday matinee."

"I'll find out for you about the Sunday matinee." James pushed his chair away from the table. "That was good Jackie. Now I need to do some exercise to keep from falling asleep. Michael, do you have a football? Would you throw a few to someone old and slow?"

The three men took equidistant positions in the front yard and street. James threw the ball with a decent spiral about thirty yards. "I won't be able to throw any farther than that until my arm limbers up."

Theo caught the ball and ran to a new position with Michael and James now in a line with James thirty yards away and Michael thirty yards beyond James. Theo threw the ball. It sailed in a beautiful spiraling arc high in the air. Michael had to jump to catch it. "Damn, Theo. You should be playing professionally."

Michael threw the ball thirty yards to James, who threw it another thirty yards to Theo. "Scoot back another ten, Mike. I want to see how far this piece of cowhide can fly."

After twenty minutes, James had to quit. His arm was hanging limp at his side. Michael said he and Betty were going for a ride and Theo patted James on his shoulder as they headed back into the house. "James, I'm glad you got to see the boy. He's a good kid. Maybe too smart to be working in a garage but a pleasure to have around."

"Yeah, I'm fortunate Jackie let me come by."

CHAPTER 14
January 14, 1946

Edwin swiveled his head so he could watch Issie and Laurie. They were looking for the book and had finally made it to his closet. Gladys had given him the one big closet and taken the rest for herself. When Laurie moved in, Gladys had to move her clothes out of the closet in Laurie's room into his. Now there were entirely too many clothes, hat boxes, and shoes in his closet. Of course, there was only one pair of shoes of any importance. Every other pair belonged to Gladys. Edwin sat in his wheelchair and watched the two girls dismantle his hiding place.

"Issie, it has to be in here. We've sifted through every drawer, every box, every nook and cranny in this house. If his book is not in here then, there is no book."

"Why don't you sweet talk the old man into telling you where it is?"

"Ssh. Old man? Edwin's not an old man. And that's no way to refer to him anyway. You know he can hear you and understands every word you say, even if he can't talk."

"Yeah, I keep forgetting. Why do we need the book anyway? We got the play. Isn't that just as good?"

"No. It's not. There'll be a lot more detail in the book. And better dialog. Plus, Edwin is probably a better writer than Miss Parker. We got to find that book so we can decide for ourselves if the characters were figments of his imagination or glossed over images of the people he came into contact with."

"Well, those glossed over images would not include you and I. We arrived on the scene after the book had been written."

"To tell you the truth, Issie. I really want to know if Agnes and Gladys is the same person. We'll find the book and read it for the truth of the matter. And we won't tell Gladys unless we're real sure there is no connection."

"Okay. It better show up fast. We've taken almost everything out of that dinky little closet and filled up half the room. I don't think all this will fit back in there. How do you reckon Gladys finds what she needs?"

"Look, Issie. Here's a box—locked. Edwin, is this your treasure? Edwin?"

"It must be. He's turned his head so we can't see him. Isn't it funny how he can get his point across with the ability to do two things— wink and wiggle his head?"

"Turn his head, Issie. Edwin turns his head. But look, he can do three things. That's a tear rolling down his cheek. Edwin, this has been a good week for you. Your ability to do things is gradually coming back. Besides we're not going to let Gladys see the book if we think it will hurt her feelings."

"How are we going to open it up? Edwin's right here and he's not helping any. And we can't pry it open. See how pretty the box is. It was probably given to him by his mother before she passed away. We can't damage something like that."

"Issie, you are so melodramatic. We'll find the key."

"That's a tiny lock. It'll require a tiny key."

"Edwin, would you like for Issie and me to push you down the sidewalk to Eudy's for a strawberry soda? You would? Well, we'll do that right after we find the key. Would you nod your head in the direction we should be looking?"

"He's not going to do that."

"Edwin, I'll read it to you. And you can decide if we should show it to Gladys."

"Laurie . . . Laurie, I think he's going to tell. Look Laurie, he's smiling."

"Nicole got home just as the sun was sending its last rays over the horizon. Nicole wondered what Oren had been doing all day. Before she left this morning, she had gone through the house re-hiding every bottle of booze she could find. During her absence, he usually recovered a bottle or two she had hidden so lately she'd been pouring every opened bottle down the sink. And hiding the full bottles under the front steps.

"Good Lord, there he is dead. Nicole leaned over her husband lying in the grass between the sidewalk and a flower bed. If he's dead, he won't be breathing. Nicole took off her glasses and held them close to Oren's nose and then his mouth. She held them up. Good grief, he's not dead—he's dead drunk. Nicole opened her front door and went inside to think what to do.

"From the refrigerator she fixed a plate of cheese and crackers and a bowl of homemade vegetable soup. Let him stew in his own pot. Nicole turned on the radio and locked the front door. She sat in his favorite chair and ate her evening meal. I can handle this. So much peace; so quiet. It might not be bad to be by myself. No one slamming me into the refrigerator. No jackass telling me that it's my place to please his appetite. After living with Oren, it appears man needs three things: booze, sex, and an outlet for his anger. Maybe I would be better off taking Richard's advice. I certainly don't make a good sparring partner. It would probably be better for Oren if I weren't around. Without me—and my paycheck—he'd have to shape up or move back to his parents."

Laurie turned the page. "What do you think, Issie?"

"I think we better quit for the day and take Edwin to Eudy's. If we don't live up to our end of the bargain, we'll never get him to help us again."

"You think I should grow a mustache?" Sam closed the case she had been working on and looked at James to see if he had already started growing a hairy upper lip. "Let me see. Uh . . . I don't know. The only people I've ever been around who wore a mustache wore one to disguise what they looked like. What if it comes in gray?"

"I was just wondering. I've never had a mustache. You women change your hair styles on occasion and I thought I'd do something similar. I looked in the mirror this morning and said, 'James, why don't you give yourself a new image.' A mustache was just an idea. What about getting my hair permed?"

"Or you could dye your hair or use an eyebrow pencil to sketch in a few wrinkles. Are you looking to improve your looks or scare the children?"

"I just want something different."

"From what I've heard, the women like you because of the way you explain things. Isn't that enough? They think you're some romanticist visiting from a time when men talked to a woman's heart. Why change what works?"

"I have no idea where that came from. One day I decided to be me and quit trying to be someone I thought people wanted me to be. I started saying only what I believed to be true. I didn't add insincere flattery or defer my asides to a time when my audience would be more receptive. It must be that the women want to see a man for what he is and not for some sort of image he wants to flaunt."

"Mr. Dandae, you may have hit on something. Isn't that what the knowledgeable father told his son before the boy went on his first date? 'Son, just be yourself.'"

"So, what about the mustache?"

"Absolutely not."

Sam and James kept working on the files. After two weeks they were half-way through and both were getting a little cranky with the work. It was tedious. There was too much detail. And crime was depressing.

"James, did you say your son's name was Michael and he lives in Lindale?"

"Yeah."

"Here's a juvenile case with a Michael Hershey from Lindale caught shoplifting."

"Let me see it."

"Pretty cut and dry. He pleaded out and had to go to a juvenile detention house for a month. Then he had twenty hours of community service."

James reached for the file. He spent the next ten minutes reading all of the particulars. When he finished, he gave it back to Sam to let her finish entering the data onto a columnar pad.

"I guess living with a single mom doesn't provide enough money for a kid to have the clothes or other things his friends have. He was caught stealing a pair of pants."

"Yeah, I saw. And it was three years ago—probably before he got a job at the garage."

James opened another case and started feverishly putting down the data. He needed to get this job finished so he and Sam could get paid. He now had a use for his money.

That night he took a chair to the telephone and dialed the mayor's house. "Hello. May I talk with Margo, please? James Dandae . . . she knows who I am. Thank you, ma'am."

"Hello, Jim. How have you been?"

"I've been lonely. Margo, did you think I moved away?"

"No. I just wanted to give you time to reflect."

"And to see how stupid it was to take Agatha to lunch at your father's restaurant?"

"Jim, I've almost come to the conclusion that you were being nice to Agatha before she had to leave for her next town. It was New Year's Day and neither of you had plans. It was just natural for you to show how a gentleman treats a lady by herself when everyone else is enjoying the day with their family."

"You said almost. Should I call back when you've migrated further down the road of forgiveness?"

"No. Now that you've called I think we ought to dispense with the hostility and find some common interest to participate in. Do you have any ideas?"

"I thought I'd leave that up to you."

"I see. Well, I'm free every night other than tomorrow."

"And what do you have planned for tomorrow night?"

"I have to bowl on Dad's team. One of the men broke his arm on a piece of farm machinery and I've been filling in while he mends. The other bowlers wouldn't let just anyone be a substitute because Dad's teammate is such a poor performer. Anyone else and they would claim Dad had brought in a ringer. No one complains if I help out."

"That might be interesting. Could I come and watch?"

"Now, Jim. I'm not very good."

"Okay, but I was planning on taking Dad bowling tomorrow night anyway."

"Have you made arrangements? The bowling alley closes all but four lanes when they have league competition."

"I thought if I called early enough I could reserve one of the free lanes."

"Then I'll see you there."

James went looking for his dad. He was asleep in his recliner. "Dad, you ever go bowling?"

"What? Jeff, you tell your brother to march himself in here right this minute and tell me what's going on. I don't want the neighbors calling the police. Go on . . . go tell him."

"Dad . . . wake up. You're talking in your sleep."

"What? Oh, it's you. I must've dozed off. I spend some of my best hours in this chair. What do you need, James?"

"Do you ever go bowling?"

"No. Never saw the need to sling a heavy sphere at some arranged sticks."

"Would you mind giving it a shot tomorrow night?"

"I was supposed to play dominoes with Ruth tomorrow night."

"Could you change your domino party to the next night?"

"How about if we ask Ruth to go with us? I think she knows how to bowl."

"Okay, but I think I'm being manipulated."

CHAPTER 15

January 15, 1946

Laurie turned the page.

"'Richard, if you so much as breathe a word of this to anyone I will hold you down while Mother beats you with a stick. You hear me?'

"'Agnes, why do you have to be so mean? I won't say anything. I mean it was perfectly understandable. The back looked as pretty as the front.'"

"'Shut up. When Loretta said, I had the thing on backward every woman in the store laughed. I'll never be able to wear it again. And if you bring it up in front of Portia or say anything about it at the office the next person you can tell will be the devil himself because I'll damn you to hell—and Mother will take care of the bludgeoning.'"

"Laurie, I don't think Gladys will believe Mr. Stanky wrote that about her. The way she babies him, I can't imagine her being as cruel as Agnes."

"Edwin, what do you think?" Both girls looked at Edwin. His eyes rolled up and a reddish tint filled his cheeks. "Edwin, you are in a world of hurt.

"Issie, Gladys told me she went through a long portion of their marriage when she didn't treat Edwin very nice. She said at first she took him for granted. Then she blamed him for not giving her all the material things other women had. When she finally figured out that Edwin had given her what he had and loved her more than anything in this world, she said it was almost too late. She changed but had not talked to Edwin about why. Nor did she receive any assurance from Edwin that he knew. She told me Edwin was always the same genial and loving man whether she treated him bad or not. And now she tells him all the time, but he still can't tell her how he feels."

"What should we do, Laurie?"

"Agnes is mean to Richard in the play. And Gladys might have thought there were some parallels to her put in by Miss Parker, but she hasn't said anything and it looked like she enjoyed the story—especially the end where Agnes tried to figure out why all the women were weeping over Richard's death. But in the book Agnes is much worse. And Richard's mother-in-law is a real witch. If there was some way we could find out if any of those instances where Agnes treated Richard so badly actually happened. Then we'd have proof positive that Agnes is characterized from Gladys—and we'd have to hide the book."

"Let's keep the book hidden until we decide."

"What do you think, Edwin?"

"He's trying to tell us something. See how his mouth is open and he's moving his tongue. And look at his hands. They're clutching his armrests so tightly his fingers are white from lack of oxygen."

"Tell us, Edwin. What do you want us to do?" After a moment of silence Laurie continued, "He does not want Gladys to see the book."

"Laurie, you must really be able to communicate with Edwin. He's closed his mouth and loosened his grip. I think the tension in his face has even relaxed. I'll never doubt you again."

Laurie and Issie were a hundred pages into the novel when they had to quit for the day and hide it before Gladys got home. Both were in the kitchen preparing the evening meal when Gladys came through the front door. She walked straight to Edwin and kissed his face.

"I'm home, handsome. Did you miss me?"

CHAPTER 16

January 16, 1946

"Margo, they gave us lane number one. We are all the way over to the side—completely away from the action."

"Who's the woman?"

"A friend of Dad's. She's helping him find a ball. He and I rented shoes, but Ruth has her own ball and shoes. Is there another league?"

"There might be a woman's league that bowls on weekdays. Jim, I'll come check on you between games."

James located a ball that would work with the size of his thumb and sat down to write the names on the score card. "Dad, do you or Ruth know how to keep score?"

"James, I'll do that. I can't believe you've actually talked Henry into trying his hand at bowling. I've been after him to give it a shot for a year."

"So what are the arrows on the floor for?"

"Try and roll your ball over one of the arrows. If you hit the pins left of center try it again using an arrow farther right."

"Sounds easy enough," said James. "I'll go first since I've already got my shoes on and both of you are lagging behind."

"Go ahead, son. We're not in any hurry. Ruth, point me to the men's room."

James walked to a line across his alley where the gutter started. He underhanded the ball but let it go too high above the floor giving a loud thud when it hit. The ball trickled down the lane and fell into the gutter half-way to the pins.

"Good grief. It's not that difficult." He threw his ball a second time with the same result. James walked back dejected.

Ruth picked up her ball, walked to a mark on the floor, took a step, dropped her arm, and skipped three more steps. While Ruth was dancing those last three steps the ball went down, swept back like a pendulum, and was set free when swinging forward, it reached the bottom of its arc. With her back bent, Ruth let the ball slide off her hand. It rolled down the alley directly over a diamond in one of the hardboards and sailed toward impact. James thought the ball might fall into the gutter but ten feet before reaching the pins it started curving toward the center. The projectile collided with the headpin. All fell except one directly in the center. It teetered but stayed upright. Ruth waited for her ball to return. With her second effort, she threw directly at the remaining pin. This time the ball did not curve before hitting the obstinate pin directly on point.

Ruth walked back with a smile on her face. James said, "That was marvelous. Are we playing for money?"

"You want to?"

"Good heavens no."

Henry returned. "My turn?"

James said, "Yeah. You wagering anything?"

Henry looked at Ruth. "How much do you owe me?"

"Twelve dollars and twenty-five cents."

"So if we played for a dime a point and you won by a hundred points I'd lose ten dollars. Let's go for a nickel a point."

"Always Mr. Conservative."

"Dad, are you sure? The woman is semi-pro."

"It couldn't be that hard. Looks like you hit one and they'll start colliding until they all fall over."

"Uh, Dad. Maybe you should play the first game for free then settle on a bet."

"Nonsense. I beat Ruth at croquet, gin rummy, and dominoes. She normally wins at canasta. I think I can hold my own in this simple, little game."

James faced Ruth. "Ma'am, do you take checks?"

When Margo's team finished their first game, her father announced there would be a fifteen minute break before starting game number two. Margo headed to the end of the floor where one woman was heaping a sizeable amount of humility on two inept men.

"Son, I've got a blister developing on my thumb, these shoes are killing my feet, and my arm has lost all sensation. I think this will be our last game."

"Dad, this is our first game."

"Yeah, but look at the score. Ruth's knocking down every last one of those sticks. Sometimes it takes both balls but each time she walks back to write down the score there's not one sentinel standing. And that stupid grin. James, I can't stand that stupid grin."

"Dad, it's just a game. Besides I think, she's starting to get tired. I've noticed she's not snatching her ball up as fast as when we first started. Her arm's probably aching from having to swing a heavy ball."

"So James, how's it going?"

"Margo! Listen babe can you give Dad and me a lesson or two?"

"Sure. How bad are you boys losing?"

"Bad."

After three games for Ruth, James, and Henry, the trio put away their equipment, paid the bill, and sat behind Margo's team. Ruth had asked the man at the counter for the score sheet. She folded it in thirds and told Henry she planned on having it matted and framed for hanging. Henry was not talking. For the three games played he had lost more than twenty dollars and now his account receivable had a negative balance.

James watched Margo's lithesome silhouette as she fluidly glided along the alley. She didn't score as well as Ruth, but James thought her style was far more exciting. To such a manly dominated sport, Margo added a touch of femininity. He was glad she had decided not to continue her hostility for his indiscretion.

CHAPTER 17
February 4, 1946

For the rest of January, James and Sam worked long hours to organize the data suffocating the West Larimore Police Department. On Monday morning, they were slated to showcase their work on the case folders to John Pauline, the mayor, and Patrick York, head of the police department.

James stood at the end of a long table. Aligned down its breadth and facing Sam were eight library-style index card files made of gleaming oak. The mayor and Patrick sat opposite Sam, ready to be impressed.

James looked at Sam. She nodded. "Gentlemen, Miss Crocker and I are prepared to demonstrate the organization we've made of the case data. First," James pointed to the wall to his right where seventeen metal filing cabinets lined the wall, "these are the solved cases. The unsolved cases are separated, with the active ones still having data being entered by the assigned detectives. The non-active ones, waiting for links to other cases or more information to be entered that might lead them to being solved, are on the opposing wall." James pointed to ten additional filing cabinets. "Sometimes the data in the solved cases will give an insight that helps solve an open or a cold case. So let's look at what data might be available.

"Let's say, for example, an open case involves a hit and run. A suspect has been apprehended and his case entered on the docket. Sam, if the suspect's name is Sid Spade, what information could you come up with?"

Sam slid open one of the file card boxes and pulled out a three by five index card. "Sid Spade has been arrested three times for driving while drunk, once for evading arrest, and once for assaulting a minor."

"Any convictions?"

"No, but the trial for assaulting the minor starts next week. The charges were dropped for the other four offenses."

"Do you have the numbers for the five cases?"

"I do." Sam walked to the wall of filing cabinets holding the solved cases with her index card and then across the room to the files containing the open cases. Soon she had retrieved all five files.

"From the first folder tell me who the presiding judge was."

"This case was for drunk driving. It was in Judge Jack Scott's court. He threw the case out for lack of sufficient evidence."

"Did Judge Scott preside over any of Mr. Spade's other trials?"

"I can find that out by opening each of the remaining four case folders or an easier way would be to look in the Judge's file. There I have a list of every case by every judge." Sam opened a second card file and removed two cards. "Judge Scott presided over the other two Drunk Driving Charges and the Evading Arrest. All three were dismissed before trial."

"And the remaining case?"

"Let's see. Judge Arnold."

"Are there any other links you can find between the four closed cases and the current assault of a minor?"

"In the case file we have the name of the prosecuting attorney, the defendant's lawyer, the name of the assaulted minor, and the names of witnesses."

"How long would it take you to check to see if there are any common denominators?"

Sam's hands flew. "Mr. Spade used the same defending lawyer in all five cases. For the assault case I have the name of the minor and the single witness. Now let me check the current file being worked on." Sam walked a second time to the open case file cabinets and brought back to the table a folder with loose papers inside.

"It appears the hit and run victim is also the witness in the assault case. In this particular instance, the charges should probably be changed as it now appears the hit and run was premeditated."

"And there might be a link between the defendant's lawyer and Judge Scott." Added James.

"Hot damn! Patrick, this is just what we asked for." The mayor stood and offered his hand first to Sam and then to James. "I understand you want partial payment for the work done so far. Bring to my office a progress statement and I'll make arrangements for payment."

"Thank you, sir."

"No. Thank you, James. And you, Sam. You've both done an excellent job."

Patrick slowly rose from his chair. The door shut as the mayor left for another appointment. Patrick said, "I guess I better talk to the judge and get the charges changed."

"Patrick, this wasn't an actual case. We were demonstrating what could be done with the new data organizer—this time it was fictitious—for show."

"That's a relief. But what about all that data Sam looked up?"

"Sleight of hand."

"I might one day put the both of you in jail, but right now I have to go stop the mayor. He's headed to a meeting with Judge Scott."

"We've been working hard, Patrick. We didn't finish till late last night. Now Sam has to get to the library and I'm taking the rest of the day off. We'll get going again tomorrow on the personnel files."

"When can we start using it?"

"Sam has to make a procedural manual. You should make everyone read it and initial that not only have they read it, but they understand it. We'll have it ready to use by the end of the week."

"James, I am impressed. I thought you might be trying to pull something over on me, so I've kept a wary eye, but this was exceptionally well done."

"And you wouldn't mind telling that very thing to another police department checking our expertise?" Sam was standing directly in front of Patrick.

"I would do that. I think you've earned it. Of course, if the mayor makes a scene with Judge Scott, then, I'll have to take that into consideration as well."

CHAPTER 18

February 9, 1946

Margo reached for James' hand. In the dark of the theater, she couldn't take her eyes off the facial silhouette in profile of the man who had kissed her in the garden at midnight. "I'm so glad you asked me, Jim."

"Ssh. I've found talking in a library or theater is frowned upon."

"Okay. Are you taking me somewhere after the show?"

"Maybe."

Two hours later Margo and James were seated in Pauline's Café. The waitress had just brought coffee for James and a cup of hot chocolate for Margo. She had also managed two giant wedges of lemon meringue pie.

"Tell me how the play is coming along."

"Everything's going fine except for my makeup. As Nicole, I am battered and bruised and as Michelle, I start off not wearing any makeup at all. Later, again as Michelle, I start applying more makeup one scene at a time until the final scene when I am completely revamped into a beautiful woman with enough nerve and rebuilt self-esteem to actually tell Richard I love him. I'm using cold cream by the bucket."

"Nobody but you could handle both parts so expertly."

"And Agatha."

"So you think Agatha acts her part?"

"I don't want to say anything bad about the woman. But I do believe she is not the same person she portrays."

"And Reginald? How's he doing?"

"As long as he sticks to the lines he does adequately. Addy has told him more than once not to add or deduct anything from his lines. I have to admit that Agatha did a first-rate job with the dialog."

"Margo, would you hate me if I didn't come to the opening performance on Valentine's Day?"

"But that's the most important night of all. Mr. Stanky will be there with his wife, caretaker, and adopted daughter. After the play, we always have a party on opening night. The actors and the audience mix with *hors d'oeuvres* and wine. I was planning on speaking to our patrons while holding on to your arm."

"I thought as much. What do you know about Mr. Stanky's condition?"

"Just what I read in the paper. He was shot by a bank robber—almost died. Since he's come out of his coma, he hasn't been able to talk or do much of anything."

"What do you think of his daughter's claim that they communicate telepathically?"

"I'd like to see that. Maybe we could talk them into proving it somehow."

"But do you think it's even possible?"

"I have no idea. I'd like to think things like that can happen. Isn't it marvelous that the author of our play has such an interesting story of his own? Suppose Mr. Stanky is the only person who can identify the bank robber and has to tell someone. If his daughter came forth with that information then, everyone would have to admit that she and her dad communicate somehow. I'd like to see that happen."

"Not me. I find it spooky. And I don't think it would be evidence admissible in court."

"Maybe not but think about the stories that would appear in newspapers across the country. Our play would be talked about from Charleston to Seattle. Our pictures would be in all of the papers. We'd be interviewed. Whew . . . it makes me giddy just to think about it."

"So Margo. If I couldn't make the premiere would it ruin our relationship?"

"Why can't you be there?"

"I have to do something for my son."

"James, you have a son? You've been married?"

"Not quite. When I left twenty years ago my girlfriend's father was looking for me with a shotgun. I was still a kid. I didn't know what to do so I ran. When I finally came to my senses years had passed. I eventually came home to check on my parents. During my absence my mother had died and my father had become a lonely, old man. I've stayed to take care of him and to repent of my sins. I even looked up my old girlfriend."

"The woman in Lindale?"

"Yeah. I've now met my son, but he doesn't know I'm his father. He thinks I'm an old school buddy of his mother. And the tickets for the opening performance have completely sold out. I want to give the two I bought for Dad and me to my son and his girlfriend. It's not like I wouldn't see you perform. In fact, I'll see every other performance after the premier."

"Jim Dandae, you are truly a good man. You don't have to miss the first show. I'll get you a backstage pass."

"Now Margo, I don't want you to go to that much trouble for me."

"Nonsense. Jim, there is not another person I'd rather do it for. Besides, I want to. You're important to me."

James placed his hand on Margo's. "Someday you may find out things about me you'll not like. I have not always been the nicest person. In fact, I once had an angry, destructive side. Do you believe a person like that can change?"

"I do." Margo reached for a napkin to wipe a tear starting to gather in the corner of her eye. "Jim, I know you. You wouldn't do anything to hurt another person."

"Maybe not now. But there was a time when I played the game by different rules."

The hostess approached their table. "Miss Pauline, it's time for us to close. Do you need a few more minutes?"

"No. I think Mr. Dandae and I'll be leaving. Will you bring us the check, please?"

On the drive to Margo's home, James had several scenarios running through his head. None of them ended in a way that would allow him to remain un-implicated. Margo interrupted his thoughts by scooting across the seat to sit by his side.

"I've always liked winter. I don't think there is anything I'd rather do than sit by a fire and read a good book. And if it's snowing or raining outside so much the better. Did I tell you Agatha left Mr. Stanky's book? I have to give it back when she comes for the play, but would you like to read it first?"

"I would."

"It's not bound or anything so you have to be careful not to lose any pages. Agatha, or maybe Mr. Stanky, cut holes in the pages and put them in a ring binder. I think a lot of people have read it because some of the pages have had their holes ripped and are now in their rightful place but loose."

"I'll be careful."

"Come in, Jim. Mom and Dad went to bed ages ago. You can tell me about those times when you were not the model man you are now."

CHAPTER 19

February 10, 1946

"Dad, let's let Ruth read awhile. While she's getting settled, do either of you want something from the refrigerator?"

James brought back three glasses of iced tea. Ruth took a sip and placed her glass on a crocheted coaster. "Let's see. This is chapter sixteen.

"Agnes was trying on a new hat when she overheard two women closer to the front door talk about a friend they had in common.

"'Have you seen him work? He had all his tools laid out in a logical arrangement on the floor and when he needed something he'd say, 'Millie, would you be a dear and hand me the pliers?' Can you imagine? He was so polite it made me want to crawl down there and hold the flashlight. I just wanted to do something for the man.'

"'Let me tell you what he did for me. My son was trying to mow the yard but couldn't get the mower through the tall grass. The man was walking home after work and stopped to help Tommy get the mower going. He raised the blades and oiled the gears and then told my boy that it should work now, but he'd have to go over the yard twice. Mow the entire yard at the higher height and then mow it again in two days after he had lowered the blades back to their original position. Of course, Tommy never finished that first time. So the next day when it was time for the man to walk by, I went outside and started pushing the mower. He ended up mowing my entire front yard.'

"'You should not have taken advantage of him like that. He's a good man. There's not many like him around.'

"'I didn't take advantage of him. I've now fixed him two meals and bought him a new hat. And he hasn't mowed the yard anymore; he hasn't had to. He showed Tommy how to make a game out of the mowing, and Tommy thinks it's fun. My yard looks a little weird if

Tommy has to quit before he gets finished, but so what, he finishes the next day.'

"'How does your yard look weird?'

"'The man showed Tommy how he could use the mower to cut patterns in the grass. Tommy has cut squares, rectangles, triangles, circles, cylinders, cones, and wavy lines. He keeps mowing to make the patterns decrease in size until he slices through to obliterate them and starts over. The boy finally gets finished and can't wait for the grass to grow so he can do it again.'

"Agnes didn't recognize either of the two women and couldn't imagine a man going out of his way to be such a gentleman or an inspiration to a kid. That night she went through her husband's work clothes but didn't find a new hat."

James crossed his leg. "So Agnes knew all along."

Ruth said, "I don't think so. Agnes considers her husband dim-witted and easily manipulated. She only thought he might have been the man the two women were talking about because they were able to get him to do things for them with inconsequential bribes."

"Well, it's no wonder to me he finds comfort in the company of other women. I mean, look at what's waiting for him after a hard day at the office." Henry Dandae turned to face his son and continued with, "Ruth and I would like to see the opening performance, but when I called they said all the tickets have been sold."

"Let's take a short break. I've got to make a telephone call." James got up and walked into the hall carrying a chair.

"Good afternoon, Jackie. Did Theo get tickets for the play yet?"

"Yeah, third row in the center for Saturday's performance. Friday's tickets were already gone so we're going to a basketball game Friday night and to the play Saturday night."

"And the children?"

"Theo got tickets for them too. They'll be with us on both nights."

"That's good. You'll like the play. Listen Jackie, I'd like to do something nice for Michael. Would you ask Theo if he'd look around for a good used car? Nothing extravagant, just good transportation."

"Theo's already taken care of that. He bought Michael a brand new Ford Monday. One of the first off the assembly line after retooling from producing tanks. Michael has been driving the wheels off it for two days. You'll get to see the new car if you're going to Saturday's performance. Michael said he's driving."

"Okay, I'll see you there." James walked into the living room and gave his dad two tickets. "Here, take these. I plan on being sick."

"Son, these tickets are for opening night. We'll get to see Mr. Stanky. Did you hear that the mayor is giving him the keys to the city? And the police department is honoring him as one of their own with a gala at their headquarters."

"Because he got shot in an alley?"

"No, because he showed no fear to a demented criminal. You mark my words. One day he'll come face to face with the bank robber and expose him for the despicable sack of crap that he is."

CHAPTER 20

February 12, 1946

Gladys unfolded a blanket and laid it on Edwin's lap. "Laurie told me you were cold and asked me to find you a blanket. Edwin, why don't you communicate with me? Laurie says she can hear you because the two of you have brains transmitting on the same wavelength. What's she talking about?"

Gladys sat down and opened a book. In a minute, she glanced at Edwin. He was looking out the window. "Honey, this is the first train trip we've taken together. I've been from Russellville to Little Rock a few times and once from Russellville to Fort Smith, but those were day trips. Here we have a sleeping car. Are you having a good time? Issie and Laurie have been in every car from the locomotive to the caboose.

"Right now they're hidden, trying to finish your book. They don't think I know about it—but I do."

The head steward walked toward one little girl and a young woman trying their best to hide behind a floral centerpiece in the last row of the dining car. "Ahem."

The two girls looked up. "Do we really have to leave?" asked the youngest.

"Tell me the reason for wanting to stay."

"My father wrote a book when he had all his faculties. It was an expose about the mistreatment he suffered from an inattentive wife. Now he's an invalid and the wife dotes over him. She's completely reversed her behavior. We're trying to read the book without her finding out about it."

"I see. And if she finds you?"

"We'll have to own up to finding the book. She'll be devastated when she reads it."

"All right. The two of you can stay if you'll not get in the way of the workers—and you have to leave when the passengers start arriving for lunch."

"Thank you, sir."

When the head steward resumed his duties of instructing subordinates Laurie re-opened the book and began reading to Issie.

"Agnes pointed to the meat she wanted and told the butcher she wanted two servings sliced thin. In the background, she heard a woman whisper something to another woman. The second woman said, 'Her?' Agnes looked around to see who else was in the butcher's shop. Was the woman referring to her? Agnes paid for her purchase and hurried out the door.

"Earlier in the day Richard had called saying he would have to go straight from the office to his night watchman's job and asked Agnes if someone might bring his supper to the construction site. Agnes was upset for the inconvenience. Portia was going on a double date from her girlfriend's house, so Agnes would have to deliver the sandwiches herself. In retaliation, she went to the market and then to the butcher's shop. She planned on spending all of Richard's extra money on a good meal for her and her mother.

"Richard's meal was two bologna sandwiches and a pickle. Good enough for him.

"'Don't fret so much Agnes, dear. If that man of yours wants a better meal, he should work to deserve a better meal. It's the man's responsibility to provide and if all he can afford is bologna, then, he shouldn't complain when that's what he gets.'

"'I'm fine with it, Mom. I just don't want him looking in the ice box to see what the two of us are having for supper.'

"'Now think, Agnes. If he can only afford a decent meal for two people, which two people should it be for? Good manners would say that those people who he provides for should come first. You're his wife and I'm the one who gave you to him in the first place—God forgive me. I wouldn't hide the fact that we had a decent meal. He should feel gratified that he was able to supply it for us and he didn't starve in the process.'"

"Laurie, is your grandmother like Agnes' mother?"

"No. She's the kindest, most lovable woman on earth."

"Then this is not a story about the real life of Edwin Stanky."

"I'm still not convinced. Even if we can't prove it for sure, there is enough incriminating evidence to beggar the imagination. Other people will wonder and make poor Gladys embarrassed by their insinuations."

"Laurie, where do you get those words?"

"I'm going to be a writer. I've been working on my vocabulary."

"I thought you were going to be a doctor."

"I was and then I changed that to being a police officer, but I've now decided my real calling is as an author."

The head steward walked their way. "Ladies, you need to wrap it up. The passengers will be arriving any minute, but you're welcome to come back later."

On the thirteenth of February early in the afternoon the train slowed as it entered the city limits of West Larimore. In the distance, the conductor could see a multitude of people standing in groups waiting for the train's arrival. Red and white bunting decorated the train station and a giant banner welcomed Edwin Stanky. The conductor had carried important passengers before, but he had always known they were aboard and who they were. Who is this Edwin Stanky? The train conductor pulled a cord setting free a peal of steam and a shrill whistle. The town needed to know their man was arriving.

The conductor slowed the train and abruptly stopped when the doors to the passenger cars came into position next to the unloading platform. Two more whistles and the passenger doors slid open. A woman pushing a man in a wheelchair passed through the center door and was greeted by the mayor.

"You must be Mr. and Mrs. Edwin Stanky. I'm John Pauline, the Mayor of West Larimore. We're so glad you made it."

"Thank you, Mayor Pauline. Do you think we could go inside somewhere? I don't want Edwin to catch cold."

"Certainly. I've made arrangements for your transportation to the Hotel Lexington. There we've secured for you the finest lodging in our town. Please follow me. Someone will bring your luggage. We want to make you as comfortable as possible—considering this is February in

Indiana. Here we have biting wind and freezing temperatures but right friendly people."

An hour later Edwin and his family were exploring a spacious suite of rooms. "Edwin, do you feel like a big shot? West Larimore thinks you are. I could get used to this." Gladys hung her coat in an armoire. She looked to see what the girls were up to. "Laurie, what are you and Issie doing?"

"Just looking out the windows, ma'am. We're on the fifth floor. I can see most of the town from up here."

"Laurie, the paper wants to interview you and Edwin. Be careful what you say on Edwin's behalf. You don't want to appear flippant or say something that, after consideration, you'll feel the need to apologize for."

"Don't worry, Gladys. I'll only say what Edwin tells me to say."

"That's precisely what I'm afraid of. Please be careful. I'll be there to help if you need it, but he doesn't communicate with me so you'll have to be his spokesman."

After Gladys had unpacked and freshened a bit she gathered her fellow passengers and herded them aboard the elevator. The interview was held in the seating area just inside the hotel's front door. A rousing fire burned in a marble fireplace positioned in the middle of a long wall. Leather chairs were positioned in a cozy arrangement with a vacant space for Edwin's wheelchair.

After everyone had sat, the man from the paper said, "Mr. Stanky, the play was adapted from your book by Agatha Parker. Do you think Miss Parker's rendition accurately conveys what you had in mind when you wrote the novel?"

Everyone looked at Edwin for an answer. Gladys cleared her throat then said, "Edwin can't talk, but he communicates with Laurie somehow. Laurie, would you please tell the man Edwin's reply."

"I would if Edwin had one. Right now, he's thinking."

"We are in no hurry, young lady."

"Good because sometimes Edwin thinks faster than he communicates and what I get is a jumbled mess. Okay, here's what he thinks. He says he is disappointed Miss Parker had to cut so much from his story. He understands though that a play has to be performed in a period of time acceptable to an audience and to get that accomplished some important parts had to go. And there are entire scenes moved from one location in the story to another. Also, he realizes that a playwright has more difficulties to overcome than a novelist, like telling the story in a reduced number of screen sets. Overall he thinks Miss Parker did an admirable job. He doesn't believe he could have done any better and he's pleased to put his name beside Miss Parker's."

"That's remarkable, Laurie. Would you tell us how you and Mr. Stanky communicate?"

"I would if I could. I just think real hard and his words come to me like ships slipping out of the fog."

"Wonderful. Is there anything he can tell us about the bank robbery?"

"He's already told me about that." Laurie turned to Edwin. "If I say anything in error, pop in and help me get them the correct details." Laurie swiveled in her seat and said, "It was the Friday before Christmas and every store had tons of money. Edwin and the bank employee had already filled Edwin's attached satchel once and taken it to the bank for a replacement. He didn't notice anyone following but when they crossed an alley on their way to one of the last stops a man stepped out and pushed a gun into Edwin's back. It only took a few moments for the robber to get the satchel of money cut off Edwin's wrist and Edwin and the bank employee handcuffed through a building's fire escape ladder. Edwin wishes he had not yelled at the man. It was a brief exclamation to let the man know he was not home free. He would always have to be on the lookout for Edwin because Edwin was not giving up until he brought the man to justice."

"Marvelous. Tomorrow morning the Mayor has planned a tribute to Mr. Stanky. He wants to give Edwin the keys to the city and the city's police department would like to give Edwin a tour of their offices."

"We'd like to talk again with Edwin after he's seen the performance. Is that acceptable?"

"Edwin agrees. He says he'd be happy to."

James had been standing on the platform when the train pulled up. The wind was whipping with snow collecting against anything standing firm. James maintained a low profile. He was mixed in with a small

141

group of people, his head held low, and his body completely masked by a heavy coat.

In the hotel lobby, James stood in a corner while the paper interviewed the man he shot weeks before. Mr. Stanky was alert with his eyes darting around the room. He had no facial expression as his adopted daughter conveyed his answers to the paper's questions. Do those answers actually come from Mr. Stanky or is the little girl making it all up? There ought to be some way he could make a correct determination.

Is her language in the vernacular of a middle aged policeman? Does she use words and phrases an eleven-year-old girl would not have in her vocabulary? No, she'd only have the gist of what Edwin wanted her to say, not the exact words. So these words would be hers.

The little girl gave a close synopsis of the actual events as they unfolded in the robbery. Maybe she does communicate with Stanky. James wondered if Edwin remembered what he looked like. His friend, Patrick, had asked for him and Samantha to demonstrate their organizational improvements. James would soon find out if the man he shot could remember what he looked like. His game might soon be over.

CHAPTER 21

Valentine's Day, February 14, 1946

On Friday, the day of the play's premiere performance, the mayor and the West Larimore police force were scheduled to meet with Edwin at ten in the morning. James was worried.

The presentation of the city's keys at City Hall went without a hitch. The little girl must have rehearsed what she thought Mr. Stanky would say. Stanky's face was expressionless through the entire ceremony. After laying a monstrous *papier-mâché* key in Edwin Stanky's lap, the mayor patted Edwin on the back and squatted down to his level for pictures by the newspaper's photographer. For the next thirty minutes, the important people milled around City Hall in little groups.

Donuts and coffee were provided while the little girl and Edwin demonstrated their communication abilities through a game of checkers. The little girl moved her piece first then moved Mr. Stanky's piece for him. She explained she had scribbled numbers in all the squares. She was quite the showman. Several times she reached to move one of his checkers and then, at the last moment, moved her hand to a different checker. She then mildly chastised Edwin for changing his mind after she had touched a checker that did not get moved.

It did appear Mr. Stanky's moves were from a more accomplished player. Once the little girl said, "Edwin, I don't want to." She then had to take a jump and Mr. Stanky jumped three of hers all the way to the king's row. When the game was finished Mr. Stanky still had five checkers with two of them being kings.

The little girl said, "I've never won a game."

"Laurie, let me play him a game." The mayor pulled up a seat and rubbed the palms of his hands together.

It was a hard fought game with the mayor starting to perspire as Edwin Stanky surrounded the mayor's pieces and then forced him to separate his men to be picked off piece-meal. The mayor stood up from the checkerboard and said, "Young lady, I have been a little skeptical of your ability to telepathically communicate with Mr. Stanky but you have made a believer out of me. It's either that or you are the world's best eleven-year-old checker player."

James walked to the other side of the building, to police headquarters. Sam was arranging her card files. "They'll be heading here in a few more minutes. I think the little girl is a wonderful con-artist—and a damn good checker player."

"James, what's that on your lip? And your hair—it looks different somehow."

"I'm just trying to improve my looks. I thought I'd grow a mustache, but there was so much gray in it I had to buy an eyebrow pencil to color it."

"And the hair?"

"Just parted on the other side. Did I make any improvements?"

"No. You do realize that an eyebrow pencil will smear? If you happen to kiss the mayor's daughter, you'll transfer a good portion to her face."

"I'll keep that in mind."

Police officers started arriving and eventually both front doors opened for the mayor, the chief of police, and Edwin Stanky being pushed by his devoted wife and accompanied by his nurse and P. T. Barnum's granddaughter.

Patrick York said, "Mr. Stanky, a few months ago our records were in a terrible state of disarray so we hired James Dandae's company, Indiana Data Management, to organize everything for us. They've been working on it for six weeks and have finished the case files. Mr. Dandae will you give Mr. Stanky a presentation of how our records are now organized."

"I'd be happy to. Last week we finished with the correspondence files and are now putting the final touches to the personnel files. With the case files finished first that only leaves some miscellaneous records and the entire job will be completed.

Every bit of documentation except the case files is what any office manager might expect, but the case files can be searched from many different avenues of interest: by the presiding judge, the names of the prosecuting attorneys, previous felonious activities of the witnesses and the persons charged, and a dozen other particulars of the case at hand. It's the interaction of the data that makes the case files so informative to the detectives solving the case and to the prosecuting attorneys trying to prove guilt."

Laurie raised her hand. "Mr. Dandae, are there many businesses who can do this type of data organization?"

"No, young lady. I'm not aware of any company other than Indiana Data Management."

"And do you only work for police departments in the state of Indiana?"

"This is a relatively new area of expertise and so far our only customers have been within our home state but that doesn't mean we wouldn't welcome the opportunity to expand. And we are not limited to police departments. Any business with a superfluous amount of data that needs some way to organize it, so that its information is easily obtainable and relevant to the situation, could benefit. In a dynamic marketplace the companies who make the best decisions will be the ones most likely to survive and to prosper. It takes knowledge to make good decisions and that's what we make available."

The man from the newspaper raised his hand. "Mr. Dandae, may I use your comments in an editorial?"

"You certainly may. I want all companies striving to keep their heads above water to think they have someone to go to for a competitive edge."

"Sir, do you have any political aspirations? Have you thought about running for office: for mayor or for the state house of representatives?"

James looked at the mayor to see his expression. "No, not for mayor."

After the morning's festivities with Edwin and his entourage, James took his second payment to the bank for depositing. At the wooden table containing blank deposit tickets, he opened the Indiana Data Management checkbook and wrote two checks for the same amount. He and Sam had decided to take out fifteen hundred each from the four thousand earned and leave one thousand in the company for its

145

expenses and to use for marketing. James made a deposit for Sam and a similar one for himself but getting back some spending cash from his. There was one thousand of the original amount still to be earned, but it looked like they'd be finished with the entire project in another week.

Leaving the bank, James walked the few blocks to Pauline's café. He had to clear his head. What had he been thinking? Run for office? Hell, he was a criminal. He needed to keep a low profile, not be drawing attention. Running for office—any kind of office—would be to drag his past up for all to see and to scrutinize. A politician can't be hiding a skeleton in the closet. Did he want to spend the rest of his life behind bars?

A waitress showed James to a seat, gave him a menu, and brought a glass of water. Then he waited . . . and waited. After ten minutes, he went looking for the waitress.

"I am so sorry, Mr. Dandae. We have been swamped and I haven't had a chance to get back to you."

"That's okay. I want today's special."

When James returned to the table Margo was seated and looking over a menu of her own. "Hello, Jim. They must have seated you at my table."

"I'm agreeable to share. Did one of your friend's call to tell you where I was and what I was doing?"

"No. I'm in my own little world today. Tonight's the big performance after all. Jim, the planet does not revolve around you."

"No. Margo, honey, it revolves around you."

"Just so we have that straight. Do you need a backstage pass for tonight?"

"Yeah. I gave my tickets to Dad and Ruth."

"You had two tickets? Who were you planning on going with?"

"My dad."

"Oh—sorry. I keep forgetting you're not my property. And your son? Will he be there?"

"No. He's coming with his mother and her boyfriend tomorrow night."

"I've heard some of the important people are talking about you running for the state legislature. Is that true?"

"It's only talk. I'd like to, but I've got too many skeletons to hide. There is no way I could justify such an injury to our political system."

"Now, Jim. You know there have been people trying to gather information on you for weeks. So far, they've got nothing. Anyone you ran against would not be able to do better. I think you ought to consider it. Besides you don't come across as someone with something to hide. I'd vote for you."

"That's sweet of you, Margo. I could probably count on you and a few other women around town, but would that be enough to get me elected?"

"You shouldn't discount the importance of the female vote. We pool our votes to make a bigger impact. Besides, the remaining votes and how to woo them is where my dad's friends come in."

After the meal, James walked Margo to the West Larimore Convention Center and Community Playhouse where he helped with the last minute touches to the set design. Addy had opted for a spartan stage with the floor divided into quadrants, each separated by its own lighting system. Three seating sections of twelve rows each surrounded two hundred and seventy degrees of the stage. A curtain on the back wall housed additional furniture or accessories for when the kitchen, that had been in Richard's townhouse, had to double for someone else's kitchen. The back quadrant, next to the curtain, contained a breakfast area having a small table and prominent washer and dryer, a second quadrant of the stage contained four desks and a water cooler, a third had a porch swing and potted plants, and the fourth was the townhouse, minus a kitchen, where Richard lived with his wife and daughter. When the action was in one quadrant then, its lights were on and the other parts of the stage were in the dark. Sometimes actors would be sitting there but not moving. The audience could only make out their outlines and the outlines of the stage props. Sometimes the same actors would step from one quadrant into another in the dark by following luminescent markers stuck to the floor. For the last act, the porch swing was replaced with a church pew. A large wall clock with remote controlled hands kept the audience informed of the passing of time.

When the set passed Addy's inspection, she told everyone but the lighting crew to leave. She said she wanted to work on their sequencing of lighting when moving from one scene to another. James was awed by the intricacies of putting on a play. He put on his heavy coat and went home. James spent the remainder of the afternoon reading the paper and shining shoes—his dad's first, then his.

CHAPTER 22

Early Evening on February 14, 1946

"Dad, why was Mother a Democrat?"

"I've thought about that. I think it's the pull between opposites. If you were to draw a line and put the Republicans, as defined by their platform, on one end and a little further down the line toward the middle the public's Republican Party perception. Then continuing on along that line close to the middle you come to the place of political apathy. And then on toward the other end you'll find the public perception of the Democratic Party and at the far extreme the Democratic platform. Above the line let's put a bell curve graphed by the number of voters. At the two extremes you find the few die-hards who lean toward the straight ticket regardless of the people running, As you slide down the line toward the middle you'll find the voters who lean a little one way or the other but are more swayed by the charisma and speaking ability of each candidate."

"Dad for a bell curve to work in this scenario there would have to be as many republicans as democrats and with the majority of voters so apathetic that they probably would not even be voting, but I get what you're saying. You are trying to say that you tend to vote Republican but can be lured away by a slick charlatan wearing the blue of the Democrats."

"I guess so. They did not teach statistics when I went to school, but yes, I'm not an extreme Republican as I think your mother was, in that same regard, not an extreme Democrat."

"But that doesn't explain why she considered herself a Democrat in the first place."

"Okay. Let me give you the differences between the two as I see it. Republicans are for what is good for business and the Democrats are for what is good for the individual. Republicans want the government to stay out of their business and to reduce taxes. A byproduct of that is a small, unobtrusive government that places tariffs on competing products made in foreign countries and chooses the employer's side in labor disputes. Also, the Republicans do not want the government involved in any social engineering."

"What do you mean by social engineering?"

"Well, James, the Democrats believe there is a great disparity between the haves and the have-nots. These people lean toward wanting the government to redistribute the wealth, to more heavily tax the wealthy, to supply benefits to the poor, to tax inheritances so that wealth does not pass so easily from one generation to another and thus keeping the status quo so that the families of the wealthy stay wealthy and families of the poor stay poor. The Democrats believe they should share in that wealth. After all, it's the worker who makes the Republican business entrepreneur wealthy in the first place. Also, they want to force businesses to hire the disadvantaged in preference to the advantaged even when the disadvantaged are not as qualified or even as competent."

"And this second line of reasoning is from Mother's view-point?"

"To a degree. The Democrats want the government to take care of the individual. To do that requires a large intrusive government needing lots of money. Taxes supply that money so—to the Democratic viewpoint—the wealth of the nation belongs to everyone. They want social programs available for the citizen's welfare. The government calls these entitlement programs. And, since the success of business is not their primary concern, they stress the importance of environmental issues, personal privacy, and the rights of the individual over the rights of the many."

"Dad, how did you become so politically astute?"

"I found a box of your mother's articles under the bed. I've read them all. She was the astute one—not me. James, why is this important to you?"

"I was asked by our newspaper today if I would consider running for office and I wanted to know why Mom chose her Democrats over your Republicans."

"So you could pick your own affiliation?"

"I am not, I repeat, I am not running for office. I was just wondering."

"Well, before you pick the Democrats you need to know that your family has always been Republican. It was your mother who was the maverick."

CHAPTER 23

The Evening of February 14, 1946

"Ladies and Gentleman, my name is Adeline Moline. I am president of the West Larimore Thespian Society and the producer of tonight's play. But this is not just any play. This is the premiere performance of *Tell Me I'm Pretty One Last Time*.

"It was adapted for the stage by Agatha Parker. Miss Parker would you please stand?" There was enthusiastic clapping as Agatha surveyed the room and almost took a bow.

"Thank you, Miss Parker. A friend in Arkansas mailed her a copy of a novel he had just written. It has not yet been published, but we have Miss Parker's manuscript. She has donated it to our library. This unpublished manuscript is destined to be our library's most valuable treasure.

"The author of the novel is recovering from a gunshot wound he sustained during a bank robbery and presently is residing in a body not cooperating. While he travels the road to recovery, his wife, daughter, and nurse tend to his needs. He has come to us all the way from Dancing Deer, Arkansas to attend this premier performance. If the spotlight will please shine on the man in a wheelchair in the front row.

"Ladies and Gentlemen, I present to you Mr. Edwin Stanky."

There was thunderous applause which continued for ninety seconds. Then Adeline Moline continued with, "Mr. Stanky, please accept this check for a thousand dollars for your allowing us the opportunity to perform your play. He has already told us, through his adopted daughter, Laurie that there would be no charge, but we want to do something for him, so please sir, accept this check with our gratitude."

More applause.

"Miss Moline."

"Yes, Laurie. You have something to say?"

"Not me, ma'am. Edwin wants to donate the money to the West Larimore Police Department's Benevolent Fund."

"Thank you, Mr. Stanky. For those of you who couldn't hear what the young lady had to say on Mr. Stanky's behalf. She said Edwin Stanky wants to give the money to our own Police Department's Benevolent Fund."

The house roared with applause. When it died down Adeline said, "The play is about a middle-aged man yearning for a woman's true love while he manages to take care of his family where no love exists. And judging by the way Mr. Stanky's family takes care of him I'd say, if there are any allusions to real characters, they are known only to Mr. Stanky.

"Please sit back and enjoy our exciting performance of *Tell Me I'm Pretty One Last Time* adapted to the stage by Miss Agatha Parker from Mr. Edwin Stanky's unpublished novel."

James watched Addy. He stared out of an opening in the curtain behind the stage on the back wall. The space behind the back curtain was divided into three areas: two triangular actor retreats and one storage section for furniture and accent pieces needed when making scene changes. James quickly found Agatha on the front row of the left section of spectator seats. She was as beautiful as ever. His heart raced as he watched her fidget. She knew she was under close inspection from several areas. James then looked for his father and Ruth. They were on the second row of the right section. Are they just friends or is there some physical attraction between the two? James didn't want to know. Whatever the attraction, it was their own business, and he would accept the outcome no matter what.

Gladys reached for Edwin's hand. She was going to enjoy this play even if it was about her—as she had once been. She wasn't like that now, and she was beginning to believe Edwin was aware of her change. "Edwin, are you okay? Do you need a blanket around your shoulders?"

Mayor John Pauline sat on the front row of the center section. On the right side of the mayor sat Jane, his wife. On his left, in the aisle, sat Edwin Stanky in a wheelchair. Left of Edwin sat his wife, Gladys, Edwin's caretaker, and that little girl who had trounced him at checkers.

Jane Pauline said, "John, what do you know about the play?"

"Not much. I understand there is a lot more information in the book."

"Well John, dear, have you heard there are several women who want to ask the library if our daughter's boyfriend will read that book, over a series of successive nights, in one of their study rooms?"

"That's news to me."

"Ssh. It's starting."

During the first act, the male members of the audience became pompous when Richard was mistreated by Agnes, and the female members became uneasy as one of their own mistreated a very loveable fellow. Then the roles switched as Nicole was battered around by an abusive spouse. In the audience there were smirks, elbows poked in ribs, a few harrumphs, and a soft murmur or two as a particular scene struck home.

At the first intermission, there were lots of two-person conversations with the men more agitated than the women. The women were finding it harder and harder to justify Agnes' behavior. The men, on the other hand, were wondering why Richard didn't slap the tar out of Agnes. She needed it and nothing was going to be resolved until Richard took charge.

When they went back into the play from the refreshment bar, there were a lot of couples not talking. During the second act both the men and the women came to the conclusion that, for Richard to be happy, he would have to leave Agnes. And for Agnes to be happy, she would have to send the person she was most unhappy with on his way.

At the second intermission most of the patrons were through with Agnes, thinking she was a lost cause, and had begun rooting for her replacement: the men favored the prettiest and the women harbored hopes for the one with the most similarities to their own individual situation.

When the third act commenced, the audience grimaced when Richard showed an affinity to one of the female players they did not favor and smiled and murmured when possible romances commenced between Richard and someone they did favor. Then when Michelle asked Richard to tell her she was pretty one last time everyone was happy. And when the funeral took place in the fourth act the audience felt vindicated because Agnes had finally become aware of her shortcomings.

After the play, the actors and the patrons mingled with an assortment of *hors d'oeuvres* and glasses of champagne. People surrounded Edwin asking numerous questions. Edwin looked into his fans' eyes, but it was Laurie who answered their questions.

"Yes, ma'am. As far as we know this is the only book Edwin has written. Would you like to know if he will ever write again? Ma'am, you have to ask him. I only say what he wants me to say."

"Mr. Stanky, I want to know about your second book. What will it be about? Mr. Stanky? Young lady, what is he telling you?"

"Nothing yet. I'm going for a soda."

"Mr. Stanky, I'm still here."

"Hello, Mr. Stanky. That was so nice of you to give the check to our Benevolent Fund. The police officers lead a dangerous life—not that we have much dangerous crime in West Larimore but there is always the possibility. Mr. Stanky, can you hear me?"

"He hears you all right, but his mouthpiece is getting a soda. Mr. Stanky, I'm not going away."

"Edwin, I'm going after Laurie. Issie, will you tend to Edwin while I find that girl?"

"Yes, ma'am."

"Mr. Stanky, my name is James Dandae. I hope you're enjoying your stay with us. I was the first to read Richard's part and have fallen in love with the characters. When you get better I hope you will come back for a visit and get to know the people and the town more intimately. We don't have a ballpark like Dancing Deer, but then again, we also don't have an entertainment facility like the Gilded Lily."

"He can't answer you, James. Laurie has escaped leaving him speechless."

"I know." James walked away to blend in with the crowd in front of Mr. Stanky. He stayed within range to hear what Laurie had to say when she returned.

"Mr. Stanky, are you having a good time, sir? I have some friends in New York City who might be interested in publishing your book.

Here's my business card. Call me if you ever decide to share your literary efforts with the world. Mr. Stanky . . . sir?"

"Get in line. Someone has gone after the little girl he tells what to say."

"Okay, I'm back. Now who's first?"

"I am. I want to know what his next book will be about."

"Oh, yes. Edwin says that his next book will be a fictional expose on the mistreatment some patients get at an old folks home. He says that his main character is put there against his wishes and . . . wait a minute. Mr. Stanky says that will be his second new book. The one he writes immediately after he gets better will be how he finds the man who shot him. He says he has a few clues no one else is aware of. Like what the man does with his hands when he's talking, his northern accent, the way he holds his mouth when he's smiling, and the nervous tic with his right index finger when he gets agitated. He says he will hunt him down like the dog he is and he might use his friends at the West Larimore Police Department to back him up."

"Oh, there you are, Jim. Hey, what's this on your face? Ooh. I find it sexy. Let's go say hello to Mr. Stanky." Margo grabbed James hand.

"Margo, honey, I've already seen him and there is such a large crowd around his wheelchair. Why don't you go talk to him and I'll get us two glasses of champagne and meet you back here in ten minutes."

"Mom, you want to meet Mr. Stanky?"

"Honey, I want to meet Mr. Stanky and I want to talk to your beau."

"Mom, James has gone to the bar for champagne. Let's go meet Mr. Stanky."

"Nicole, tell me how you prepared for your role." A blonde woman holding the arm of a man in a blue silk suit asked while offering an extra glass of champagne.

Margo accepted the drink and a second woman said, "Yeah and how did you transition from Nicole to Michelle?"

"As for portraying Nicole, I had a girlfriend in college who had boyfriend problems. We talked about this abusive guy late into the night on numerous occasions. I just remembered how the girl was in denial. She was always offering lame excuses for him hitting her. And as for changing into Michelle, I thought about the girls at school who never got asked on a date. The ones who dressed up for the dances but sat on the sidelines while no boy walked over to ask for a dance. So if a girl was decently pretty it must be that she was extremely shy, lacking in self-confidence, not adept at presenting herself in the best possible perspective, and probably not with a wardrobe containing the latest fashions. But Michelle wanted to feel pretty; all she needed was a little nudging in the right direction. Richard did that for her. Now if you will excuse me I have to ask Mr. Stanky something before his wife whisks him away."

"Gladys, I'm getting sleepy. Having to concentrate so hard for so long is tiring."

"I know baby, but it's important to Edwin. Another few minutes and I'll let you sleep in tomorrow morning."

"Hello, Mrs. Stanky. Has Edwin had a chance to talk with Agatha Parker?"

"No, I don't believe so."

"I'll get her. She started over here several minutes ago but was waylaid by a group of admirers. Still, she and Edwin should get to talk since it is their collaborative work we're celebrating."

"Yes, well she better hurry. Edwin's main avenue of speaking is getting drowsy. Issie would you get something with caffeine in it for Laurie. Edwin has been looking forward to talking with this Parker woman."

"Mr. Stanky, this is Agatha Parker. Agatha this is Mr. and Mrs. Edwin Stanky and their daughter, Laurie Stansberry."

"Thank you, Margo. Edwin, I am so glad to meet you at last. Of course, I feel like we're old friends. Over the past few years, we have written numerous letters to each other. And your book. It was so marvelous I thought it sinful to keep it to myself. Thank you so much for allowing us to perform it."

"Miss Parker, Edwin says you did a wonderful job. You took his novel to new heights. He couldn't be more pleased."

"Edwin, if the play continues to be performed are there any changes you'd like to see made?"

"He says, Miss Parker, there are no actual people represented by any of the characters portrayed in the novel. If there was some way, this could be made known in the playbill he would appreciate it."

"I can see to that."

"Edwin, Laurie is almost asleep on her feet. If there are any more questions, we could make our address known and answer anything requested by return mail." Gladys walked to the back of Edwin's wheelchair.

"Mr. Stanky, the entire town of West Larimore is praying for your speedy recovery. Please get well and come back for another visit."

"Thank you, Miss Parker. We have had a wonderful trip and enjoyed the play immensely, but now I must take Edwin to our room. He's had a very tiring day."

As Margo and her mother walked back to where James waited, Jane Pauline said to her daughter, "Honey, you didn't get to ask Mr. Stanky your question."

"I know. How would you and Dad like to make a trip to Arkansas?"

"I guess that's possible. Is the question so important that it requires a trip so far from home?"

"Yes, Mom. It's the most important question of my life."

CHAPTER 24

February 15, 1946

"James . . . James, wake up boy. You're wanted on the telephone."

"Uh . . . hello."

"Jim, darling. It's so nice to hear your voice. I've missed you."

"Hello. Is this Agatha?"

"In the flesh."

"I'm sorry I didn't get to talk with you last night. I did see you several times, but it was always from the other side of the room. And when I headed in your direction I got caught by well-wishers who wouldn't let me pass until some inane bits of conversation had been exchanged. Then when I looked you were gone. When I spied you again, you were on my side of the room and I had traveled to yours."

"That is the most ridiculous excuse I have ever heard, so I guess, it must be true. I could give you another chance," said Agatha

"Name the place and time."

"Today for lunch at the Hotel Lexington Café."

"I'll be there with bells on."

"Would those be to alert your prey that you are on the prowl?"

"No. It's just a figure of speech to let you know how excited I am about seeing you again."

"Till twelve then."

There was a loud kiss made into the telephone and heard on James' receiver. He was immediately running down the hall to get ready.

"Son, are you okay? That's the fastest I've seen you run since you tried out for the track team. That wasn't our missionary friend was it?"

"Dad, I'm fine. And yes, that was Agatha. I'm meeting her for lunch."

"Sounds good to me but I would steer clear of Pauline's Café. That would be Margo's parents' restaurant."

"Dad, you're a little late giving me that information."

On the way to the Hotel Lexington, James walked past Elisa's Gifts. He thought he might pop in for a small gift to show Agatha the extent of his undying love.

"Good morning, Mr. Dandae. Do you need more chocolates?"

"I might. I have a lunch date at the hotel and don't want to arrive empty-handed."

"I see and this would be with that beautiful young lady, Margo Pauline?"

"Uh . . . no. A different, beautiful young lady."

"So, Mr. Dandae, you are immersed in intrigue. You must realize that Margo has eyes everywhere. I report to her on occasion."

"There is nothing clandestine in this luncheon. Margo could join us if she were not busy."

"Would you like to call her to see if she would change her plans?"

"Well no. It's not up to me. I was asked but if the young lady wants Margo to be there she'll have to be the one to ask and it would be perfectly all right with me. I mean the other woman is Margo's friend too."

"I see, so this other woman would be Agatha Parker?"

"Ma'am, I need some chocolates or, possibly, a disappearing cloak."

"I only have the chocolates. Would you like to try the Swiss box this time?"

"Why not."

"I'll be just a moment."

When the woman returned, she had wrapped the box of chocolates with a dark purple ribbon and handed the box and a sealed envelope to James. "Would you give this little note to her? It's to Seth."

"How much do I owe you?"

"You don't owe me anything. I'm still paying for that initial conversation we had where you told me about the power, the influence, and the titillation of love."

James was early for the meeting with Agatha. He sat at a small table by the window and ordered coffee while he waited. February 15th was a blustery day. Most of the snow had melted as temperatures climbed into the forties. But the main weather bandit, pummeling the land and beginning on the fifteenth, was the wind.

James opened a book he found in the lobby on his way in. It was a murder mystery. James started reading. Did he need to get some ideas? Become more knowledgeable about the current state of gathering forensic evidence? See how other perpetrators remained calm while the hero, or heroine, accumulated evidence against them? Or did he need to develop a current list of entertaining authors so he could while away his eventual incarceration reading?

James wondered how many years a convicted felon would likely get for bank robbery, for attempted murder, for armed robbery, for . . . for whatever additional crime he might be charged with.

"Oh, Jim. You look so sexy with that mustache. Have you been waiting long?"

James stood at the table and gave Agatha a welcome kiss on the cheek. Agatha dropped her purse and placed both hands on James' face. She was not through kissing.

"Jim, you got my heart thumping. I have to sit down."

"Here, I have something for you." James shoved over the box of chocolates.

Agatha winked at James and then picked up the envelope. She turned it over. James had to stop her before she opened someone else's mail.

"Agatha, that's for Seth. It's from the lady at Elisa's Gifts."

"But the chocolates are for me?"

"Yeah."

"Jim, you are such a dear. Let's open them and celebrate our reunion."

"Hello and welcome to the Café at Hotel Lexington. I'm Alexis and I'll be your waiter. We have two specials today. The first is a fired chicken salad with artichoke hearts, green olives, and romaine lettuce sprinkled with balsamic vinaigrette. The second is a tuna salad sandwich on pumpernickel. It's served with a pickle spear and chips. And we have raspberry flavored iced tea to drink."

James opened the menu. "I think I'll have a bowl of cheese broccoli soup and a loaded baked potato."

"And you, ma'am?"

"I'll have the fired chicken salad. And you can bring both of us raspberry tea to drink."

"Thank you. We also have cheesecake for dessert."

When the waitress left, Agatha opened the box and plucked out two small squares. She picked one up with her fingertips and fed it to James. "Have you thought about joining me on our tour? I am so lonely. Seth is always on the road and the workers keep their distance. I have no one to talk to, no one to eat a meal with, no one to spend a quiet evening embracing. Jim, put a little excitement in your life. Spend some time with me."

"Agatha, I have another week or so of working for the police department, but I might meet up with you after I finish. Where will you be the last week in March?"

"Bowling Green, Kentucky."

Another couple came in. James looked around the dining area. The tables were filled: some with women and some with couples. There were no unaccompanied men.

"Have our celebrities already left?" Agatha asked.

"Yes. Their train pulled out at eleven thirty. Wasn't that funny how the little girl talked for Edwin? Do you believe they could actually communicate somehow?"

"No." said Agatha.

"So, Laurie gave Edwin's thousand-dollar check away on a whim?"

"He didn't have much time to clarify his position on that, did he?"

"No. If they didn't communicate telepathically then the little girl had to be acting on her own. In my opinion, I have to think it was not faked. And I am an expert on stunts like that. I watched her play checkers. If she's faking, then, that kid ought to get an Oscar."

"Jim, let's talk about us."

CHAPTER 25

February 19, 1946

"James, do you love me?"

"Now Margo, what kind of question is that? Of course, I love you."

"Then why did you see Agatha behind my back?"

"Margo, she called me. I had no way of knowing what she wanted she just asked me to meet her for lunch."

"So you kissing her on the lips, you giving her a present, her feeding you chocolate, and you holding her hand while waiting on your meal is not true?"

"No, that happened."

"James, I can't believe you treat me this way. I must not mean anything to you."

"Now, Margo."

"Now, Margo nothing. James Merle Dandae, we are through." There was a loud click as Margo slammed down the phone.

Next day the duo of Sam Crocker and James Dandae finished their project. James handed Patrick his final bill along with Sam's list of procedures to keep the files current.

"Patrick, you might need us to check on the files periodically. In three months, we'll come back and make sure everything still works. After that, any time you need us, there will be a small hourly fee."

"How small?"

"Ten dollars per hour, per person."

"Whew, that is a lot of moola."

"It is, but we can do a lot of work in an hour."

"Okay, I'll tell the boss. In the meantime, we'll keep a list of items we need fixed or explained so that the warranty work in three months will be put to good use."

The sergeant at the information desk charged into the room. "Chief, Mr. Dandae has an important telephone call. It's about his father."

"James, you can take that in my office."

James thanked his friend over his shoulder as he ran the eighteen feet to Patrick's private office.

"This is James Dandae."

"James, this is Rudy. Your dad has had a massive heart attack. You need to come to the hospital. I don't think he has much time."

James came out of Patrick's office like a madman. He ran into a desk, knocked over the coat rack when grabbing his jacket, and raked papers to the floor while trying to put a hand through the arm sleeve. While running to the front door and getting his hand back out of his coat, James yelled over his shoulder, "I've got to get to the hospital."

"Hold on, James. Let's use a cruiser. I'll drive."

Six minutes and four harrowing miles later, Patrick and James reached the West Larimore General Hospital on the outskirts of town. James jumped out of the police car at the Emergency Room Entrance and ran to the admitting clerk.

"Where's Henry Dandae?"

"In surgery."

"Point me in the right direction."

"This nurse will take you to the waiting area. Someone will get an update and bring it to you."

"Thank you, ma'am."

When the nurse delivered James to the waiting room, Ruth walked over and gave him a big hug. "I was driving your dad to the Senior Center for an afternoon of bingo. Two blocks from your house he asked me to take him back home saying he was nauseated and his chest hurt. Before passing out his last words were, 'Tell James I'm proud of him,' I got him as comfortable as I could then sped here."

James said, "I got a call from Rudy. He said it was serious. He didn't think Dad was going to make it."

"Oh, no." Ruth sat down. "First it was my husband, then my square dancing partner, and now my best friend. I don't think the Lord wants me, just everybody I love."

James took Ruth's hand. "I'm sorry, Ruth. We have to be strong. He will be in a better place. I know he loved you but he was married to my mother for forty years and she's been waiting for him."

"You're right, James. Your dad and I had two good years as friends and I'm glad for it. A person shouldn't grow old by themselves. Henry and I played cards, board games, bingo, and one evening of bowling. I owe him seventeen dollars."

"Are you Mr. Dandae's son?"

"Yes, sir. I am."

"Your dad fought the good fight, but his heart wasn't strong enough. I lost him a few minutes ago."

CHAPTER 26

March 4, 1946

"Hello, Jackie. I'm glad you had time to meet me. I was down in the dumps this last week. Have you heard? My father passed away."

"No. I'm sorry, James. He was always nice to me. Of course, I was closer to your mother, but your dad was a kind and gentle man."

"Yeah. Michael is now the only family I have."

"I don't think he needs to know about your dad. Michael never met the man."

"Maybe not, but I have a proposition for you. Dad left me a small life insurance policy and I now own his house. If you would tell Michael that I'm his father and let me spend some time with him every once in a while, I'd use the insurance money to give him a good education."

"James, Michael doesn't want an education. He wants to get married and have a decent job working with his hands."

"As a mechanic?"

"Yes, but Theo isn't in the picture anymore, so Michael had to give the Ford back. He's now looking for another job. He hopes to work for a garage. At least, Theo gave him proper training."

"How about I go into business with Michael? I put up the money, he does the work, and we split the profits."

"Let me think about it. Will you stay in West Larimore now that you have no ties to the community?"

"I don't know. Having a house is nice. You have something of value when you own a house. I guess that gives me roots of sorts. I feel like West Larimore is my home and I've made friends, so yes, I'll be staying for now. There's a woman I'm interested in and I plan on spending a few months convincing her to marry me and come live in West Larimore. So when that's done, I'll be here on a permanent basis."

"This partnership you're proposing—would it have enough money to operate while it gets going? I've heard most small businesses close during the first year because the owners didn't have enough capital to keep them afloat while the company builds up its clientele."

"I can put up five thousand dollars."

"Okay. When do you want to talk to Michael? If he agrees to the arrangement, I'll tell him about his parentage."

"Let's do it today. The one thing I have learned from my father's death is that a person has just so much time, and no one should put off important things. There might not be enough time to get them done."

"All right, follow me home. He's there. Every day he's been looking for a job, and today he said he didn't have any more places, so I left him reading the paper."

An hour later, James and Michael sat at Jackie's kitchen table. James asked for a tablet of paper and a pencil. Jackie also gave him a cup of coffee.

"Michael, I understand you're a decent automobile mechanic."

"Yes, sir. Theo gave me an old car to work on and I fixed it up real good. He sold it for a profit."

"Well, I've recently inherited some money and I'm looking for a place to invest it. If I was to buy a garage and stock it with the necessary tools, would you consider being my partner? I supply the money, and you do the work. The garage would pay you a weekly salary and once a year we see how much money we're making. After raking a little off the top to improve our cash picture, we split the remainder down the middle."

"Would I have to do all the work?"

"At first we probably wouldn't have enough business to keep two mechanics busy, but after a while, I can see having a larger labor force."

"Mr. Dandae, there might be problems with that. Most of the mechanics around here are ancient. I'm not sure they'd do what I told them."

"I see. Let's modify our business plan. How about a used car lot. We buy old cars and you get them running then we sell them for a profit. Since they are our cars, we can be working on three or four at the same time, but without a definite date to be finished. You could eventually hire someone like yourself to help. You wouldn't have to hire a seasoned mechanic just someone who wanted to learn and you oversee his work. Or you could do all of the work yourself. We'll probably have to go several months without making a sale while we get a few cars ready for the lot. I know a little about selling, and you know a little about repairing. I'm willing to take the risk if you are."

"Mr. Dandae, you have a deal. Let's shake on it."

"That's great, Michael, now I think your mother has something to say to you."

"You mean about you being my dad and all?"

"Yeah. You already know?"

"When Mom and Theo broke up and I had to give the Ford back, she said we might be able to get you to buy me a used car. She said that you had mentioned it a few weeks back."

"Aren't you upset that I ran off and left your mother before you were born?"

"All I know is that you left to find work and started sending us a check each month after I was born. One day I ran across a bundle of notes you had included with the checks. They all said the same thing, 'Dear Jackie, here's the money I earned this month. Love James.' It came every month—until stopping about three years ago. Mom said you probably thought I was old enough to start providing for myself. Then when she introduced you as James, I knew."

"Michael, I'm not much of an emotional man but if you would give me a hug right about now I'd appreciate it, because I'll remember this day for the rest of my life."

CHAPTER 27

March 5, 1946

James drove around West Larimore looking for a run-down garage with a large parking area. What he found was a service station that had gone broke. From looking in dusty windows, James determined it had two bays—one with a hydraulic lift. It also had an office area and two public bathrooms. Outside were three gasoline pumps.

James called the number on the real estate sign and waited for the salesman to arrive. He didn't plan on making an offer just getting the facts to talk over with his new partner.

When the man arrived he was wearing a plaid sports coat and a black hat with a feather sticking out the back like a colorful bird had landed on his brim and was now eating sunflower seeds with only his tail sticking up. The man came strolling to James' car jingling a set of keys.

"Mister, this is your lucky day. I haven't made a sale this week and my baby is sick with the flue. My wife just called and said for me to pick up the baby's prescription. Sir, whatever you're offering I'm accepting, but I need some of it today."

"Then let's go inside and see what's for sale."

"You, sir, are in for a surprise. She needs a coat of paint and the gas pumps calibrated. Then you're in business. Be thinking of a catchy name and a color scheme. I've already got the telephone number of someone who can get those pumps working. Then we'll call the state department of weights and measures to get them certified as accurate and call the wholesaler to clean out the tanks in the ground and check for leaks before delivering your first order of gas. You might need to buy a safe to hold all the money you'll be making."

The man unlocked the front door and kicked some boxes out of his way as he reached for an electrical switch. "Damn, they must've turned off the electricity."

James said, "Do those big doors go up?"

173

"I think so. Let's try one."

"Better try this one. That other one's track is hanging loose."

"My good man, that's easily fixed. Oh dear, this one is stuck. Listen, I'll reduce the price to compensate you for making the necessary repairs."

"I thought you were going to take whatever I offered."

"Yes. I did say that, but you have to cover the outstanding debt at the bank and add three hundred for my commission. I was going to include a little profit for the owner but with the repairs I think he'll have to be happy with being relieved of the debt."

"So that makes it about eight hundred dollars?"

"Good heavens, man. This is prime real estate: a corner lot on a busy street. The bank wouldn't loan him but seventy-five percent of what it was worth and he paid on that for two years before the bank foreclosed. I'll have to have sixty-two hundred for the bank and three hundred for me. So you can start living the American dream for a paltry six thousand, five hundred. No, I don't want any commission. Make it sixty-two hundred to repay the loan and ten dollars for my pocket. I'll swing it at the bank."

"Here's what I'll do. I'll assume the note at the bank and give you two hundred dollars for your pocket."

"The bank won't go for that."

"Yes they will. I'll open a savings account and tie that to the collateral. Besides I'll be making repairs to the building so if something happened and they had to take it back, it would be a more saleable commodity."

"Okay. I'll take it to them."

"I'll want to see the original loan and an amortization schedule showing the payments the owner made and his telephone number. It's not that I don't trust banks. Yes, it is. I don't trust banks. And I don't trust salesmen. If you'll be on the up and up with me we'll do more business, but, if you mess with me, I'll buy your brokerage firm and fire you for incompetence."

"My wife would appreciate that. She's been after me for years to get a real job. One that pays enough for us to live on."

James reached into his vest pocket and took out a soft leather wallet. He removed two fifty-dollar bills and replaced the wallet. "I don't know your name but I'm willing to trust you for a hundred dollars. Pick up the prescription, kiss your wife, and make the offer to the bank. Here's my business card." From another pocket, James took out a sterling silver business card case and handed the man a card saying he was the president of Indiana Data Management Company.

Driving home James thought about a name for the new enterprise. He hadn't moved into the larger bedroom yet and still had to go through his dad's things but that was depressing and finding a location for him and his son's joint venture was more fun by far.

"Hello Jackie. I found a place in West Larimore. Would you put Michael on the phone, please?"

"James, West Larimore is twenty-five miles from Lindale. Why didn't you find one here?"

"Why didn't you tell me about those letters?"

"Well, I figured they were from your mom. The postmark was from West Larimore, but Michael didn't need to know what I thought. So back to my question. Why did you not find a garage in Lindale?"

"And be in competition with Theo? I've made friends here and that gives us a head start."

"Here he is. But James, I'm not happy."

"Hey, Mr. Dandae."

"Michael, if you're uncomfortable calling me Dad you can call me James. I've found us a location. Your mother is not too happy about it being in West Larimore, but we'll have to work around that. How about you and I having a strategy session. We got to come up with a good name, decide the hours we're going to be open, the color scheme for the building, and a thousand other details."

"I'd like to see it, but I don't have any wheels. Can you come get me in the morning?"

"Yeah. Pack an overnight bag. I think they're going to accept my offer, and I've never had much patience. The building needs repairs and, if the bank and I come to terms, I want to get started on those as soon as possible."

James went to the kitchen. There wasn't much in the pantry or in the refrigerator. He thought he ought to get his head back on and organize his affairs. Tomorrow he would clean out his father's closets and restock the food supply—and he'd move into the larger bedroom with a shower. Tonight he was going to tough it out. It's either a bowl of oatmeal or get in the car and drive to a restaurant. Possibly he'd see Margo. What's going on, he thought. As soon as you get this business up and running for Michael you'll be heading to Bowling Green, Kentucky and the most exciting woman you've ever met. Why in the world can you not get Margo out of your head?

What if something happens while I'm gone? Maybe I should make a will. Yep, that's a loose end I'll have to tie up before leaving.

The next morning James pulled up in front of Jackie's house. Michael was sitting on the doorstep with a small suitcase. "I'm glad you finally made it, James. The sun's been up for hours."

James looked at his watch. "I've never been an early riser. Always in too much trouble the night before. Is your mother here?"

"No. She's at work."

"That's good. I was going to assuage her misgivings. There's no need in upsetting the establishment if a kind word or a simple explanation will mollify the problem."

"She's not going to be a problem. She lets me make my own decisions. We've always been good friends, but sometimes having a good friend is not as necessary as having a good parent."

"Okay, I'll defer to your sound sensibilities. How about we start the day with breakfast? Your girlfriend's restaurant, perhaps?"

"Let's go. Betty works at the Lindale Dandy Diner. It's downtown."

Betty seated the two men, brought them water, took their orders, and dropped off two cups of coffee.

"Michael, here's what I got. A building that used to be a gas station with two bays and a decent lot. And it sits on a busy corner. I think we ought to use one of the bays for mechanical repairs and the other—the one with a hydraulic lift—for oil changes.

"Our first car is my father's Desoto. It's never been in an accident but runs sluggishly. What do you think?"

"What about the gas pumps?"

"I don't know. Do you think we should make this into a gas station, auto repair, used car lot thingamabob?"

"Theo says you have to have several strains of revenue to be prosperous. You never know where the money is lurking and looking for it in several places beats scrounging around in just one."

"Okay, multiple businesses it is. Let's figure out a name. How about Mike's Car Works?"

"No. If you ever want to sell the business, it should have a name that travels well. If either of our names is used, we lose the goodwill that provides the high price. If the new owner has to change the name and start over he won't want to pay for pie in the sky."

"Michael, why don't you go to college? You're a smart man. I'd cover all the costs."

"Betty and I want to get married and I don't want a boring job. What I'd really like to do is build race cars. Not race them mind you but build them. I want to soup up an engine and listen to it purr. I want to build a car that slides effortlessly through the gears, accelerates with power through the corners, and stops on a dime."

"We ought to do that. Let's build those cars. We'll call it the Indiana Racing Factory."

"I'd need to take some correspondence courses."

"How much salary do you need?"

"If Betty got a job waitressing and you paid me forty a week we could get married. We'd rent an apartment in West Larimore close enough to work that I could walk and . . ."

"Set your standards higher, son. How about I pay you fifty a week and give you a nice two bedroom house with a fenced backyard for a year. After we've been in business that year, you'll probably have enough profit available for you to buy your own house."

"At fifty a week, and a house to boot, Betty wouldn't have to work unless she wanted to. Suppose she operated the cash register and wrote up the repair tickets for me?"

"That might work."

Betty brought the food. "The guy two booths over wants to know if you gentlemen might need some help. And my boss told me I have to give a notice if I'm leaving. Can't you cowboys keep it down?"

James said, "I'm sorry Betty. We're so damn excited we must've let the volume knob creep up when we weren't looking."

"Babe, I'll call you tonight."

"You better. I don't want to be an after-thought."

When James and Michael pulled to the front of the gas station, Michael jumped out of the car and ran to look through the windows into the two bays. "We'll have to improve the lighting and it doesn't look like there's any heating."

"Hold on. Let's not get too carried away. I'll go across the street to the drugstore and call the agent. He might know something by now."

Fifteen minutes later James was walking back with a grin on his face. "I've got to go to the bank and sign the papers."

"You need me to come along?"

"You might as well. No telling how long it'll take. We have to open a bank account, order our checks, pay the utility deposits, have a telephone installed, and there are numerous other things to take care of. Maybe at that point we should go to the house and make a list. Then tomorrow you take your list and start working on it and I'll do the same with mine."

Michael's list contained the painting and repairs to the building while James' list contained repairing and calibrating the pumps, opening an account with a gasoline supplier, and registering their company's new name with the county clerk's office. James also had to procure insurance, obtain a sale's tax permit and a City of West Larimore license to do business. When he got home, he found Michael working on the Desoto.

"James, I hope you don't mind. I got to have some way to get around."

"No. We need to use all our resources."

"There's nothing wrong with your dad's car. I'm changing the oil and filter. And I adjusted the carburetor."

"Maybe I could get the Ford next in line. After we get the business up and running, I'll be leaving for a while."

"How long will you be gone?"

"Long enough to talk a young lady into giving up show business and come live a slow-paced life married to an old man in a hamlet."

"That might take a while."

"Tonight I'm going through my dad's stuff. You and Betty can have the house when I leave. I suppose the two of you have made plans?"

"Yep. But it's going to be a simple affair. She has an uncle who's a county judge and we'll be married by him in his chambers."

That night James and Michael piled Henry's clothes in the back of the Ford for delivery to a charity. The remaining artifacts, representing the lives of James' parents, were divided into three stacks: the items James wanted to keep for himself, the items James and Michael thought they might find useful for housekeeping or for the business, and everything else James would sell on the driveway.

CHAPTER 28

March 6, 1946

James decided to wait until the weekend to have the driveway sale, since that was still three days away, he thought he'd show Betty the house and talk to her about doing the paperwork for the new business.

"Michael, now that the building is about ready for us to open we need to purchase the tools you'll need and to decide on our operating procedure. Will you be able to work with Betty? I've heard that some marriages do better if each participant has a degree of independence. Working together requires one to be in charge, and women, these days, don't like to be told what to do."

"Betty's not like that. Still, if we were to give her tasks she's responsible for without our interference then we could help if she needed it and asked for it and I'd do the same. She ought to go for that."

"Let's talk to her about it. If she agrees then she ought to give her notice, because, two weeks from Monday is our grand opening."

"I've made a list of the tools we'll need, but I don't think we can have them delivered and installed in time. What about you and me driving to Indianapolis and pick them up. When I added their costs from the catalog, it totaled five hundred dollars. We have to go through Lindale so we could talk to Betty on the way."

"Michael, I'm a little slow on the uptake, but I now believe you've had this planned for a few days."

"Yeah."

"Okay, I'll pack a bag while you change the oil and filter on the Ford and we'll drive to Lindale, talk to Betty, and let you pick up some clean clothes."

"I'll take care of the Ford, but I want to drive to Indianapolis in the Desoto. If it's going to be our test car, I need a good idea of where we're starting from."

"Like I said, I'm a little slow on the uptake, so you have to let me know ahead of time what's going to happen."

At ten, James and Michael sat in a booth with Betty at Lindale's Dandy Diner.

"Betty, we need your organizational expertise in managing the Indiana Racing Factory."

"You do? I thought you and Michael were going to run it together."

"Since I don't know anything about cars, Michael's going to do most of the work. Actually, I have another business to run, and I've made plans to be out of town for the first six or eight months. What he and I have decided is to hire you to manage the office, schedule the work, handle the customers, deposit the money, and pay the bills. Michael and I haven't talked yet about your salary, but I imagine it will be about what you're making here.

"Michael has probably already spoke to you about this, so I just want to be privy to what the particulars are and find out who will be responsible for what."

"Yes, we've talked, and I'm as excited as he is. Would it be all right if I came to look at the house?"

"Sure. Have you set a date for the wedding?

"The second Saturday in March."

"Wow. That's a week and three days from now and only one week before we open on the twenty-fifth."

"I know. Everything is happening so fast. I'll tell my boss today.

"And you'll be happy working in an auto repair shop, used car lot, and gas station thingamabob?"

"Yep."

James had the driveway sale on Saturday. Quite a few of his friends came by to see what he might be selling. Margo made an appearance but got something in her eye after purchasing the telescope James had received as a Christmas present thirty years prior. Her mother took her home. James made enough money from the items sold to purchase a three hundred dollar gift certificate to the nicest furniture store in West Larimore. It would be his wedding present to his son and new daughter-in-law.

Michael and Betty got married in a small ceremony a week later. The only people invited were Jacqueline and her parents, Theo, Betty's parents, and James. Betty was pretty in a white dress. After the wedding, the new couple drove to West Larimore. They had agreed to work hard the first year and to use their share of the first year's distributed profits for a postponed honeymoon.

James moved to the Hotel Lexington for his last week in town. He'd be leaving for Bowling Green after the opening day festivities at the Indiana Racing Factory. James spent a good portion of that last week preparing the advertising in the local paper and placing flyers on every available billboard. He also helped Michael dress the building in festive colors.

When the opening day came, a radio station set up their broadcast in the parking lot and everyone stopping by received a baseball cap with an Indiana Racing Factory insignia. James even hired a vending truck to hand out free hotdogs and beverages.

John Pauline and his daughter, Margo, stood by the front door. Each had a hotdog in one hand and a beverage in the other. John said, "So James. Are you going to be building cars for the crooks so they can outrun our police cruisers?"

"No, sir. We're going to make improvements to cars so that all law-abiding citizens will start to look at his automobile as something fun to drive, something exhilarating to drive. But you might want to consider making alterations to the police cruisers so that the criminal element doesn't become our primary source of business."

"How about building a car for the Indianapolis five hundred?"

"Now that's an idea. But I think we'll start off on a more practical track. My son, Michael wants to build a safer car. One with improved cornering and braking abilities. He's the one with the talent. I just put up the money."

Margo said, "Jim, I'm sorry about your father. How's Ruth taking it?"

"Thank you, Margo. Ruth is handling it better than me. At her age, she's already lost several friends. She says you can never get used to losing someone close, but she already knows how to deal with the pain and the sorrow. Ruth checks on me every few days.

"And I want to thank both of you for the flowers and the food your restaurant delivered. I have never been good at taking care of details. My mind tends to wander when depressing things creep in."

"Jim, that happens to everybody. You have to let your friends be a source of refuge, to offer a helping hand, to help you manage the pain. Your dad lived a good life. He was well thought of in West Larimore."

"That's right, James. But it was your mother who told me I should run for mayor. She became my campaign manager and I knew her better than I did your father. Now, you don't have either. Son, if there is anything I can do, we're here for you."

"Thank you, sir. I knew my mother was politically involved but not that she helped get you elected. I keep learning new things about her. And I appreciate your concern, but I'll be all right."

John Pauline smiled and then walked to where Michael had prepared his working area.

Margo stayed behind. She said, "Have you made any decisions on what you're going to do now?"

"Margo, I need to get away. To clear my head. I'm going to catch up with Agatha and help with her evangelism. She told me she was heading south into Kentucky and then west through Missouri or Oklahoma."

Margo had tears in her eyes as she said, "That means we are truly through and I don't get to use my last wish."

"It depends. What is your last wish?"

"Jim, I can't ask for anything selfish, so I'll just ask that you find peace for your soul and love for your heart." Margo wiped her eye and put her hands in her pockets. She said, "Goodbye, Jim" and went looking for her dad.

At the end of the first day in business, Michael had pumped a hundred gallons of gas and been promised one customer's car for an oil change later in the week. Not much money made it into the till, but a lot of potential customers now knew the Indiana Racing Factory was open for business.

CHAPTER 29

March 26, 1946

James thought he was on the right track. Agatha was waiting for him. He'd tour the Midwest and points beyond with a beautiful woman. James decided he'd be on his best behavior as he strutted his stuff. He had once watched a bird strut his stuff. The bird fluffed up his wings, puffed out his chest, and danced in circles while a female bird tittered nearby. James planned his strategy: he'd start out slow, being always handy, interesting to talk to, pleasant to be around, friendly, lovable, and a little mysterious. He wondered how long it would take for him to convince Agatha that she needed to settle down, let a man take care of her for a change, and learn the advantages of being a loved woman.

The towns flew by as James traveled through Indiana. By nine in the evening, he was sore, had developed a cramp in his leg, and his backside was uncomfortable from being in the same contorted position for several hundred miles. James pulled into a motel inside the Kentucky State Line.

The next morning James was up early, showered, and on the road. Before escaping the confines of another small town, James stopped at a diner for breakfast. In his previous life when he stopped at a diner, it was usually to case the joint for a possible robbery. That was behind him now.

Thursday afternoon James pulled into Bowling Green. At a café on Main Street, he asked the waitress if they were having a revival in town.

"A few weeks ago there was a rumor of one coming to town but they never showed."

"No revival at all?"

"Not the first one. I heard the city council wouldn't grant them a permit."

"Why not? Bowling Green got something against missionaries?"

"Certainly not, but I can't rightly say why they didn't get their permit."

James checked into a hotel. Tomorrow he'd scout around and find where they might've headed instead of coming here. That night James had a weird dream. Margo and Agatha were teeter-totting. They were having fun, giggling, and waving their arms in the air. It was a big teeter-totter—maybe sixteen feet in length. Margo said she needed to add a sack of flour to her side so that their weights would be more equal. The next time Margo was high in the air Agatha jumped off. She walked away as Margo came crashing down. James woke in a sweat. He could only remember bits and pieces of the dream but was not happy with Agatha for some reason.

After a bowl of oatmeal and two pieces of toast James headed to the city clerk's office. "Good morning, sir. I'm trying to catch up with a lady evangelist. She told me Bowling Green was her next stop. But I understand she didn't make it. Can you help me? Did someone come to town to purchase a permit? A tall skinny man in a frock coat, perhaps?"

"Yep. Sold him one too."

"But they didn't use it?"

"Nope. Asked me to point him in the direction of the post office. In thirty minutes, he wanted his money back."

"Did he tell you why?"

"I told him the town appreciated his purchase, but it was non-refundable. He stormed out without giving a reason."

"Did he say where he was headed next?"

"No. You might check with the police department."

The Bowling Green City Police Department was located in a two-story white painted brick building. James entered through two glass paneled doors into a maze of public servants, ringing telephones, filing cabinets, whirring fans, and desks piled high with work. James continued to the information desk.

"I was supposed to meet up in your town with a group of evangelists. The city clerk's office thought someone here might know where they went when they bypassed Bowling Green."

"Let me call Detective Sandoval. Have a seat it won't be but a minute."

James waited in a place where he felt uncomfortable. He had dreamed of being interrogated in a place just like this then being led to a cell in handcuffs. James started sweating under the collar.

"You the one asking about the revivalists?"

"Yeah. Is the police department keeping up with them?"

"We just like knowing who's coming to our town and why."

"Do you know why they didn't have their revival after getting a permit?"

"No."

"Do you know where they might be now?"

"No. We do know the towns they came through before getting here. Here's the list of the ones we got. Mind if I ask you some questions?"

"Sure. What can I help you with?"

"What do you know about Seth Holman?"

"I've met him. He doesn't talk much. Pretty much keeps to himself. Kind of slithers when he walks."

"We've heard he talks a lot. You know anything about his insurance company?"

"No, nothing."

"Mr. Dandae, why are you trying to find them?"

"I'm a friend of Miss Parker's, the evangelist. I'm going to donate some of my time to help her."

"I see. Here, take my card. When you catch up with them, I'd like you to report back. We think this Seth character might be a person of interest."

"Did he do anything in your town?"

"No. We had an inquiry from the FBI and I have to respond to their request for information."

"Yes, sir. I thought there might be something wrong with him. I'll find out what I can. Now about this insurance company, is there any information you can give me?"

"No. That's what you'll have to find out. Now let's take that list of towns and figure where they might have gone."

James pulled into Hopkinsville worried for Agatha's safety. He had never been a fighter, but if the situation called for it, he thought he could take Seth. Any average, physically fit man should be able to handle a sickly, emaciated, beanpole. From a downtown, café James found that Agatha's revival was about to start and she was staying at the Belvedere Hotel a few blocks down the street.

After securing his room, James had the desk clerk connect him with Agatha's room. "Hello. I'd like to schedule one of them revival things. Do you charge by the hour or the number of converts?"

"Jim, I don't find that funny. How'd you find me?"

"I asked the waitress at the first restaurant I came to."

"Here in Hopkinsville?"

"Yep. I haven't eaten yet. You want to meet me downstairs in the hotel's restaurant?"

"Ten minutes."

Ten minutes later James was sitting across from a woman who made his heartbeat race. "Agatha, you look beautiful."

"Thank you, Jim. Have you come to keep me company?"

"To help in whatever capacity I can."

During the course of the meal, it was determined that James would help with the tent and collection of donations. And in return for his services, she would pay for his lodging and the gasoline for his car—but no salary.

"How's Seth?"

"About the same. He's also here in the Belvedere. Tonight is our second service and it's in a pasture at the edge of town. I'm sure glad we haven't had any rain for a while. With you here, Seth can leave so he's there an hour before we begin to make sure everything's all set. You and I can go in your car and arrive about six forty-five. The service usually lasts an hour."

"Agatha, do you worry that Seth manages your money properly?"

"I have complete confidence in him. He's been with me since halfway through my first road trip. At first I didn't do so well handling the bills, or even paying the men, so he asked if he could take over that responsibility. He's done very well. So well, I have not had the first complaint."

"Does he have any side business?"

"Let's not talk about him. Let's talk about us."

"Okay."

"Jim, I heard your father died?"

"Yeah. At first I took it bad. For a week, I was so depressed I thought I couldn't go on. Then I got a telephone call from one of my dad's church friends saying Dad had a life insurance policy listing me as the beneficiary."

"I set my son up in a business. That must have been therapeutic, because, I instantly started feeling better. Michael never met his grandfather, but it's grandfather's money that has changed his life."

"Did you spend all of your inheritance?"

"Not all of it and I still have the house."

"Okay, I need to cut this short. There is still some polishing I have to do on my sermon. How about I meet you here at six-thirty?"

When they arrived at the tent, Seth and three men were arranging chairs and a podium. There was a low hum that could be heard when it wasn't being drowned out by the men bickering or Seth barking out orders.

In ten minutes, people started arriving. James went outside the tent and observed the men directing traffic with flashlights. Actually it wasn't dark yet but the flashlights were needed to point out lanes and empty parking spaces. Each man wore a purple jacket embroidered in gold with "Agatha Parker Ministries."

James went back inside the tent. Where was Agatha? At the back of the podium, an interior curtain cordoned off a section of the main tent. James looked for an opening. Stepping through, he found Agatha sitting at a table with her bible open and a briefcase at her feet. It must be where the men slept, because besides the table, there was a small refrigerator and a portable stove with extension cords snaking to the floor and out the back of the tent toward the humming noise. In the corner were several, stacked, twin-sized mattresses and a few randomly placed folding chairs. James didn't remember Agatha carrying a briefcase when he brought her from the hotel. It must be Seth's.

"What can I do to help?"

"Stay out of the way until it's time to pass the hat. We'll be more instructive about your duties tomorrow before our next service."

"I can do that." James sat in a neighboring chair, then got up and walked to a stack of bibles. He picked one up and returned to his chair. Beside the table of bibles was a record player with wires going to a box and then more wires traveling from the box under the canvas flooring. He thought those last wires must be running to speakers.

A few minutes before seven, a man in a purple jacket sat down in front of the record player. In just a minute or so of fiddling, he had the entire tent filled with organ music. At seven, he heard from the other side of the curtain, the same man tell the people in attendance that they were appreciated and they would soon be hearing a revival message from one of the newest and most accomplished of all traveling evangelists. He asked everyone to bow their heads, and then led them in a short prayer. For the next five minutes he talked about the towns the Parker Ministries had been through and a summarization of the life story of Agatha.

"Now let me introduce you to Miss Agatha Parker, emissary from The Glorious Council of Traveling Evangelists. Ladies and Gentlemen, Agatha Parker."

James heard a sizeable amount of applause when Agatha stepped through the overlapping of the curtain.

"Is anyone here worried about getting into heaven when your time comes? Let's talk about why you don't want to be cast into the alternative."

James took a chair and went to the farthest edge of the curtain. From a small crack, he could see the audience and if he opened the crack a little bit more he could see the podium and Agatha. He really didn't have to worry about being discovered because every eye in the house was on the beautiful Agatha Parker with the flashing eyes.

Who brought the briefcase? It wasn't Agatha's.

Through the curtain, James could hear applause, occasional moments of complete silence, short bouts of singing accompanying a guitar followed by hand-clapping—or was that foot stomping, and shouts of "Amen, sister." But James was more interested in what was in the briefcase. It had a small lock. Years ago when his fingers were more flexible, a lock of this sort would not have been a problem, but now James needed a new pair of glasses and his fingers had developed a touch of arthritis.

"Damn, I may have to cut this thing off."

From the corner of the stage, the curtain opened a bit and a man whispered, "Mr. Dandae, it's almost time to pass the plate. After the service, we give the plate to Jerry and then stand ready to help anyone who might need assistance getting to the door."

"You guys have a regular routine. I'm happy to help any way I can, just let me know what I'm supposed to be doing."

"Right. There's our cue."

From the far edge of the stage, the two men descended three steps. James held an offering plate as his fellow worker walked to the other side of the front row of attendees. Agatha gave a short prayer and then the guitar player began playing slowly as Agatha talked over the loudspeakers in a soft persuasive voice.

"Please give what you can. We depend on your donations to keep our ministry going." Agatha walked to the left area of the stage. Looking straight at the attendees on that side of the audience she continued with, "When you stand at the pearly gates the angel holding the keys will look into your heart. Jesus said he loves a cheerful giver." Agatha slowly made her way to the right area of the stage and made eye contact with the members of her audience on that side. "You are not allowed to take any of your riches with you. Don't let anyone think you were a miser with your money. God knows and sees everything." Agatha then moved back to the center. "If you fold a dollar so that it looks like it might be a ten, or more bills than you actually put in the plate, no one will know but you and God. Give what you can but don't give if it means a hardship on you or the ones you love. We need some of your extra money, but not the portion you need to feed your family. Think of us as you might an emissary from Christ. We don't use the money for our benefit but to keep our ministry going.

"All right, please stand and hold the hand of the person standing next to you as we close our service with an old favorite everyone knows."

Fifteen minutes later the tent was empty, the last of the cars were leaving the parking lot, and the workers were walking back with their flashlights. One of the returning workers asked James. "Sir, do you have a bedroll?"

"James, have you met Tom and Frank? Besides erecting the tent, they direct traffic and pass the offering plate. Jerry helps, but his main duty is to operate the organ music and the loudspeakers. He also plays the guitar when I sing or pray. Boys, this is James Dandae. He'll be staying in town and giving me a lift every day for the service. Seth, can you tell how we did? Any large bills?"

"No. I don't think so. There's probably a hundred maybe a hundred and fifty. Not bad for a tent with fifty empty seats."

"Yes, but our mark is two hundred." She looked at James. "That's what it takes to break even."

That evening Jerry cooked supper on a camp stove. He served everyone on paper plates and gave them iced tea to drink from paper cups. The workers seemed a happy lot with only the stern countenance of Seth to keep the group focused and a little uneasy. Frank unfolded a chair for James and pushed it up to a long skinny table. It was plain fare but seasoned well. James decided that Seth was the odd one with everyone else good-natured and pleasant to be around. After a few bites, Agatha asked James what he thought of the service.

James was chewing on something he didn't quite recognize and waited till he swallowed before answering. "You are the first lady preacher I've heard. After the opening prayer and a few songs, I forgot the differences that a woman brings to the pulpit and started concentrating on your message. Is there not some way of incorporating your need for donations without offending those less liberal minded? I think there were a lot of people here who came out of boredom wanting to be entertained or to find out if a woman could actually fit into a man's shoes."

"Jim, are you playing the devil's advocate: baiting me into a tirade against an unfair accusation?"

"No, ma'am. I think you did an admirable job. Still, if two hundred is your goal then one-fifty is fifty too little. Have you had services that exceeded your benchmark?"

"Occasionally. We usually arrive in town Saturday night or early Sunday morning and spend the day erecting the tent. Monday and Tuesday we go into town and separate with each trying to make as many friends and acquaintances as possible. Our first service is Wednesday night with most chairs taken by a minister or two bringing his entire mid-week congregation with him. That first night most of our audience is long in the tooth and short in the pocketbook. On Thursday and Friday nights we have a younger audience and I sing songs more to their liking and preach on topics they find more interesting. Our big night is

Saturday. That evening we have our biggest audience and largest donation. Then, after the service, we take down the tent, pack things up and head to the next town. Tonight is Thursday and it routinely has the lowest attendance and amount donated."

"So two days mustering support and four services and you've worn out your welcome?"

"No, Jim. We make friends wherever we go, but the newness wears off and we find the audience and our collections decrease after that first week."

Jerry asked, "Mr. Dandae, have you any suggestions. We'd like to stay longer. Putting the tent up and taking it down every week gets old. And we're never in a town long enough for any of us to receive mail—everyone except Seth. Somehow his friends can find him."

"And increase our donations. Agatha gives us half of the money that exceeds two hundred dollars."

"Let me think on it."

CHAPTER 30
May 12, 1946

In the middle of May, the Agatha Parker Ministries arrived in a small town not far from the center of Missouri. It started raining Saturday night and their trip from the previous town had been a slow and wet process. Sunday the workers sat under a piece of stretched canvas waiting for the rain to stop so they could erect the tent. It would be a few more days before the tent would be needed for the revival, but the men were really interested in getting it up and settling in with the kerosene stoves lit for themselves—the tent was their home.

It was late in the afternoon before the last tie-down was made. During the entire process the rain would pause for an hour, or so, and when the men thought they were making headway, the clouds would gather, argue with boisterous bickering, and end in a battle using lighted sabers punctuated with cannon-fire.

A clothesline was stretched. Draped over with wet clothing, the cord sagged to the floor. Each hanging article dribbled remnants from the previous battle. Tom lounged in a round tub filled with heated water. Frank waited his turn with a towel draped over a naked shoulder. "James, if you'd like a hot bath before going to that cozy bed in town I wouldn't mind waiting."

"I wouldn't deprive you of your one luxury. I'll just borrow a towel to sit on so my car seat doesn't mildew."

"James, thank you for your help. You could have gone into town and checked in the hotel with Agatha. We would have understood," added Jerry.

"Nonsense. For the past month, I've helped put up the tent the first night and take it down on the last. I'm not going to cut and run at a small inconvenience. By the way, how were we so lucky to find a place with gravel? That's now three towns in a row. Even with all this rain there shouldn't be any problems with stuck cars."

"Seth started asking if we could set up shop in the towns' fairgrounds or rodeo arenas. He's found they aren't commonly used in the winter and early spring. And if he signs that we will be responsible for cleaning up we get the use of bathroom facilities."

"Kudos for Seth."

That night James wrote a letter to the police detective in Bowling Green, Kentucky.

Dear Detective Sandoval:

I've been working for the Parker Ministries for the past six weeks. Everything seems to be on the up and up. We make a few converts every service but the donations aren't enough to cover our expenses. Miss Parker says she supplements the income from her personal funds.

So far no one knows anything about an insurance company but I haven't been around Seth too much. He's the front man staying on the road most of the time making arrangements for our next venue. He carries a locked briefcase. I'll try to find what he keeps in it the next time he shows up.

I am only interested in Miss Parker, so if you find anything on Seth I could use to sever her from this evangelizing, I would appreciate it.

James Dandae

James thought about writing to Margo but decided against it. No need checking the depth when you're tied to an anchor. Of course, Agatha wasn't an anchor. No, she was a spirited woman who made his blood shoot through venial highways under massive pressure. And to accomplish that scenario she just had to walk into the room. No, the anchor was this entire slow-moving wagon train.

The next morning James was reading the local newspaper and drinking a cup of coffee as the hotel desk clerk walked up to his table saying he had a telephone call. When James answered, he was surprised to be talking to Sam Crocker. A police department close to Indianapolis wanted a quote and Sam was insistent he use his skills to get Indiana Data Management a second job. She said she'd do the work all he had to do was to make the sale. He didn't want to leave Agatha, not even for a few days, but then again, they wouldn't have to pick up the slack but just for this one town. And it looked like there would not be much of a turn-out anyway. The weather was bad, the people were hoity-toity, and someone had pulled down most of their posters.

While he thought about his options, Agatha stepped off the last rung of stairs with an umbrella in her hand. "Jim, have you eaten yet?"

"No. I've been waiting for you."

"Good. Pay for your coffee and let's go meet some people. I've got a few good ideas to add interesting information in my sermons. I may have gotten a little boring. Let's find the most frequented café in town and talk about it."

"Okay, but it's still raining and the wind has picked up. You'll have to hold onto your parasol with both hands."

"It's an umbrella, but it's too small for two people. You'll have to cover your head with a newspaper."

"Agatha, I think you're not so good about sharing."

At a downtown café, several people looked up when Agatha and James hung their jackets on a crowded hall tree and leaned one wet umbrella against the wall behind. They slid into a comfortable booth.

A waitress bringing two glasses of water and two paper menus asked if they needed a minute to look over the items listed. When Agatha nodded, the waitress went to another table.

"This is the same menu as the last diner we ate at. What does it take to get a little variety in our diet?"

"Probably adding larger towns to the itinerary. People buy what they're comfortable with and businesses stock what's in demand. So, in a larger town, there would be a greater diversity to its citizenry. And since ethnic groups tend to congregate together you'll find that a town with a sizeable Chinese population has abundant Chinese restaurants. That also holds true for costs. In areas where cattle are raised the area restaurants have a greater demand and a lower cost of providing beef. It works the same for seafood in coastal cities."

"Jim, sometimes you can be so boring."

"Really? I thought I was perceptive."

"I want to talk about the changes I plan on making to spruce up our performance."

"Okay. What have you got in mind?"

"First, I want to know what you bring to the table?"

James squirmed. "Me?"

"Yes. Can you play a musical instrument?"

"No."

"Sing?"

"Not the first note."

"Juggle, do acrobatics, tell stories?"

"I know a few card tricks and have a light touch when something needs pilfering."

"Now, Jim. Don't be sarcastic. I was just looking for a little help in entertaining our visitors."

The rest of the day James and Agatha introduced themselves to the people of another small town in middle-America. Several people swore they would be attending services, but James thought most were skeptical and leery of strangers. This town might be a bust. Agatha needed his help.

That afternoon after dropping Agatha off at her room with a headache James asked the hotel desk clerk if he could make a long distance telephone call. The clerk said the charge would be added to his bill and asked for the number. The desk clerk called the operator, gave the number, and asked her to call him back with the time and charges. He then handed the telephone to James.

James stretched the cord to its maximum length and pulled a chair close enough to sit down. "Hello, my good man. Have you sold any properties lately? No? Then I have a business proposition for you."

On Tuesday morning, Agatha told James at breakfast that she had made arrangements to see a doctor. After being in the rain all day the day before, she now had the sniffles and a runny nose. They made arrangements to get together in the early afternoon.

James aimlessly ambled down the sidewalk looking in the retail store windows. In one store offering general merchandise, James walked inside and struck up a conversation with the salesman.

"You got any books?"

"Yeah. Hundreds against that back wall. You looking for anything in particular?"

"I need one to make me less boring to an attractive young lady?"

"You got a particular young lady in mind? I mean, I have an older sister who might not find you boring."

"Thanks but I've been following this woman around like a puppy with eyes on a food bowl. Yesterday, she said I was boring."

"Maybe, you need a new presence. If you made a devilish appearance in stylish clothes, some changes to your hairstyle, and handled yourself in a mysterious, self-assured manner you'd be turning heads of the fairer sex. And a man in demand is anything but boring."

"You, sir, might have something. Do you sell those stylish clothes?"

"No. But my brother Bob does and he has a seamstress who can alter anything that doesn't fit just right."

"And the barber? Can you recommend anyone in particular?"

"We have three barbers in town and they are all the same with similar conservative haircuts. What you need is a hair stylist and the best one anywhere is my older sister."

"Could I hire your services to oversee the transformation?"

When it was time to meet Agatha, James was sitting in a ladies hair salon chair having two beauty operators and three female customers make a collaborative effort to change his coiffeur into one sported by the handsome devil women dream about.

"Joyce, if he had a touch of gray in the sideburns it would give an air of sophistication."

"Well, I think he ought to have a don't-care, tousled look."

"Oh, yeah. I like that."

"How about leaving his sideburns long and combed forward like Napoleon. Ouwee, now that's what I'm talking about."

"Okay, girls. Opinions only, please. This is my masterpiece. Helen, quit running your fingers through his hair. Has no one seen a man up close before? James, do you have any input? Are we out of control here?"

Joyce moved so she could appraise her work from a second angle. "I'm seriously considering giving you a spot perm for a few locks we'll pull to the side."

"Joyce, I'm enjoying the fuss. Use your own judgment about the perm."

One of the customers walked around James' chair, her finger playing with an earring. She announced, "I'm calling my sister. She says there are no good-looking men in our town. And here's one right here, right now."

"Mr. Dandae, is there any particular criteria you're looking for in a woman? An age preference perhaps? Proven abilities at anything? Piano? Cooking? Foreign languages? Does size matter?"

"Eleanor, maybe he likes to dance."

"Ladies, the only requirement I have is for the woman of my life to be able to calm the savage beast raging in my heart."

"Good God, I can do that—or, maybe, I can't. Just exactly how does someone do that?"

"I can't give you any more clues, but if you would like to see the front runner you'll have to attend the revival. For she is Miss Agatha Parker."

When it was time for the evening meal, James knocked on Agatha's door. From inside he heard a faint "Come in."

James turned the knob and walked inside a dimly lit bedroom.

"I'm sorry I missed our meeting this afternoon. The doctor sent me to bed. He said I was coming down with a bronchial infection and gave me some pills. I don't know what to do. We've already posted flyers and received a notice that the Southern Baptist Church would be bringing all of their Wednesday service attendees."

If I could keep some food down, I think I could speak long enough to satisfy our naysayers and I'd be back to normal in another day or two."

"How about me officiating at the service tomorrow night. My dad was a Methodist minister. I've had to sit through thousands of his—he called them 'Sermons in the Making.' And after listening to you for these last few months, I think I could do a creditable job. Certainly not as good as you but good enough to buy you some time."

"You are such a help, Jim." Agatha stared. "What have you done to your hair?"

"It's nothing. Just a new style. I decided it was time for a change. Do you like it?"

"I'll have to get back to you on that."

CHAPTER 31

May 12, 1946

Margo re-read the letter from Agatha. She's gloating. That woman is gloating about convincing Jim to leave me and catch up with her. Why can't Jim see Agatha for the woman she really is? He talks like a man who knows what a woman wants but the gist is he's only an onlooker piecing together a ridiculous puzzle with fragments and a rational way of deciphering clues. The man makes good guesses, but right now he's in over his head. Agatha will cast him off when he begins to bore her—just like she did Reginald Howard, and that Conan character before him, and poor Alonzo even before that. To Agatha it's a game. A game with no winners—no male winners anyway.

Margo went looking for her dad. "So, Daddy, have you heard anything about those missionaries?"

"A little. Our newspaper editor lets me know whenever anything comes in about them over the wire. As they get farther away, the news becomes less available. I wish James Dandae would come back. We've received a couple of inquiries about his work at the police department. If he came back, he might have another job or two."

"Dad, I'll come by your office later today and pick up those names and contact details. His associate is probably in touch with him and could use your information to lure him back. The man needs to clear his head."

"Honey, he's not going to see it that way until he gets over his infatuation with Miss Parker."

"You know about that?"

"Not really. But it doesn't take much intelligence to figure out why you were so happy for a time and then moped around like you'd lost your best friend when he left. You got to have a little patience. It'll all work out."

"Dad, I want to help it along the way. Why don't you take a short vacation? The three of us could catch up with them in Missouri to see how things are progressing. There's no need to wonder, not if we can check it out first hand."

"I don't think that would be a wise move. Chasing after love has a way of backfiring. He'll just think you're trying to keep up with his activities—to shackle his freedom. I can't think of a faster way to lose the man you love than to act like a clingy woman."

"Suppose we don't let him know we're there. There's got to be a lot of people in the audience. And he won't be expecting to see us—that's for sure. We could even disguise ourselves."

"Honey, there's no way of talking you out of this is there?"

Next day Margo arrived at the library just as Sam was unlocking the front door. "Good morning, Miss Crocker."

"Margo, what are you doing out so early? You having trouble sleeping at night and need a good book?"

"I usually buy mine, so I can dog-ear the pages. No, I came to ask about James Dandae. Have you been in contact with him?"

"No, I haven't and, to tell you the truth, I'm a little worried. We talked about continuing our business, and I had dreams of being self-employed. But I can't make it on my own. He's the salesman between the two of us. I'm just a worker drone."

"He told me you were the brains in the outfit. If I can get a telephone number, would you call him? He needs to come home to the ones who love him. And besides, I have more business for the two of you. Bleiberville, a small town just outside Indianapolis, is asking for someone to look at their records and give a quote for organizing them in a similar way to what you did here. And there's another town, but Dad can't find his notes. He's looking."

"Margo, that's great. Give me the number, and I'll give it a shot. He's probably had all he can take from that floozy with the raven black mane and flashing eyes. I bet he's already thinking of some way he could come back without admitting failure."

"Okay, but don't tell him how you came by the number. I received a letter from Agatha and had our police chief track him down from the postmark. He's staying at the Odessa Hotel at this number." Margo handed Sam a folded note. "If he asks how you found him, tell him you had Patrick York's help. Our poor police chief thinks you were the one on the phone asking anyway."

"You got it. I'll call right now. If you would like to listen in, I've got two telephones on the same line."

"Will he be able to hear me?"

"Not if you don't say anything."

It was a blustery day, and Sam didn't expect any customers for another hour or so. She took Margo to the check-out desk and said she'd motion when she wanted Margo to pick up the telephone. Sam then walked to the information desk and called the number on the piece of paper. "I'd like to speak with Mr. James Dandae, please. Yes, I'll hold." Sam then pointed at Margo who picked up the second telephone. The women could hear papers rustling, a metal clank, a swinging door creak, and shoes marching across a wooden floor. A moment later they heard the same noises in reverse order.

"Hello. This is James Dandae."

"James, don't you think it's time you came home?"

"Sam? Is that you?"

"It is."

"How did you find me?"

"Had your friend at the police department put out a missing persons bulletin."

"Ha, ha. That's funny. I actually think you're a better detective than he. So, how are things in Indiana?"

"James, we got one police department close to Indianapolis, who wants a quote and possibly another. It will just snowball from there, so you better tidy things up and get back here pronto. Indiana Data Management is on the verge of big things."

"Sam, I would like to, but I'm in the middle of something. Don't you think you could talk to them? Give a quote comparable to the one I prepared for West Larimore."

"James Dandae, you're the salesman—not me. You need to figure something out because I really want to get rolling. Don't you think you could take a short break? After you get the particulars worked out, I'll hire a couple of workers and get the job done. All you have to do is make the sale and rake in the money."

"Sam, give me a day to conjure up a solution."

"Okay. Write my number down so you can call me back with your plan. You are the man with the plan, aren't you?"

"Yeah, Sam. That's me."

Sam Crocker hung up the telephone and shirked her head at Margo. "We'll have to wait for him to realize the opportunity he would be missing by staying with Miss Parker."

"Call me, Sam. Just as soon as he gets back to you."

A few minutes before closing, a man in a plaid sports coat came through the front door of the library in a big hurry. "Ma'am, are you Sam Crocker?"

"I am."

"James Dandae called me earlier today. He said to go to the library and talk to you about a job."

"What kind of job?"

"Miss Crocker, I'm a salesman. Mr. Dandae said I'd also have to learn how to file and do a lot of other things like bring you chocolate." The salesman set a box of Swiss chocolates on the counter. "He said you would fill me in."

"Why did you wait until five minutes before closing?"

"I had to talk my wife into letting me. I was on the verge of getting a job for the city. She's been after me for years to give up sales and get a real job."

"So, installing sewer lines would be a step up for you?"

"Uh, no. I was applying for a city inspector's job."

"I'm sorry, I didn't mean to be rude. I was just disappointed that James decided to send somebody instead of doing it himself."

"Ma'am, I'm a good salesman."

"I'm sure you are. Have a seat and write down your address, telephone number, last place of employment, and two references. I have to make a telephone call. I'll be right back."

At the information desk, Sam Crocker called Margo with the bad news and Margo promptly went into the kitchen to enlist help from her mother who was supervising the cook.

CHAPTER 32

May 15, 1946

James spent Wednesday morning in the hotel coffee shop. He had gone through two pads of paper and was working on his third pencil. Wood shavings littered the floor. While James was deep in thought, Seth walked over and sat opposite with a frown on his face.

"I think it's a bad idea."

James looked up with a blank expression on his face.

Seth continued with, "Agatha thinks you're going to make an ass of yourself. We've decided if you do we'll take down the tent and move on—maybe even skipping the next town to get farther away from your debacle."

"Really? There's not going to be many people in attendance as it is. Almost all of the people I've met have had frowns on their faces. Isn't Missouri the skeptical state with the self-imposed motto of 'Show me?'"

"Dandae, what makes you think you can lead a revival? Do you actually have anything to say? Agatha has worked on her sermons for five years, and still some people heckle or walk out during the service."

"I'm just trying to buy her some time."

"Okay, we'll give it a shot, but if you create a riot, no one's got your back. It'll be every man for himself. I'd park that car of yours in a convenient spot behind the tent, and I'd pull up one of the tent pegs so I could slip under if I had to leave quickly. You do what you want, I'm just saying."

"Seth, you're not much for giving a person a slap on the back while telling him everything will be okay, are you?"

"No." Seth picked up the top sheet of paper in a neat stack. After reading the first paragraph, he said, "This is rubbish. You, sir, are going to make us the laughing stock." Abruptly Seth stood up and stormed out.

James went to refill his coffee. When he got back to the table, he reshuffled his stack of papers with the bottom sheet now on top. He started reading, re-writing, editing, inserting, deleting, and eventually wadded up the whole mess and started over.

When lunch rolled around James had a big bowl of chicken noodle soup and hot jasmine tea prepared on a tray. He carried it to Agatha's room. She was in a sitting area by the window while two housekeepers were changing sheets and cleaning the bathroom.

"How do you feel?"

"Like I've been drugged. My throat hurts. I can barely talk." She dipped a spoon into the soup. "Jim, are you sure this is going to work?"

"After talking with Seth, I'm having second thoughts. But yes, I can pull this off."

Agatha poured a cup of tea for herself and another for James. She ended up spilling a good portion when the lid of the teapot tumbled onto a folded napkin. "Maid, maid. Get over here and clean this up."

James went after a towel but ended up leaving when Agatha snatched it away and started giving the maid verbal abuse for her lack of organization.

At one o'clock James went to the clothier's store to pick up his new suit after the seamstress had finished the alterations. And he had decided to pick out a new tie. The suit was a light tan with narrow, beige stripes. The tie he picked out was striped in two shades of Kelly green. "I also want a new pair of shoes. Do you have any brown ones in soft leather?"

"I've got just the thing. They're two-tone brown and white dancing shoes."

"What makes them dancing shoes?"

"I first saw a pair like them on a spirited band leader in Harlem. He danced all over that stage. Took me most of the next day to find a wholesaler carrying his kind of clothing and shoes. They're not too popular here. Too *avant-garde* for our little town. So I carry a small selection for the few men who know style and fill the rest of the store with the conservative stuff that sells."

"I have found when women get depressed they go shopping. Maybe I could learn something from their remedy. So now that we have a complete ensemble for this evening's services, let's add a blue blazer with polished brass buttons, a few pair of slacks in contrasting colors, and two cashmere cardigans. Do you have those dancing shoes in black? And, I need a few more ties."

"Mr. Dandae, if anyone asks where you get your clothes would you give them one of my business cards?"

After leaving the clothier, James decided to check on the girls at Joyce's Hair Salon. "Joyce, you have wonderful hands. Would you mind showing me the best way to get my hair to look the way you had it yesterday afternoon?"

"By all means." She turned to the other women being tended to. "Ladies, this is Mr. James Dandae. He's with the missionaries who are starting their revival this evening and running through Saturday evening. James, what time do we need to be there?"

"Seven o'clock. But you might be disappointed. Miss Parker is sick so I'll be filling in—and it's my first time to do so."

"Nonsense. You'll do just fine. What are you going to talk about?"

"Love."

"Sounds like something dear to every woman's heart. Tell us more."

"Then there wouldn't be any reason for you ladies to attend the service. Let me say that I will make it worth your while."

One lady poked her head out from under a dryer. "Mr. Dandae, will you be serving chocolate?"

"Ha ha. I hadn't thought of that. I'll have to make arrangements to do that the next time Agatha gets sick."

"Mr. Dandae, what does your wife think about you traveling over the countryside with another woman?"

"I'm not married."

"I've seen other men in town from your troupe. Are they single as well?"

"I don't know. But I've been traveling with them for the past two months and no one has made mention of having a wife or family."

"Okay, James. Sit down here and let me show you how to redo my *tour de force*. Have you had many stares or comments?"

"I did yesterday but not so many today."

At seven, the last car parked, the last visitor seated, the last moment of possible escape passed. Jerry played the organ music on the phonograph and then stepped to the microphone, "Hello, Evansville."

He was welcomed with a resounding, "Hello."

"Tonight we have James Dandae presenting the service while Miss Agatha Parker recovers from a head cold. She hopes to return tomorrow night so listen up because the esteemed Mr. Dandae has some important insights to give you. Please welcome, Mr. James Dandae."

James shook Jerry's hand as he walked to the microphone. He took the microphone from the stand and looked out over the audience. The seats were about three-quarters full with many more women than men. The front two rows were filled with the ladies from Joyce's Hair Salon and their friends.

"I'm not the gifted speaker Miss Parker is. However, there are some things on my heart you might find interesting. Tonight I want to talk to you about love. Everyone knows the words of *John* 3:16 where it says, 'For God so loved the world that he gave his only son, that whoever believes in him should not perish but have eternal life.' The word 'loved' that John uses is a translation of the Greek word *agapao* which is a past-tense version of *agape*.

"The Greeks have several words for love. To them *agape* is the love a man has for his wife, a mother for her children, a woman for her father, and so on. John used a version of this word to communicate God's love for all mankind. A second Greek word for love is *philia* meaning affection, friendship, and brotherhood. It's one of the roots for philosophy which means the love of wisdom. And a third is *eros* which is love in a more sexual setting.

"The bible has lots more instances of the Greek word *agape* translated as 'love.' In *Matthew* 5:43 through 44, 'Ye have heard that it hath been said, Thou shall love thy neighbor and hate thine enemy. But I say unto you, love your enemies.'

"In *Timothy* 4:10 Paul says, 'For Demas hath forsaken me, having loved this present world, and is departed unto Thessalonica.'

In the thirteenth chapter of *Corinthians,* the translators of the King James Version changed what William Tyndale and others before him had used for the Greek word *agape*. They changed the translated English equivalent from the word, 'love,' to the word, 'charity.'

"If you brought your bible would you raise your hand?" James looked around the room. About half the people in attendance had their hands raised. "Okay, if you have a version of the bible that is not the King James Version keep your hand up." All hands went down.

"Okay. Let me read to you *First Corinthians* Chapter 13 with the word 'charity' as used in your bible changed to what most authorities believe is a more accurate translation—the word 'love.'

"'Though I speak with the tongues of men and of angels, and have not love, I am become as sounding brass, or a tinkling cymbal.

"'And though I have the gift of prophecy, and understand all mysteries, and all knowledge; and though I have all faith, so that I could remove mountains, and have not love, I am nothing.

"'And though I bestow all my goods to feed the poor, and though I give my body to be burned, and have not love, it profiteth me nothing.

"'Love suffereth long, and is kind, love envieth not; love vaunteth not itself, is not puffed up.

"'Doth not behave itself unseemly, seeketh not her own, is not easily provoked, thinketh no evil.

"'Rejoiceth not in iniquity, but rejoiceth in the truth;

"'Beareth all things, believeth all things, hopeth all things, endureth all things.

"'Love never faileth: but whether there be prophecies, they shall fail; whether there be tongues, they shall cease; whether there be knowledge, it shall vanish away.

"'For we know in part, and we prophesy in part.

"'But when that which is perfect is come, then that which is in part shall be done away.

"'When I was a child, I spake as a child, I understood as a child, I thought as a child; but when I became a man, I put away childish things.

"'For now we see through a glass darkly; but then face to face, now I know in part but then shall I know even as also I am known.

"'And now abideth faith, hope, love, these three; but the greatest of these is love.'"

James paused. He closed his bible and sat it on a small shelf of the microphone stand. He looked out over his audience to see if anyone had been listening, if anyone was still in attendance.

"Now that we have the proper word inserted, let's look at some of its usage to see what we can take into our hearts from this passage." For the next fifteen minutes James dissected the biblical passage like his father had done so many times in James' youth.

To finish James said, "In my humble opinion this says to me that no matter how important I am, how rich I become, how much knowledge, influence, or abilities I acquire that if I have not love I have nothing—a tinkling cymbal. And these earthly things profit me not for they will all pass away. That I have to seek love which is true, which will abide with me forever. I have to change my childish attitude from wanting things of this earth to loving what is perfect and what will make me whole and give me life eternal.

"Please stand and sing our closing hymn. The words are in the leaflet you found on your seat when first arriving." Jerry played the phonograph. The congregation sang.

"We didn't take an offering tonight but if you feel in your heart that you want to help our ministry then, you may drop something in the plate as you leave. Please bow your heads. Go in the grace of God, for he loves you, he protects you, and he is preparing a place for you. Amen."

James descended the stage and held out his hand to Joyce. "I am so glad you came."

"I'm glad as well. I think most of us will be back tomorrow night. Do you think you will be giving another sermon?"

"It all depends on how Agatha feels."

"Mr. Dandae, you did such a wonderful job. My heart is overflowing."

"Mine too."

From the back row three people James did not recognize, but should have had he taken a closer look, slipped out. One of the three dropped a ten dollar bill into a myrtle wood bowl sitting on a chair.

Later that evening when the last car had left and the last chair repositioned for the next day's service, the men gathered around a table to count the evening's offering. Jerry was more or less in charge. He exclaimed, after putting the bills into a neat stack and adding the total of the change from Tom, "We received two hundred and twelve dollars tonight. And that, gentlemen, is from a town in Missouri—a state where everyone is money conscious."

Frank said, "Jerry, why do you think we received the large donation?"

"I think it was James' sermon. He touched a chord. I overheard Agatha telling Seth that women see something in James." Jerry looked straight at James. "I don't see it, but I think we ought to run with what we're given."

"Well, I do. James, you got new clothes, two-tone gangster shoes, and you got your hair fixed like a movie star. What's not to like?"

"Hey, I got it." Frank sat down at the table. "Let's get Agatha to include James in her services. Give the ladies something to look at, some reason to dip into their purses."

"I'm not going to stand on the stage like a mannequin. I need to have a job to do." James looked around at his buddies who were now thinking he would be adding dollars to their purses.

"James, we all have different talents. And we have to use those talents to advance God's work. Some are teachers, some give sermons, others heal, and then there are those who help by taking care of the mundane and the administrative duties so those that teach, lecture, or heal can focus on their primary area of expertise."

James shifted his weight around a bit. "I don't want to replace Agatha. I don't think Agatha would allow anyone to replace her. This is her operation. I only gave this one lecture to help her out while she was sick."

"And teaching does not fit in with our short time spent in each locality. So how do you feel about listening to people's problems and offering to heal them? We could make it into the finishing part of our service each night."

"I don't know. Agatha would have to be okay with the idea."

Jerry said, "Let's talk about it tomorrow."

CHAPTER 33

August 15, 1946

Laurie put her pen down and went for Edwin's glass of water. When she came back, she held it up to Edwin's face and inserted the straw into his mouth. "We've only got five pages written so far. What else can we say about the old folk's home?"

"Issie, can you help me out here? I don't know the day to day routines that go on in a place like that? And Edwin's a blank slate."

"Are you sure Edwin wants you to write a story about an old folks home?"

"No. He's being difficult. I tried first to write about his job as a policeman and didn't get very far there either."

"Didn't he say he wanted to write about catching the man who shot him? He said that he'd write the expose about the old folk's home second. Maybe, he's not communicating with you, because, you're traveling the wrong road."

"Okay, smarty pants, how do I write about catching the criminal before we do catch him?"

"Laurie, I'm not the author here, but if I were, I'd gather all the facts and make a likely scenario that fits, sprinkling in the actual details as I wrote. He gave the money back, so the authorities aren't looking for him very hard. I think you ought to talk with the boys who stayed with him in that cabin, get a picture of the man—you know, how he thinks. Have a human interest in it. Maybe, a love interest with a waitress at the diner."

"Issie, usually your advice is not logical or even reasonable. Normally I listen for a minute and then tune you out, but this time—this one time—your advice is perceptive, maybe intuitive even."

"And you, young lady, are a condescending know-it-all. I don't like the way you pigeon-hole people based on the slimmest bits of information."

"*Touché*. But we'll have to put this difference of opinion on a back burner, because right now, we're taking Edwin on a field trip." Laurie turned to Edwin and said. "Let's gather all the known facts about the bank robber, and see if we can turn it into a story. I think we ought to start with Chief Trent. What do you think, Edwin?"

"I think he agrees, Laurie. Look at that smile."

In less than ten minutes, the girls had man-handled Edwin's wheelchair through the front door and were strolling down the sidewalk to the Dancing Deer Police Station. When they passed the Dancing Deer Mercantile, Laurie suggested they go inside and get a hat for Edwin. It was ninety degrees and the sun was out, wreaking havoc on any unprotected patch of skin.

"Good morning, Harry. We're out and about with Edwin and I think I'd like to buy the man a hat. What do you have?"

"I have Stetsons, baseball caps, and a brand new selection of Panamas. What's his size?"

"I don't know. Just stick one on and see if he smiles. That's how he communicates."

"I thought you communicated with him through telepathy?"

"Normally I do, but lately, he's closed the pathways. Guess he got tired of exposing his innermost thoughts. Edwin, would you like a baseball cap, a Stetson, or one of these straw hats from Panama?"

"I see what you mean. When you mentioned the straw hat, he had a grin that went from ear to ear." Harry took out a paper tape and wrapped it around Edwin's head. "Okay, he wears a seven and a quarter."

Harry was gone for just a minute, and when he returned, he was carrying three boxes. "I stock three styles and have his size in all three." He opened the first box, lifted the hat, and placed it on Edwin's head.

Issie pushed Edwin in front of a floor length mirror. "Edwin, you look like a movie star in that hat. Don't you think so, Laurie?"

Laurie was looking at the box. "This isn't from Panama. It says on the box it's made in Ecuador."

Harry said, "That's true but these hats were made popular by the American workers coming back from building the Panama Canal. And the name stuck."

"And this price. Harry, is this the price of the hat?"

"Yes. It is. But don't worry about that. Edwin has always been a special friend of mine. He checked on me every day he walked his beat. It was a comfort when he popped his head in to make sure everything was all right. I want to give Edwin the hat. Let's allow him to try on all three before he makes up his mind."

Back on the sidewalk, the three continued to the police station. Laurie patted Edwin on his shoulder. "Edwin, you have friends like Harry all over this town. It's hard to imagine how one person could impact so many people in such positive ways."

At the police station, one officer held the door while another relieved Issie at the wheelchair handles. Chief Trent came out of his office to tell Edwin how much he was missed. Then the police chief asked Laurie if she had brought Edwin by for a social visit or police business.

"Chief Trent, Edwin wants to know what progress you've made in finding the man who shot him."

"I was afraid that was it. We haven't made much headway. I can show Edwin the case file."

"Will you make Edwin a copy? He says he wants to solve the case before the crook dies of old age."

"He said that? You do know the FBI has taken over?"

"Chief, I don't get his words. It comes to me as a general idea. The harder we concentrate, the more detailed the idea is."

"I see. Well let me copy the file for you. It'll be just like the one we put together for the FBI."

"And give us what you have on the bank robbery in Skunk Hollow."

"We stuck that in as well."

With a copy of the case file stuck under Laurie's arm, the three continued to their next stop which was to see Lacy at St Bartholomew's Holy Catholic Church.

In each new town James shopped for items to add to his new wardrobe. In fact, the proprietor for the men's clothing store where James made his first purchase had decided James was not only his best customer but also his best advertising. After James started sporting the high fashion clothing, more men began stepping forward—at the request of their wives—to make radical changes in their conservative manner of dress. But then again, some people are resistant to change.

"James, I think we need to sprinkle the people needing to be healed throughout the house instead of having them all congregate on the front row. When I stand on stage and look into the audience, I see all those hurting people and start thinking about war, expecting sirens to start blaring."

"Agatha, we need to talk about the healing. I don't think I'm healing anyone. I touch them on the forehead, say a few words, and they fall to the floor like it was rehearsed the day before. One man stood up from his chair holding a crutch high in the air and yelled he'd been cured. It's all a bit much. In the first town it was only that one boy who stuttered, in the second a woman who was depressed over the death of her son and two people with sore feet, and then in the third they asked if I would make a side trip to their hospital. What's going on? I can't heal anyone."

"It's the power of suggestion, James. The people think you can and they want to be healed in the worst way. Our donations have soared. The men have made mention that they may have to start tying you up between sermons so you can't escape and thereby letting their pay go back to the previous amounts."

"Well, the authorities may decide to take matters into their own hands and lock me up for fraud."

"Now James, we don't advertize that you can heal. We don't tie it into our requests for donations. In fact, lately, we haven't even had to beg for money. We pass the offering plate because it's expected and keep an extra one on both sides of the two exits in case they feel personally blessed."

"I know. But what if they're giving us their rent money or what they've put back for an emergency? Or giving us what should be going for regular medical care? Agatha, I'm getting a little nervous about the whole thing."

"Oh, pooh on that. We've gone from losing money to making money and you feel guilty—and you're not even profiting from the extra loot. Maybe we should give you a cut so you could wallow in your own success."

"Agatha, what I'd like to do is take a leave of absence for a couple of weeks to let the brouhaha wear down and then join back up, down the road a piece, playing a down-sized role."

"I'll think about it. Our next town is Dancing Deer and your name and picture is smeared all over town so it would have to be after next week before we could make any changes."

"Next week is Dancing Deer? Nobody told me. What would happen if I packed my bags and went back to Indiana?"

"The men would store the tent and search you out. Then they would start tying you up between performances."

"Mrs. Holloway, may Edwin and I speak with Lacy?"

"Certainly. I'll see if I can find him. He's the only one left and spins most of his days in Father Don's study. Laurie, you know where it's at. Why don't you and Issie wheel Mr. Stanky in there, and I'll have the cook fix a plate of sweets. If Lacy's not there, I'll fetch him."

"Thank you, Mrs. Holloway." Issie and Laurie managed to push Edwin's wheelchair down the hall and into the study. Most of the books in the entire church had somehow found their way into Father Donovan O'Reilly's study. It now resembled a library or a place of research, more so, than a place of repose. On a massive dark, wood table lay several open books and loose sheets of paper. Lacy was standing in front of a bookcase pondering some great mystery.

"Well, good morning, Laurie. Are you and Mr. Stanky on a field trip?"

"More or less. Lacy, this is Issie, Edwin's caretaker."

"Pleased to meet you, ma'am. And you, sir. Mr. Stanky, you're starting to look better. You now have color in your cheeks. They must be taking good care of you."

"He says, 'Thank you, Lacy. They are.'"

"Laurie, I heard you beat the mayor of West Larimore at checkers."

"No. That was Edwin who beat him."

"But you could have had you wanted to. Father Don says you're the best checker player he's ever seen for someone your age. You routinely beat all of us—except Spencer."

"Yes, well, Edwin has beaten me every time we've played. So it was no surprise to me that he took the mayor so easily. But Lacy, what we've come here for is some information on the bank robber. Edwin is going to bring him to justice himself."

"Are the police not working hard enough?"

"He doesn't think so now that the money has been given back, and the perpetrator has fled their jurisdiction."

"Okay, but I don't know much. He was of medium build, about six feet tall, not fat nor skinny, and had no distinguishing features. He did talk a little different like he might have come from somewhere up north. He had a big coat, a hat pulled down to his nose, and wore gloves."

"Did he introduce himself?"

"No."

"So, how did you refer to him?"

"We called him our new friend or the stranger."

"Did he have a limp? Was he left handed? Wear any jewelry? Anything different about him? Anything at all?"

"Nope. None of that. He did tell us he hadn't seen his family for twenty years, and that he had a brother named Jeff. I've tried to reconstruct the events and haven't come up with anything else. Have you read the note he left?"

"Yeah, we have a copy of the case file. It's in there."

"Who else have you talked with?"

"No one. We plan on talking with Terrell and Spencer since they had separate instances where they talked with him by themselves. And then there is Mr. Bell. His reporters interviewed everybody right after the robbery."

"You might check with Mr. Potter to see if the robber mailed the bank any of the gas money he kept. And I'd like to be kept informed on your progress."

"Okay, Lacy. Edwin and I are going to write a book on our capture. Would it be all right if we mentioned your name and credit you with giving us some of the information?"

"Sure."

"Edwin, let's stop by the post office to see if you've received any more mail. What if the bank robber has tried to get hold of you?

Suppose he wants a duel, at noon, on Main Street?" Laurie looked at Edwin. He had his mouth open and rolled his eyes.

"I was just being funny."

"Yeah, melodramatic might be a more descriptive term. Laurie, I think Edwin is having a good time with this. Look how he's leaning forward in the wheelchair. It's like he can't wait to get to the next place. Whoa, look at this." Issie stopped the wheelchair directly in front of an electrical pole with a paper poster attached at eye level.

"The Agatha Parker Ministries will be in town to start a revival on the 21st of August, 1946. She was that pretty lady who turned Edwin's book into a play. Do you think Edwin would want to go?"

Both girls turned to look at Edwin. His eyes relaxed and a grin extended across his face. "Do you think we'll need tickets?"

"I don't know, Issie. But I bet there will be mail for Edwin."

When they reached the post office, the woman behind the counter retrieved a stack of mail and handed it to Laurie. "Couldn't you find the mailbox key?"

"Not yet." Laurie shuffled through the mail. "Edwin, you got a letter from Miss Parker and one from Mayor Pauline's daughter. You also got two magazines from *American Writer's Gazette*, one envelope with a pink dun enclosed, and several *Grit* newspapers. We need to start including a stop at the post office every time we wheel you around town."

Outside the post office was a wide place in the sidewalk with a bench and a bright yellow trash receptacle. Several people went out of their way to check on Edwin, and extend their wishes for a speedy recovery. Laurie sat down while Issie set the parking brake for Edwin and then sat beside Laurie.

"Edwin, the bill is for the *American Writer's Gazette* magazine. They say your subscription is about to end. Which one of the letters do you want me to open first?"

"Okay, the one from Mayor Pauline's daughter. It says:

Dear Mr. Stanky:

I will be arriving in Dancing Deer sometime during late August and would like to meet with you. I'll call when I get into town to find out when would be the most convenient time.

Thank you,
Margo Pauline

"Edwin, do you have any idea why she wants to meet with you? I guess we'll find out soon enough. The revival starts next week so she must be traveling with them. Whew, Edwin, you got some major events about to occur. Are you up to it?

"Okay, here is the letter from Miss Parker

Dear Edwin:

I thought I'd let you know we have scheduled our arrival in Dancing Deer for the third week in August.

We have finally turned the corner and have begun having enough donations to pay the expenses. Mr. James Dandae has joined us and has added a new dimension to our ministry.

I would like to sit with you sometime during our stay. And I have a copy of the play's manuscript. Do you have a thespian group in Dancing Deer?

Yours in Christ,
Agatha Parker

"Do you know this James Dandae? What could he be adding to her revival that would bring in more money? I guess we'll find out."

"Laurie, let's stop at Eudy's before heading home."

CHAPTER 34

August 19, 2013

"Chief, two FBI agents want to talk with you."

"Send them in, Sergeant." Chief Trent put down the paper he was reading as the day dispatcher left and two men dressed in business suits came in. "Good morning, gentlemen. It's not often we get the pleasure of offering Ozark hospitality to our federal friends. Are you here on business or is this a social visit?"

"Good morning, Chief Trent. It's business I'm afraid. But we'll be in and out before you know it. And we'll keep a low profile while we're here. We just thought we'd make our presence known and let you know there is no cause for alarm. It's just a little administrative action, nothing for you to worry about. Nothing at all."

"Well, if there is anything we can do just let us know. How long will you boys be in town?"

"Probably for a week. We should have everything tied up by Friday evening and headed back to Little Rock."

"I see. Is there not anything else you can tell me?"

"Not yet. However, if something out of the ordinary appears on your radar, we're staying at the Ritz Grand Hotel and Ballroom."

Chief Trent waited for the two FBI agents to exit the building before he called in Frank Howard, his deputy chief, and Detective Albert Savanova. "Men, we got anything out of the ordinary going on in town? Two FBI agents just left after announcing their presence."

"Uh . . . no. Bill just got back from Wyoming, a group of evangelists has arrived for a revival starting Wednesday, and two executives from the railroad are in town—they're talking about bringing a spur in from Russellville. Oh, and three wives of our sitting city council have announced they're going to run against their husbands at the next election."

"Clarice has already announced she's running for mayor against her husband, Mayor Bob. Do we not live in interesting times or what?"

"Yes, sir. We do. But I can't see how any of that would bring the feds down on us. How about that bank robbery a while back. Edwin was here earlier today asking for the information we have. Maybe he's come up with some new incriminating information and wants the feds here to slap on handcuffs and haul the culprit off."

"But, he's one of us."

"I know and I think he would ask for our help if he wasn't so influenced by that young girl. She says whatever pops into her mind and tells us that it's Edwin doing the talking. I'm not buying it."

Chief Trent shook his head while biting his lower lip. "Is there anything missing from the evidence room?"

"No, sir. Not to my knowledge, but I'll check to make sure."

"Better round up a couple of people and take an inventory. And let's keep our ears open."

It took James an hour with a paper clip and stretched spring to open Seth's briefcase. He found it with the other items needing to be packed for moving to another town. In a truck stop parking lot on the way to Dancing Deer James stopped and finally got the non-cooperating locks to dance his tune.

Inside James found several blank applications for insurance coverage, a few that had been filled out, and a ledger book listing names, addresses, policy numbers, and amounts paid—$1,000 on every line. There was one more column and this one was labeled Bonus. Between blank lines, a few values were entered from $1,000 to $5,000.

James copied the ledger page and the names and addresses of the filled in insurance applications before relocking the briefcase. When he drove through Harrison, he stopped at the Western Union to send two telegrams before getting something to eat and heading on to Dancing Deer. He'd be there in two hours.

At four o'clock on Monday afternoon, August 19, 1946, James arrived at the town where he had committed his last crime. After checking into the Ritz Grand Hotel and Ballroom and delivering his luggage to a cozy room on the second floor, James unpacked. It was time to get his new wardrobe dry cleaned or washed and ironed—whatever the fabric required.

At the concierge's desk James asked, "Where can I get my laundry done?"

"Good afternoon, sir. There's someone I can ring who will come pick it up and deliver it back to your room in one day."

"But some of it needs dry cleaning."

"Yes, sir. She'll separate it. Wash and iron some and dry clean the rest."

"Fantastic."

"And your room number is?"

"207."

"There are sacks on the closet shelf to place the laundry in. Would you like for me to call the lady now?"

After retreating to his room and preparing his clothes for the laundry woman, James left to find something to eat. On his last stay in Dancing Deer, James had found the hotel bistro to be more than adequate in that department.

Six tables over sat Agatha and Seth. James had been giving Agatha more space after their talk about reducing his role in her service. Actually, she had slipped a few notches in his esteem. Now he was wondering how he could extricate himself from his entanglement.

A waiter brought a menu. "Good evening, sir. Could I bring you something to drink—a glass of wine possibly?"

"No, but a glass of iced tea would work." As the waiter scurried away, James surveyed the room. Was there anyone who might recognize him from his previous visit? He hoped he had made sufficient changes to his appearance that no one could make the assessment he was the one who robbed their bank and shot Officer Stanky. At a table at the edge of the seating area sat three people huddled together whispering. James thought they might be up to something clandestine, so he focused on them every time he glanced about the room like he was looking for someone in particular.

The man looked directly at James then turned his face to the older woman and away from James. Besides the man there sat two women, one older than the other. James thought the presence of the three to be extremely odd. They sat at a circular table and each of the three was glancing in a direction that did not allow James a good look at their faces. Then they would all lean toward the center of the table and talk in hushed voices. Very odd.

James' food came, and then Agatha and Seth finished their meal. They walked by his table without saying anything. Agatha had a slight smile with Seth keeping a stone-cold demeanor.

After the meal James paid, then spent the rest of the afternoon walking around the downtown area. He was wearing casual clothing, a large-brimmed straw hat, and aviator sunglasses. When he found the address he was looking for, James took in everything he could from the sidewalk. He was trying to form an opinion, but the only thing he could see was an outer office with everything neat and tidy. No papers left in a jumbled mess, no magazines laying in a disorganized pattern for waiting clients. James still had two days before their Wednesday opening performance. This would have to work.

Tuesday morning at two a.m. James stole out of his room with Seth's briefcase. He drove to Dancing Deer's baseball stadium and parked a good ways from the tent set up in the parking lot. With a small flashlight James managed to negotiate through the tent to the cordoned off area the employees used for their living quarters. Through the canvas partition, he could hear abundant snoring. He listened a period long enough for him to feel comfortable everyone was in a deep sleep, then he stole through a riff in the partition into the enemies' stronghold and left the briefcase in a semi-hidden location. Back in his hotel room, James tried to determine if the information he had copied was sufficient. He'd have more information the next day.

When James signed his ticket and exited the bistro, the three assumed desperadoes at the back table paid their ticket and snuck upstairs to their room. "Dad, do you think he recognized us?"

"Hard to say. He didn't act like it, but I did see him stare at us from time to time. With these getups, he was probably trying to find a category to stick us in. Actually, I more resemble Buster Keaton with this silly hat, hairpiece, and funny looking glasses than a respected city official. Why aren't the two of you in comparable getup? Do you think wigs are a good enough deception?"

"Dad, we're on an adventure here. You should enjoy the opportunity to act out of character. This morning mom did a creditable Gracie Allen, while I acted the straight part. But instead of George Burns, I was more like Carole Lombard."

"Well, if you ask me, this beau of yours is the best actor of us all. He mesmerizes the women with his easy manner and choice of clothes. I think he somehow tunes in to what women want to hear, and it just rolls off his tongue. I now know why we're here. Honey, do you think there is any substance behind all his subterfuge?"

"James is a kind man who is able to make sense of all those things that confuse us women. Right now, he is simply trying to help Agatha receive enough donations for her to pay her bills."

Jane Pauline said, "I don't like all this bickering. I, for one, am having a wonderful time. We have now been to four revival services and I've enjoyed every one. However, I don't believe he's actually cured anyone. I think they are all actors—just like us.

"And between services, we've traveled through the most picturesque forests, rolling high meadows, and pristine rivers. There are flowers everywhere; the people are friendly—until they hear us speak. And every one of these little towns looks like it should be a picture on a postcard. I'm having a great time and I'm glad we came. What I don't understand is how we can convince James into coming home with us if we don't even let him know we're here.

"And what's with those clothes he's wearing. He looks like he's a New York runway model advertising the new fall line."

"Okay girls, here's what we do. Tomorrow I'll go to the hardware store and buy some rope and a shovel. We'll catch him walking down the sidewalk with me shadowing. Gracie you pull up to him right before he crosses an intersection. I'll bean him with the shovel and shove him into the back seat. Gracie, you step on the gas. You'll peel out of town while Carole Lombard and I tie his hands behind his back. He'll wake up about the time we cross into Missouri stretched out in the back seat with his head in Miss Lombard's lap. Young lady, you'll be applying a bandage to his head, and cooing about how, it was a miracle your dad was able to fight off those tough looking farmers while you and your mother manhandled him into the car. And we all are escaping to the friendly confines of Indiana."

"What about his hands?"

"Just tell him you haven't been able to untie the knot, but when we stop for lunch, we'll find some way to cut him loose if he'll be nice."

"Dad, you are too funny."

CHAPTER 35

August 20, 1946

"I gotta go to Silver Springs. Just got word." Seth held up an envelope with a torn, uneven edge.

"Seth, Silver Springs is in Missouri. We'll have to go back over some of the same roads we just traveled."

"I know and I don't like it any more than you. But like the boss says, 'It's not ours to reason why, just to do or die.'"

"I'm seriously thinking of doing the preaching thing full-time. With the increase in donations, we can now make it on our own. Seth, wouldn't you rather be our front man only and take it easy for a while—not to be constantly looking over your shoulder to see if the law is creeping up from the shadows, or worse, someone from Philadelphia?"

"I've thought about that, sis, but the guys in Philadelphia wouldn't let us walk away quietly. And, besides, I like the adrenalin rush I get when I'm working the other job."

"Well, I think it's gruesome. They wouldn't do anything against me would they? I mean, I've never talked with any of them. As far as they know, I'm not even in the loop."

"Who's to know for sure? They may even have one of our men keeping an eye on us and reporting back. For now, I say we continue with the game, but I'll start giving some thought to escaping. There might be a way we could break free—especially for you. I'm in too far for them not to consider me a loose end that would have to be tidied up."

"Don't say that, Seth. You could take your share of the money and leave the country. Go to South America or somewhere in Europe. I could make them believe me when I told them we had a big argument and I kicked you out, and then hired another front man. I don't want to lose Jim, he's our cash cow, but someone else would work. Why don't you hire an assistant, get him properly trained, and then you and I could have a conspicuous argument, break a lamp or two. You could give me a black eye. We could yell at each other in front of a few witnesses and then you leave, with me still here trying to struggle through. Let's think on it, refine our plot, and then put it into action somewhere in Texas. You could skip over the border into Mexico and start a new life. Then in a few years, I'll retire and meet up with you in Spain or France with the rest of the money."

"All right, high noon at the top of the Eifel Tower on your fortieth birthday. We'll have to develop a plan. I'll think on it, but right now I got to head to Silver Springs. There's another town about forty miles farther west that we've never been to, Davenport, I think. After I finish the job in Silver Springs, I'll start making arrangements for us to go there."

Tuesday morning James ate breakfast at the Ritz Bistro and then, with a paper under his arm, strolled down Main Street. On a side street two blocks past the courthouse James entered the office of Michael Jellico, Attorney at Law.

"Ma'am, would you tell Mr. Jellico his ten o'clock has arrived."

"And your name?"

"John Smith."

After a few minutes of James twiddling his thumbs, the receptionist returned and asked him to follow her. Along the way, she asked if he would care for a cup of coffee. Michael Jellico was standing at the entrance to his private office and held out his hand as James approached.

"Come in, Mr. Smith." After both men were seated Jellico continued with, "Now, how may I be of assistance?"

"Mr. Jellico, I'm not going to beat around the bush. I robbed the First Bank and Trust of Dancing Deer and shot Officer Edwin Stanky. I want to exchange some information to the FBI for leniency and I want to hire you to broker a deal."

"Hmm. Quite a startling pronouncement. But you did give the money back."

"And I returned the gas money I took when I left those boys in their shack. And I returned the four hundred and fifty I took from the bank in Skunk Hollow."

"That still leaves Edwin. He's a town hero. The citizens of Dancing Deer would want something out of that."

"I could apologize."

"You'll be lucky if the town doesn't roust you out of jail and take you to the live oak at the edge of town. Let me see the information you have to trade."

James pulled out three sheets of paper from his inside breast pocket. "I'm not sure what it is but the FBI has had Seth and the Agatha Parker Ministries under scrutiny for some time. And I've been supplying them information through Police Officer Sandoval of Bowling Green, Kentucky.

"Two days ago I took the liberty of bypassing Officer Sandoval and sent a telegram straight to the FBI guys saying someone would be giving them the information they were looking for. I also mentioned that they should stay at the Ritz Grand Hotel and Ballroom and be in the Ritz Bistro at two p.m. on Friday afternoon. That gives us two full days and two half days to polish up the sale and, maybe, to determine what this information is in the first place."

"Mr. Smith, I applaud you for your attention to detail, but you can't expect to walk away a free man."

"No. I just don't want to spend the rest of my life behind bars. Mr. Jellico, I've changed my life around, and since this last Christmas Eve, I've been righting my wrongs. I just don't know what I can do for Mr. Stanky."

"Okay, let's look at these papers. They're not the originals— except for this one blank application. I suppose you included it because it has the insurance company's name, address, and telephone number."

"Yes, sir."

"And this insurance company specializes in annuities. My guess is they're taking President Roosevelt's Social Security plan to the elderly who don't have the opportunity to build up a nest egg like younger workers.

"Mr. Smith, I've never heard of the Philadelphia Patriot Acceptance and Annuities Insurance Company. But, I assume, they are located in Philadelphia and doing something not exactly within the law. What would have been nice was one of the filled out policies. I think it would be interesting to see how much a purchaser would have to pay and what his expected payout would be."

"I do remember the numbers on one of the policies. A widow aged fifty-five was going to pay in one hundred a month. When she reached seventy, she would be receiving five hundred a month for the rest of her life. I calculated that she would be paying twelve hundred a year for fifteen years or eighteen thousand dollars. And she would receive back six thousand per year. She would be recouping her investment in three years. If she lived to be seventy-three, she would be breaking even and for every additional three years she'd make another eighteen thousand.

"So if the insurance company sold their policies to people who died young or not long after getting to be seventy then the company would make a killing and if it sold policies to people who lived into their eighties, and beyond, they'd go broke.

"It looks to me like the insurance company would want to make sure their clients died soon after they started receiving their monthly annuity."

"Mr. Smith, you may have figured it out. I'll work on it and spend some time rehearsing how I'll present it to the feds. Do you want to be there? I'd suggest against it—not for the first meeting anyway. They may not be in a dealing mood. So I'll play the attorney-client privilege card in an effort to buy some time. I assume you are in the revivalist's entourage and want to keep things hush-hush during the negotiations."

"Yes, sir."

"Where are you staying?"

"On the second floor of the Ritz, room 207."

"Okay, you stay by the telephone on Friday and I'll call you on the house phone as soon as I've talked with them. By the way Mr. Smith, I charge a hundred per hour—whether I'm researching, practicing, following up on a lead, or dickering. Are you comfortable with that?

"That's a rather steep fee."

Mr. Smith, in matters of law you get what you pay for. And I'll need a five hundred dollar retainer."

"Mr. Jellico, I thought I was the thief."

CHAPTER 36

Wednesday Evening, August 21, 1946

James and Agatha sat behind the curtain. Agatha swirled a tiny brush against a circular cake, then applied it to her eyelid.

"Agatha, I have to go back to West Larimore for a week or so. My company has landed another contract, and I have to check on it."

"I thought you had a woman taking care of things for you."

"I do, but she wants to hire more people, and I don't think we have enough business. I'll come right back."

"Have you said anything to Seth?"

"No. Should I? You're the one in charge."

"Yes, I'm in charge, but Seth likes to stay abreast of things. Our next town is Davenport—back in Missouri."

"I thought our next town was Russellville."

"There's been a slight change. We're still going to Russellville but now it'll be in late September. I'll call you at the Lexington Hotel and let you know exactly where we'll be."

"Agatha, do you work the year around? Is there not time for a vacation?"

"Before you started healing people, we had to work every week to pay the bills. But we might schedule some time off this year."

Jerry popped his head through the overlap in the stage curtain. "Looks like we're going to have a full house. I put the Baptists on the right and the Church of Christ members on the left. I hope we don't have a melee."

James turned the page in his father's bible. Lately, he'd been going from one page with a corner turned down to another and using his father's notes for the few instances in each performance where he was called on to say something to the audience. Tonight he was studying Paul's letter to the Romans.

Jerry came through the curtain and started fiddling with the phonograph. Soon, the entire tent was filled with organ music. Over his shoulder he said, "Showtime."

In the audience, Michael Jellico was attending his first ever revival meeting as were two suited men from Little Rock two rows closer to the stage. Jellico had not thought to bring a bible, so he now turned the pages in the one he had found in his chair.

The two men from Little Rock also did not bring a bible. They set the ones they found in their chairs on the floor. Erik, the larger of the two men, crossed his leg and folded over his arms. He looked around at all of the attendees. "I wonder if the Agatha Parker Ministries has achieved non-profit status. Maybe, we should notify our brothers at the IRS."

"Yeah, if they've got this many people attending their service, then donations should be pretty good." Will, the second of the suited men, checked his back pocket to see if he still had his wallet. He had once been to a circus where every seat was filled, and a pick pocket among the multitude had relieved him of everything—including his badge.

"Who do you think the snitch is?"

Will said, "Could be any one of them, but probably, the lowest paid parking attendant. A person jealous of someone else getting more money for putting out less work."

"Just like in the FBI," said Erik.

"Yeah, but what does he want in return?"

"Maybe, justice—and immunity for his own sins."

Jellico and the two men from Little Rock were thoroughly entertained. Will reached to the floor looking for the bible. He wanted to look up a passage used by the guy in the blue blazer. And now several people had walked or hobbled up front to stand beside the same guy. He had promised a special blessing on anyone suffering. Each person needing healing was handed the microphone to make his request.

The first one said he had a speech impediment. The guy in the blue blazer told the man to sing what he wanted to say or he could try to talk with marbles in his mouth. He said God would help, but the man should try to meet God halfway. The guy in the blue blazer said something in a low voice to the man, while holding the microphone down to his side. He then raised the microphone to his mouth, asked the Lord to help the man, and placed his free hand on the man's forehead. The man fell to the floor, then got up saying everything had gone black for a second, but he now felt he was on the road to recovery.

A second person had sugar diabetes, a third was lame, and a fourth said he had a son at home too sick to attend the services. The guy in the blue blazer prayed hard with that man. In a moment the man grew weak in the knees and had to be led to an empty chair by the guy in the blue blazer where he continued to pray for the boy with his hand on the man's forehead. After he was finished, he said that was all he could do tonight, and one of the parking attendants had to help him back on stage. The guy in the blue blazer looked physically exhausted. The pretty lady said a closing prayer. People were now lined up to put money into the offering plates placed in various strategic locations—this was after they had already put money into the plates when they were passed during the service.

Walking to their car Will asked, "How much did you place in that wooden bowl?"

"One at first, then a fiver after the healing. I thought he earned it."

John and Jane Pauline stayed up late Wednesday night playing gin rummy, while Margo read a book. Thursday morning John ordered breakfast to be delivered to their room along with a copy of Wednesday's *Marsden County Meteor*. Just ten minutes after placing the order, there was a knock on the door. John couldn't believe the kitchen's efficiency and hurried to the door before the waiters decided no one was home and began offering the meal to more appreciative people down the hall. But when he opened the door it was a maid pushing a cart laden with clean towels, new bars of soap, and other items necessary for cleaning their room.

"Good lady, could you possibly come back in a couple of hours? We stayed up late last night and now everyone, except for me, is still slumbering."

After receiving an affirmation to his request and closing the door, John Pauline walked onto his balcony and stretched. From two floors up he had a good view of a bustling Dancing Deer. A morning breeze flapped the lapel of his housecoat, but that would dissipate as the morning waned. He wished he had coffee and a newspaper. John sat in a wrought iron chair and began watching the people walk by twenty feet below on the sidewalk. In ten more minutes, John had not moved. Then he heard a second knock on the door. This time Margo answered and John thought he had better go in, so the waiter delivering would be adequately tipped.

In minutes, a third chair had been taken to the balcony and the food carefully placed on a small circular table. Both women were in terry cloth bathrobes with Jane pouring her husband a cup of steaming coffee. Margo drank orange juice.

"Dad, yesterday I followed Jim down the street. He went into a lawyer's office. He must've been there for more than an hour. What business could he possibly be transacting with a lawyer here in Dancing Deer?"

"I'll bet he's trying to buy part ownership in the Agatha Parker Ministries. Every time we've attended one of their services the donations have increased."

"I haven't noticed those little bowls being fuller than usual."

"Then you also haven't noticed there are now twice as many of those little bowls to fill. I wouldn't doubt they're taking in five hundred or more each night. This evangelizing has become a profitable business. I counted two hundred seats. They are usually about three-quarters full on Wednesday nights, a little less on Thursday nights, and completely full on Friday and Saturday nights with some people standing in the back."

"Then we have to do something. Jim has to come home to Indiana and take care of his businesses there. Indiana Data Management has just started overhauling some police department's files above Indianapolis and the Indiana Racing Factory has six cars for sale and is doing a thriving business selling gas and changing oil and I . . . I need him.

"Honey, how would you feel traveling around the country helping him with his evangelizing? I think he's making enough money to put you up each night in a fancy hotel and feed you in good restaurants. And you could talk him into buying a traveling piano so they could replace that dreadful phonograph."

"No, that won't work. I want a family; I want to take care of him in our own house, to fix his meals in my kitchen, to . . ."

"Pumpkin, you don't always get what you want. Sometimes there are hardships to overcome, potholes in the road to maneuver around. Sometimes it takes time to achieve your goals. Everything can't always be accomplished right now and everything can't be what you want anyway. A happy marriage is one involving compromise and communication—lots of communication. You need to find out what James wants and weasel your way into one of those roles."

"Dad, you are so right. Maybe, Jim needed to do this to hone his ability to sway public opinion. Just think how much better he would be giving a public speech when running for office with this under his belt."

"Honey, I know how hard it is for you to let go and let destiny happen on its own. You are just like your mother, always manipulating events to your own taste. Maybe you should write down on paper what the problem is, break it down into its component parts, and start solving them one at a time."

"All right, I'll put down how things stand right now, and how I eventually want things to be. Then my problem is navigating between the two. I feel so empowered."

"Jane, I think I've started something here. Why didn't you head me off at the pass?"

"John, do you really think I'm a manipulator?"

Edwin had been tapping his toe all morning. Sometimes he got into a tapping frenzy between his right index finger on the armrest and the toes of his right foot against the floor. At first everyone was amazed that he was able to accomplish movement with other parts of his body than just his head. But after a day and a night the newness had worn off, and everyone now wanted peace and quiet for a change. Then he mastered a rhythmic syncopation between the two and that elated him beyond measure.

Gladys finally stepped in and solved their problem. "Edwin, we are so happy you finally have movement somewhere other than your head, but we feel like a family with a child who has just received a set of drums for his birthday. You just keep on tapping, but I'm going to muffle the noise a little with these gloves and two pair of socks. You can still make noise but not quite as much."

"Gladys, if we put a rug under his chair you could dispense with the socks."

"Good idea, young lady. I don't know how we ever got through the day before you came along."

"Oh shoo, you're just saying that."

"No, I mean it. You've added energy to our day. The entire house is brighter and more cheery with you in it. And Edwin, when he can talk again, will thank you from the bottom of his heart for taking care of him through his journey."

Gladys adjusted her scarf. "Honey, how are you doing on your writing?"

"Better. I've read most of those writing magazines Edwin had stuffed under the bed. Now, when I read him something I've written, he doesn't roll his eyes like he used to. But the problem is I can't think of anything interesting to write about.

"My girlfriends at school are only interested in boys. They swoon over any boy with curly hair. The giggling, hushed remarks made under cupped hands, and constant chattering is more than I can stand. When they get in a group they all talk at the same time. I don't want to write about the things they're interested in I want something with more substance. My problem is I haven't been anywhere nor did anything, and I have no experience with any death defying or life defining events."

"Why don't you make up a story? It doesn't have to be true. How about a girl detective? Or you could solve the case of the anonymous benefactor. The town is still receiving presents from someone."

"I've thought about that. I now believe that if I knew who it was, I wouldn't tell anyone. No, I'd want to help him—or her—decide on the next thing the town needed. He hasn't come forward so he must have some good reason and telling everyone who he was would be a betrayal. It would be the story of the century, but I'd have to keep it under my hat."

"Laurie, you never cease to amaze me. Well, I'm off to work. Have you and Issie anything planned to do with our guy today?"

"We're taking him to City Park to let him dangle his toes in the water, then we're gonna feed a few ducks, and finish up at Eudy's for ice cream."

"That's wonderful. I'd like to do that myself. Do you have any money?"

"Yes ma'am. But usually no one will let us pay. Edwin has a whole town wanting to do something for him."

"Yes I know, and if you hesitate they look so sad that they couldn't do anything. I usually give in and let them, but of course, nothing major."

"Do you think a fifty dollar hat would be major?"

"Is that what that thing cost?"

"Yes, ma'am. Harry said it was a Montecristo. I think that is a type of Panama hat. And Harry was so happy when he saw Edwin's big grin that we had to hurry out of there before he rampaged through his store looking for something else he could give."

CHAPTER 37

August 23, 1946

Margo was not a happy woman. She had followed James Dandae from somewhere in Missouri all the way to Dancing Deer with her parents in tow. But this morning they informed her they were ready to go home. It was Friday and, if they left Saturday morning, her father could start the week at work on time Monday morning. So far, James had not discovered that he was being stalked by a disguised and determined woman. A woman commander bolstered by friendly troops obeying her every command—almost every command.

Margo had to step up her campaign. She had one day to get what she had set out to acquire and the outlook was dismal. James seemed to be in his element with the evangelizing. And Agatha was as beautiful, as manipulative, as deceitful as ever. Margo had to find a chink in Agatha's armor. Margo knew that when Agatha's parents died she had fallen into a deep depression and was only able to break free through the insight and persuasive advice of a man Agatha had never met. That man knew more about Agatha Parker than any man alive. But could she stoop so low as to use secret information to sway the one she loved from the woman he was infatuated with.

Over the telephone Margo said, "Hello, Miss Stansberry. My name is Margo Pauline. I need to speak with Mr. Stanky."

"Miss Pauline, Edwin can't talk. He communicates through me." After an awkward pause Laurie continued with, "Why don't you come by and I'll try to help."

Fifteen minutes later Margo was knocking on the Stanky front door. "Come in, Miss Pauline. Edwin is in his usual place. After his morning bath, Issie sets him by the front window so he can see people walking by."

"Good morning, Mr. Stanky."

Laurie said, "Edwin says you look pretty and that he would prefer you to call him, Edwin."

"So, Edwin, how are you coming on bringing your assailant to justice?"

"He says he's having a difficult time but should have better use of his faculties by the end of the year and then nothing will stand in his way. And I, Miss Pauline, will be right there with him."

"I know you will, Laurie. The man I love said he once passed through Dancing Deer. He and Agatha Parker are the two reasons I've come to talk with you. James has returned to West Larimore after being gone for twenty years. He and I were seeing each other until Agatha Parker stepped in and stole him away. She disrupted his thoughts and my plans. He has now left me and West Larimore to join up with the Agatha Parker Ministries. But I know the woman to be other than she appears. If James could see the true Agatha Parker then I think he could break free from the hold she has over him and come back with me to West Larimore.

"What I was hoping was that you could give me some information about Agatha. I know that she hates men and only uses them as playthings and then casts them off when they start to bore her. I also know that she wrote to you when her parents died. She was in a nose dive dipping into a deep depression. Is there anything you can tell me that would explain her current behavior?"

Margo waited. It was two minutes before Laurie said, "Miss Pauline. Edwin says you are mistaken. He was aware of her depression and gave her consolation for a grieving heart, but he is not aware of any character flaws she might have. Before our trip to Indiana, Edwin had never met Miss Parker except through a few letters. And to make an opinion as to her moral integrity on such flimsy evidence would not do justice to their relationship. He says he can't help you."

"I understand."

On the way back to the Ritz Grand Hotel and Ballroom, Margo's mood changed from one of militancy to one of complaisance. If she couldn't have James for her very own, then it was not meant to be. And she had no right to ask for Edwin's help—or anyone's, for that matter. Maybe, she would go back to West Larimore and start a business, or join the West Larimore Garden Club, or do charity work, or move to Charleston and live with one of her cousins, or join the church choir.

Maybe she would instead write that book she had threatened to pen, *Jim Dandy, the man your mother warned you about.*

When she arrived at Main Street, Margo turned right, toward her hotel. A few blocks farther she stepped inside Ava's Dresses. Maybe a new purse or pair of shoes would improve her spirits.

Gladys approached and said. "Hello, are you looking for anything in particular? Our sale items are pretty well picked over, but we received a new delivery of shoes this morning. I don't have them displayed yet, but in our order catalog they were stunning. And hats were delivered a couple of days ago. I've got some of them put out. Do you need new fall fashions?"

"I don't know what I need. Yes, I do. I need for my man to take me in his arms and say, 'Let's run away. Let me love you and take care of you.' Ma'am, do you have that on display?"

"I keep it under lock and key, and only bring it out to my very best customers."

"Is it expensive?"

"Not expensive in money but it does cost a lot in determination, patience, and putting his interests ahead of yours."

"How does a woman make her interests known?"

"He's not aware of your passion for him?"

"No. I've left everything up to chance. Tell me, how did you and your husband . . . Oh, I am so sorry. My name is Margo Pauline." Margo held out her hand.

"I'm pleased to meet you, Margo. My name is Gladys Stanky."

"Edwin Stanky's wife?"

"Yes. I don't believe I recognize you. Do you live in Dancing Deer?"

"No. I live in West Larimore, Indiana. I was one, no two, of the actors in your husband's play. I think we have already met. I introduced Agatha to Mr. Stanky at the party after the play."

"Yes, we have. And you're here in Dancing Deer to see Edwin?"

"Partly. Also, I've come to kidnap a man before he does something he'll regret the rest of his life."

"This man. Has he run to Dancing Deer to get away from you?"

"Oh, no. He doesn't know I'm here. In fact, he thinks I won't have anything to do with him when I find out the terrible things he's done before he met me."

"Honey, there's nothing he could have done that he can't be forgiven of if he's truly repentant."

"Well, I know him now and he's a good man. He's even joined up with Agatha Parker and goes around the country healing people. And he doesn't even know how to do that. At least, I don't think he does. There have been a few people who swear he's cured them of various ailments. I saw one man hold a crutch high in the air yelling he was cured. He then propped the crutch against a church pew and danced a jig before falling down exhausted."

"How do you know that, if he's not even aware you're here?"

"I wear a wig and baggy clothing to his sermons."

"Margo, may I tell you something? You need to tell him how you feel. Don't let another day go by without pouring out your heart. Edwin and I went through some hard times. For over ten years, I never told Edwin I loved him. And when I woke up, I changed my ways but it was hard to actually say the words. I kissed him and we were intimate a few times but I never said 'Edwin, I love you.' Then I almost lost him. And it was my own stupidity and my own preoccupation with myself that kept me from that one act of love. Now not a day goes by that I don't tell him I love him. We women want that from the men in our lives, so why should we hold it from them."

"And telling him how mean spirited Agatha is would not advance my position?"

"No. He has to make that assessment on his own. You should hold yourself above such demeaning actions. A woman never builds herself up by belittling her competition. Jump out of the fray and let him see you as you truly are: a kind, considerate, passionate woman who loves him with all her heart. A woman like that who is unspoiled and as pretty as you won't have anything to worry about. Now, let's find you a new outfit to blow his mind."

Michael Jellico was in the Ritz Grand Hotel Bistro a few minutes before the two p.m. time John Smith had asked for the FBI's interview. Jellico knew most of the people in Dancing Deer, so he only had to find the FBI agent from among those seated he didn't recognize. A nice looking, middle-aged man in a smart looking suit sat by himself. A middle-aged man with a bad haircut. Under his breath Jellico said, "Well that was a lot easier than I had anticipated." Jellico walked over and introduced himself.

"Hello, my name is Michael Jellico. Are you the government agent I've been waiting for?"

"Yes. I guess it's possible."

Jellico pulled out a chair and sat his large frame on a seat almost too small. "I have been approached by the man who sent you the telegram requesting your presence. I have the information you need, but I want to see what you can do for my client in return."

The middle-aged man had been looking through the menu but promptly closed it and leaned forward. "Are you propositioning me in some way?"

"Uh . . . no. You can use this information to further your investigation. My client is offering it because he thinks it is the right thing to do, but hopes you will take into consideration the risks he has undertaken in its procurement. He is a man who has suffered through a life changing epiphany and has been righting the wrongs he's perpetrated for the last twenty years. He just wants a recommendation from you in the sentencing phase. He doesn't expect to go scott-free but does want to trade years off his sentence for risking his life. You should be able to use this information to bring your criminal and the company he works for to justice."

"Let me stop you right there. My wife and daughter are standing behind you and we don't understand in the least what you're talking about."

"You're not an FBI Agent?"

"Good heavens no. I'm the mayor of West Larimore, Indiana here on vacation."

"My God. I was supposed to meet with an FBI Agent at two p.m. and I know everybody in here. You had to be the man."

"I'm sorry to disappoint you, but if you would continue the story, I am sure the FBI man will be here shortly, and I promise not to divulge any of the facts to anyone. I just want to know who this man is, what he's done, and then, of course, what you have in the package."

Jellico was red in the face as he apologized and stood to let the two women be seated. As he walked back to his table, Jellico mumbled, "I hope I live long enough to live this down."

Jellico ordered iced tea and waited. Fifteen minutes later two men were seated who also fit the image of supposed FBI Agents. This time Jellico made eye contact and withdrew the envelope from his breast pocket, setting it on the table. The larger of the two men walked over and stood in front of Jellico.

"Sir, we were told to meet someone here at two. Are you that person?"

"I am if you're with the FBI."

"We are." The agent turned and motioned for his friend to join them. The man sat down in a chair opposite a flustered Michael Jellico, Attorney at Law.

"We were told that you would be supplying us with some incriminating evidence. Let's see what you've got."

Jellico looked toward the table of the Mayor of West Larimore. Three faces were staring his way. Jellico picked the envelope up and held it in both hands. "The procurement of this material took considerable patience, a highly calibrated plan, and a measure of ingenious deception. And it was achieved by a man risking his life while doing so. The man, who accomplished the feat, wants you to recommend a lenient sentence for a crime he committed several months ago and for which he wishes to make amends. He robbed a bank and shot a guard—without killing him. The bank guard was an off-duty policeman. The man I represent has now returned the money he stole and will plead guilty to the crime." With that said, Jellico handed the envelope to the larger of the two agents.

"We can't promise anything."

"I completely understand. Please, look at the information and tell me if it is what you require. The man's position has not yet been compromised in case you need additional incriminating evidence."

"We need to cross check these names against a list we have in the case file. Do you think we could meet tomorrow morning again?"

"I was hoping we might meet again later tonight."

"We have a revival meeting to go to tonight. How about ten in the morning right here in the bistro?"

"Is there anything I can tell my client?"

"You can tell him that he shouldn't go around robbing banks and certainly not shooting a fellow member of law enforcement. However, if these names are in our database, he will have done the FBI, and his nation, a great service. And I have no problem stating as much to my superiors."

"Okay. Tomorrow morning at ten."

CHAPTER 38

Friday Afternoon, August 23, 1946

Jellico called his client's room right after talking with the FBI agents saying he had another interview Saturday morning and that the agents would be in attendance at Friday's revival service. James had set the wheels of justice in motion. He was now officially past the point of backing out.

After Jellico's call, James paced the floor, hashed and re-hashed the events leading up to the point of no return, and wondered how he could have improved his chances. James intensely disliked being at the mercy of someone he didn't know. But he was also resigned to the fact that his life had changed and he needed to make amends for past transgressions.

The organ music stopped and from the other side of the curtain came, "Welcome, Dancing Deer. We have a wonderful program for you tonight. Miss Agatha Parker will be telling you that it's not too late to get yourself right with the Lord and what the consequences are for putting it off until it's too late. Also, we have Mr. James Dandae talking to you about his walk with the Lord and what a change it has made in his life. Then we'll ask for the infirm among you to step forward for a special blessing: Mr. Dandae will pray to our Savior that he restore your health. So please stand while I give thanks for the opportunity to minister to you in beautiful Arkansas."

Agatha was looking through a slit in the curtain. Over her shoulder she said, "Another full house. You have certainly been a prayer answered, Jim. You're just going to miss the one week, right? You'll catch up with us after Davenport? We have a few more stops in Arkansas, and then we'll go to either Oklahoma or Texas. Have you ever ridden a horse?"

"Ladies and gentlemen, Miss Agatha Parker."

"Showtime, Jim."

For the next forty-five minutes Agatha talked about the second coming of Christ, of the faithful being lifted into heaven, of the non-believers being cast into hell, of the torment and miserable conditions they would have to endure for time *ad infinitum*. A few songs were interspersed: one by Agatha accompanied by a guitar and two more by Jerry leading the congregation. At the end of Agatha's portion of the program, the offering was collected.

"I will now ask Mr. James Dandae to say a few words, James."

James stepped through the curtain and received a warm welcome from the people in attendance. "I've been to Dancing Deer once before. You have a beautiful town and real friendly people. I especially liked your City Park with its thermal spring. But as good and as hospitable as Dancing Deer is it pales in comparison to heaven. There you will be in the presence of God.

"I was raised in a Christian home. My father was a Methodist minister and I was required to read a chapter of the bible each night before going to bed. I rebelled against that strict regimen and left at my first opportunity. I thought my father's sermons were nonsense and I was not the only one to criticize them. He often told the story about an argument he had with my mother when they first got married.

"You see, my mother complained that his sermons lacked energy. She told him flat out that they were boring. Now, she was a young woman still trying to find her position of authority in their relationship.

"My father, on the other hand, was an organized and methodical man. He was constantly going behind my mother shutting her dresser drawers, reshuffling items in her purse when he saw something protruding out the top, and rearranging items on her kitchen countertop. This infuriated my mother until they reached an understanding. My mother would refrain from criticizing his sermons, no matter how boring they were, and my father would not mess with my mother's things. It worked for many years. When I left, I was eighteen and they had been married for twenty blissful years.

"My father told me many years later that he was assigned another church, and the congregation of the church he was leaving gave a big send-off party. He was elated with the attitude of his flock and the love he had for his wife, but that night when they were getting ready for bed he noticed there was a piece of lingerie sticking out of my mother's top dresser drawer. My father couldn't stand it. After years of controlling his compulsion to organize, he gave in and opened her dresser drawer to stuff back in the undergarment. Inside the drawer, he found three eggs and a sack of money. My mother had over a thousand dollars stuffed in a big envelope. My father was flabbergasted and immediately went to ask my mother about it.

"She calmly said that instead of complaining, she placed an egg in the drawer each time he gave a dreadful sermon."

"My father was impressed. He said, 'Twenty years and only three eggs. I must have improved. But what about all that money?'"

"She replied, 'Each time I got a dozen eggs I sold them.'"

James received several laughs and felt like he'd struck a friendship with the audience. He glanced around to see if there was anyone in attendance who did not appreciate his whimsy. That's when he saw her. The most beautiful woman there. The woman he saw when he closed his eyes. The same woman he reached for in his dreams. The woman who would soon be unattainable. When she found out what a scumbag he really was, there would be no way her feelings for him would not be altered. And sitting next to her was her father and mother. How humbling.

James tried to get through the remainder of his talk but did a lot of stammering with awkward pauses where he couldn't remember what he was supposed to say next. James and Margo locked eyes and he gradually grew strength from her smile. James talked about the roles of husbands and wives, of how they had to work together as a team, and how the love between them is only second to the love God has for each. James finally came to the end of his talk with how love transcends all obstacles and nothing can stand before a strong marriage's united front.

"I would like for any couple needing healing in their marriage to stand. I'll ask God to show them the way to a blissful and meaningful relationship."

As soon as he had finished with that prayer, several people started making their way to the stage. Word had gotten out that James would be doing a healing ceremony at the end of his talk and they felt like they had waited long enough. The first man was handed the microphone. He said how he had terrible back pains. James put his hand on the man's forehead and asked Jesus to cure this man of his ailment. He then leaned forward and whispered, "See a chiropractor." James gave the man a slight push. He crumbled at James' feet and had to be helped up by Jerry and James.

The next person was a woman who complained of headaches. While James was talking with her, the eight or ten people who had gathered in front of the stage parted and let Gladys approach pushing Edwin Stanky in a wheelchair. James stood stock-still. He finally handed Gladys the microphone.

"Mr. Dandae, please ask the Lord to heal Eddie. I have prayed for his recovery for nine months and he has made some progress but still can't talk. Please, Mr. Dandae."

"Ma'am, whether I can help with Mr. Stanky's infirmities or not is totally up to God, but what I can say is that it is quite apparent that you and Edwin have a deep love for each other. You have a blessed marriage."

Edwin was powerless. He recognized the man standing before him as the bank robber who shot him, but Edwin couldn't tell anyone. His hands grew white from the tight grip he had on his armrest, his mouth opened, air moved across his tongue, his head quivered as he willed speech. Edwin decided if he couldn't talk, he'd try to stand. He pushed on the armrest, perspiration accumulated on his forehead; his hands shook as he pushed down. Then it came—from somewhere deep inside his body it grew and swirled and headed up gaining momentum with each centimeter of travel. James put his hand on Edwin's forehead and was about to say something when Edwin's entire body shook.

"He's the one!" The words were loud, stretched out, and gnarled. Drool slid down Edwin's chin. He fell back in the wheelchair; his eyes wide in wonder.

CHAPTER 39

Saturday Morning, August 24, 1946

At 10 a.m., Michael Jellico sat in Dancing Deer's most celebrated restaurant, the Ritz Grand Hotel Bistro. With him were two FBI agents from Little Rock. They were discussing how James Dandae would spend the rest of his life.

Will, the smaller of the two FBI agents, said, "Okay, here's what we have: one, James Dandae does not contest that he robbed both banks and shot a bank guard at the one here in Dancing Deer. And, according to Mr. Jimmerson, our contact at the local bank, all of the money from both banks has been returned. Two, this morning Edwin Stanky informed us through his spokesperson that he has forgiven Mr. Dandae for shooting him and, according to his wife, Edwin is gradually recovering from the temporary paralysis he sustained. Also, that Dandae has an index finger on his right hand that is in constant movement when he's agitated. Three, as soon as Edwin left, this Margo Pauline showed up to tell us how Dandae has changed. He is now a successful businessman with two profitable businesses, a local actor in the West Larimore Thespian Society, and has plans to run for the West Larimore City Council."

Erik, the other agent added, "And the man is a gifted speaker, he somehow gives hope to sick people that they can improve their chances of getting well if they'll meet their maker half-way, and has risked his life to deliver incriminating information against Seth Holman."

"What else can he do?" said Jellico.

"He can serve time to pay society for his crimes."

Will added, "I agree with Erik. This evidence will probably lead to the successful prosecution of Holman, but we can't tie it to the insurance company. Mr. Jellico, the best we can hope for Dandae, is ten years for the bank in Skunk Hollow and fifteen for the one here—because he shot Stanky."

"Is that all?"

"If all goes well convicting Holman, we'll recommend that the sentences run concurrently."

"And?"

"And nothing. Sentencing for a federal crime is a lot more cut and dry than what can be worked out at the city, county, or state level."

"Suppose he offered to infiltrate the insurance company?"

"We'd have to check with our supervisor, but that would be a game changer. If he got a job for the insurance company, found the information we needed to bring it down, and he testified, then he might be eligible for our witness protection program."

Jellico was rolling. "And not be prosecuted for the two bank robberies?"

"Probably."

"And any other crime he may have committed prior to the bank robberies?"

"Now see here, Jellico. How many banks has the man robbed?"

"None that I know of and no one else has been shot on purpose, or by accident—because of a nervous trigger finger. But there might be other indiscretions of a lesser nature leading up to the bank heists."

"I imagine those would be covered as well."

"And then the last thing I want for James Dandae is the ability to run for political office. He would have to have his record purged clean."

"Good lord, Jellico. Do you really want criminals running the country?"

"My good man, I would feel safer with this reformed man in office than the ones we have there now."

"I'll have to talk with my supervisor. And we may have to school him in actuarial science, so he can get a job of sufficient importance."

"We'll agree with that but will need the agreement in writing. Oh, and witness protection if he thinks it's necessary after testifying."

Erik took a drink of water and motioned for the *maître d.* "I'll call my boss."

CHAPTER 40

Saturday Afternoon, August 23, 1946

"James Dandae, pack your suitcase. You need to come with us."

"I have a couple of loose ends to tie up. Do you think I could have two hours? And I'll need to drive my car. You can follow."

Erick said, "I'll allow you until three o'clock, but you better not provide us with any trouble or the deal's off."

"I won't, but I will have to make up a lie to the Agatha Parker Ministries."

"Okay. However, I'd caution you not to mislead that young lady who helped Jellico put this together. She might be the best thing you got going."

"Yes, I'm harboring that same opinion."

"We'll be in the lobby."

James sat on a small wrought iron chair on Agatha's balcony. "Agatha, I won't be coming back. The law has told me to quit or they'd prosecute me for fraud."

Agatha dabbed at her eye with a wadded up napkin. "They can't do that."

"I've hired a lawyer and he says it all depends on the judge. He thinks my only hope is to raise a big stink and let the newspapers, and the public, pressure the court. Evidently, I have been curing the same people one town after another. Jerry and Seth have been paying several people to follow us around and act as if I healed them. The law has affidavits sworn by these people to that effect. So I'm quitting the evangelism circuit, because making a stink would not be in your best interest and being prosecuted not in mine."

Agatha had a tear rolling down her cheek.

"You don't need to cry on my behalf, I'll be okay."

"I'm not crying for you. Seth hasn't called and he never showed up in Davenport to pay for our permit. I don't know what's happened to him."

"You and Seth? I wasn't aware . . ."

"Seth is my brother. When our dad ran off, Mother let her drinking get out of hand. She would go days without changing my diaper, we didn't have food in the house, and our landlord was about to kick us out. So Seth wrapped me in a blanket and deposited me on the doorstep of a minister's house in a neighboring town. He then left to make his way in the world. He found me on my first evangelistic tour and has been looking out for me ever since. But now, something must've happened. I still have Tom and Jerry, but Frank is also missing.

"Tom and Jerry have taken down the tent and loaded it on the truck. We're going to take a couple of weeks off and consider our options. I'm just afraid something dreadful has happened to Seth." With that said, she dabbed at her eyes again.

James got up, gave Agatha a hug, and left to see Michael Jellico.

"Mr. Jellico, sir. I can't tell you how pleased I am with the arrangements you've made for me. But Erik said that Margo Pauline was involved."

"Yeah, Margo loves you, James. She's the one, with help from Gladys, who talked Edwin into saying he forgave you to the IRS agents. She also convinced them that you accidentally shot Edwin because of something you do with your trigger finger. She then painted you as a changed man: someone who wants to help law enforcement by modernizing their offices and your commitment to combating crime through a career in local government. Young man you owe that woman."

"Yep. She and I will form a united front—if she agrees."

Margo waited. Earlier that morning Jim had called saying he'd like to talk to her and asked if she would be in the bistro a few minutes before two p.m. She got there at one-thirty and was into a second glass of iced tea when James entered. He walked straight to her table and bent to kiss her on the lips. She remained seated, wishing but not knowing what to expect.

"Whew, Jim. You still remember how to sweep a woman off her feet."

"Margo, honey, I only have a few minutes before they'll be carting me off to Little Rock. Will you wait for me? I have a work assignment that might take as long as a year. But after that, I will be a free man, not carrying extra baggage. It will be a huge load lifted from my shoulders, and I am looking forward to coming back to West Larimore, to coming back to you. You don't think a year is too long?"

"James, I'll be there waiting. Now that I've found you and cleaned you up, you are mine."

"Margo, I think you're a lot like my mother. She was always taking care of what was hers."

"Did you love your mother?"

"Second only to you."

"Hmm. I can accept that but would rather have heard my name in it somehow and the word 'love' incorporated. And a few more terms like 'forever.' And did I say, 'love?' There, that would make me happy and I need more passion, lots of passion, Jim. So now, with that bit of information, is there anything you want to say to me?"

James took Margo's hand in both of his and leaned forward almost touching her face. In a quiet, intimate voice he said, "Margo, I love thee, I love only thee. With a love that shall not die. Till the sun goes cold, and the stars grow old."

The End

Author Bio

Ron Lambert, an Examined Life

As an accountant in a small West Texas town, I spend my days studying the bank statements and tax returns of other people's businesses. I classify, summarize, and display their financial transactions in some meaningful format. I love creating order out of chaos.

I'm middle-aged and twice married—with the second blessed from heaven. Four grown children, their children, two bobbing tails of barking energy, and one sly cat round out my cache of treasure.

Over the years, I have owned and operated two boutique retail stores, several service businesses, one ranch, and one restaurant. I have been prosperous and poor, with wild fluctuations in between. At present, being neither rich nor poor, I consider my status as deeply entrenched in middle class—a term bandied about by politicians and economists.

In an effort to restore my youth, I purchased an old sofa on two wheels. Since that initial existential groping, I have occasionally strapped sacks of clothes, maps, and a compass that doesn't seem to work onto the back cushion. After kissing my wife, I set out for adventure and story. Usually, after only a week or so, I realize what I left behind was more important than what I set out to find and drive a day and a night hell-bent-for-leather back home.

I then settle into an old and comfortable routine. I read a few books, attend a few plays, daydream of new horizons, and plan my next adventure. I kept a journal on my first excursion. It was such an exhilarating experience: rewriting the journal and incorporating the pictures I took that I became intoxicated to the point I wrote a novel.

At present, with pen on fire, I am working on my eighth book—actually swimming in untested waters by writing a book for young adults. I'll win prestigious awards and be asked to speak at the local library if someone would read what I have written.

If you're looking for an evening spent with colorful and mesmerizing characters, if you want to immerse yourself in a rollicking good story, enthrall yourself to the point of madness, go two days without bathing, then have I got a story for you.

Additional Novels

The Dancing Deer Story

All books are available as Trade Paperbacks in perfect binding at www.printersguildpublishing.com and from several fine retailers in Columbus and Weimar, Texas.

Dancing Deer (Book 1)

Dancing Deer is the embodiment of small-town America. When asked, she sent her sons to war. This is the story of The Calhoun—one of those boys. Its also about his fellow combatants, the men he served, the men he fought, and the women he loved.

There is the French Resistance, the German Gestapo, Midge at the Mike, Anzio Annie, the Gustav Line, and the US Army's Forty-Fifth Infantry campaigning from Sicily through Italy, France, and Germany to push back the formidable Germans. But this story is so much more.

Find a comfortable chair and settle in with a great new book. You won't be disappointed.

The Last Dance (Book 2)

Bill Potter is charged with murdering his Friday night squeeze. His bumbling lawyer steps out of a dead-end job of contracts and leases to save Bill from being strapped to "Old Spanky." Bill's wife returns after a twenty-year absence to muddy the waters and it's up to her and Pepe, the womanizing Resistance fighter and WWI spy from France, to solve the case.

The Measure of a Man (Book 3)

A group of Cuban immigrants decides to barnstorm the Midwest, entertaining the towns they come to with a game of ball. When they get to Dancing Deer, the men on the city council con Bill Potter into a wager for more than they could afford to lose. Bill's position is that the Men from Dancing Deer will prevail. With a team of misfits and one win under their belts, Bill goes searching for a new manager. His ex-wife is traveling throughout the Western US with Pepe, the French womanizer. She knows more about ball than anyone and he has to convince her to come back and once again save him from the wolves at the door.

Lost in Appalachia (Book 4)

The head of Dancing Deer's Police Department is lost in the mountains of West Virginia. Suffering from an injury, he can't remember who he is or why he's lost. Two kids take him in and hide him from a determined fiancée. The chief of police is in the process of teaching the kids how to read when the fiancée posts a big reward for knowledge of his whereabouts. The chief thinks he must have committed a major crime for someone to pony up such a large bounty.

While the chief awaits the inevitable and worries about what kind of person he really is and what crimes he's committed, the children take measures into their own hands. Their rationale is there will be no one to teach them to read if their new friend is carted off to jail.

Christmas in Dancing Deer (Book 5)

St. Bartholomew's is consolidating its orphanage, but the children don't want to be separated. They come up with an alternative plan to present to the church, but the women of Dancing Deer bring the orphan girls into their homes for the holidays. The orphan boys leave on their own in the snow three days before Christmas and spend a night with a burdened bank robber in a desolated cabin.

Beggarman, Thief (Book 6)

A story of a bank robber who finds his moment of epiphany in a shack with six lost little boys. He goes home after twenty years on the lamb to have Christmas with his family and to right his wrongs. But he finds his past is in hot pursuit and the new life he has found is in jeopardy. He runs away in the clutches of a pretty lady evangelist who is taking her show on the road to the very town where he committed his last crime.

Toe to Toe with A Drunken Philosopher (Book 7)

This is really one story in three parts. First we have a high school philosophy teacher who has to resign his position much as Aristotle had to when the authorities in Athens came looking for him. Part number two is of an indigent Irish family who emigrates from the Emerald Isle. The little Irish boy in the family grows up to become a priest. The third part pits the philosopher and the priest in a contest of wits.

Racing the Wind (Book 8, Written for young adults, but not yet finished)

The story of a boy with plans someday to build bridges or design skyscrapers. He decides to pay for his education by building a racer and winning the Soapbox Derby. Problems, orchestrated by his main adversary, creep into the racer's production. The boy has to rely on the help of a fellow classmate—a girl—to find the source of his problem and to finish the racer and the race.

For All the Marbles (Book 9, Written for children but just now seeping into my consciousness)

Eston's best friend, Ben, is a little older, a little bigger, and a lot slower. The other kids have always taken advantage of Ben. Now a bully has won all of Ben's marbles. Eston promised he'd win them back but ended up losing his as well. This is the story of how Eston takes a dangerous new course of action: one that will cleanse the schoolyard of bullying and win back the lost loot.